TO FACE A SAVAGE MOUNTAIN

ALSO BY JOHN LEGG

TO FACE A SAVAGE MOUNTAIN

SAVAGE LAND
BOOK 3

JOHN LEGG

WOLFPACK
PUBLISHING
— EST 2013 —

To Face a Savage Mountain
Paperback Edition
Copyright © 2023 John Legg

Wolfpack Publishing
9850 S. Maryland Parkway, Suite A-5 #323
Las Vegas, Nevada 89183

wolfpackpublishing.com

Paperback ISBN 978-1-63977-866-9
eBook ISBN 978-1-63977-867-6
LCCN 2023946615

TO FACE A SAVAGE
MOUNTAIN

PROLOGUE

Summer 1834

THEY MADE A DRAB SPECTACLE, a sorry-looking lot of men who, now that they were away from the rendezvous site, could relax and slump in the saddle, letting the sickness of two weeks of revelry wash over them in stomach-turning waves.

Hawley Copper leaned over and vomited, the bile spewing out, making his horse stutter-step. Cooper groaned as the retching and the horse's movement jarred his sickness-racked insides. He spit out the last of the vomit and straightened up in the saddle, feeling like the entire Blackfoot Confederacy was dancing on his head. His temples throbbed and his eyes felt ready to pop out. His tongue felt like it was coated with buffalo dung, and his stomach churned and tried to roll over on him with each step.

Gingerly he looked around, blinking in the sun as sweat beaded under his wide-brimmed felt hat and trickled down into his eyes. There were more than fifty men, most of them now remnants of what had been the Rocky Mountain Company boys under Milt Sublette. A few, like Cooper and the men he rode with, captained by Elson Brooks, were free trappers, traveling alongside Sublette and Henry Fraeb's brigade. And there were perhaps a dozen women, Indian wives of some of the free trappers and almost as many half-breed children. Nathaniel Wyeth and his green New Englanders were along as well.

Cooper looked behind him and managed a smile, then grimaced as the biliousness splashed over him anew. He quickly spun his head to the side and vomited again, his stomach roiling on him.

A few yards behind Cooper, a young Nez Perce woman watched impassively. Goes Far had been with Cooper for two and a half years now, and she was already used to this. He would be over it soon, she knew. Until then, she was content to ride along in his wake, her hand holding the rope to the Cooper's four pack mules.

She felt bad for her man, but there was little she could do. Her medicines and herbs and such did not hold a cure for what was ailing Cooper. But come tomorrow, he would be better, and he would be apologetic for having been that way. She smiled at the thought. Unlike many of the white trappers who took Indian brides, Cooper truly cared for her, and showed it, not only in the foofaraw he bought for her, but also in the way he treated her—both when they were alone in their comfortable, warm lodge and in front of others.

She smiled again, thinking back to the first time she saw him three years ago. With Brooks's men, as was usual, he had come into her village near the confluence of the Salmon River and its East Fork. She was sixteen; he was twenty-three; she learned later. Her name then was Butterfly, and she was ready to take a man. Indeed, three of the finest young warriors of the village had been courting her, playing their flutes near her father's tipi at night, waiting along the paths that led to the river in hopes that she would pass and acknowledge them.

Her lithe grace and delicate features, though seen briefly, caught Cooper's eye. But he was not ready to marry again, not with the killing by Crows of his first wife, the Shoshoni Black Moon Woman, still fresh in his mind. But he kept her in his thoughts through the fall.

As she rode, she absentmindedly patted her stomach. It was time, she thought. She knew the ways of keeping from getting pregnant, and she had used them faithfully since she had been with Cooper. She had wanted to be sure he was not one of the many white men who, when tired of their Indian women, lodge-poled them somewhere and left them or traded them to some other trapper or to an Indian. Now, she was sure. This winter it would be time to change that, she thought, *Yes, for sure this winter...*

Brooks rode up alongside Cooper, who looked at his friend with bleary, bloodshot eyes. "You look a sight," Brooks said, trying to grin with little success.

"You ain't lookin' so good your own self." Cooper squinted into the sun, then said softly, "Damn, I am feelin' some poorly, that's certain."

"You ain't the onliest one," Brooks said. "Just look at the rest of the boys."

With a glance at the men with Milt Sublette and

Henry Fraeb, he figured they just as hungover and aching as he was, though the captains might not be.

He turned his blurry gaze back to his own partners and saw that none of the men was in any better shape than he was. All of them—Brooks, Zeke Potts, Bill White, Two-Faces Beaubien, Duncan MacTavish, Jacques Dubois, Luis Gamez, Paddy Murphy, Alistair Wentworth, Sam Bacon, George Miles, Dan Anderson, and the two newcomers, Dave wheeler, and Malachi Webster—looked ragged, each as sick as Cooper.

"Hell," Brooks growled, "we'll all get over it." He tried to grin again but mostly failed. "'Course. it ain't gettin' easier for an ol' coon like me." Brooks was tall and gangling, loose jointed, with a long, thin face and pointed, crooked nose. He was thirty-four, or thereabouts, and had been a mountain man for almost ten years now. He was the elected leader of their small band.

"You ain't that old. Just a crusty ol' critter." Cooper spit, then wiped his hand across his thin-lipped mouth.

"Mayhap you're right."

Cooper managed a weak smile. He was in his midtwenties now, and some thought him handsome. Long, straw-colored hair peeked out from the high, round-crowned hat, bunching on his shoulders. He was a little over medium height and build, with a strong, firm jawline and high cheekbones. "Might not be so bad if at least one didn't get over it none too soon."

"Webster?" Brooks asked.

Cooper nodded. "He's been nothin' but trouble since he hooked up with us last year. And it's gettin' worse." He had still not fully forgiven Brooks for allowing Gamez and Anderson to talk him into allowing Webster and Wheeler to join their small group of free trappers. Of course, they did not know at the time what incorrigible men Webster and Wheeler were, though Cooper had had his suspicions, especially about Webster, when the two had joined at last year's rendezvous. He had even asked why Brooks had allowed it.

"There's enough men with us now without takin' on a few more, especially with one havin' a reputation like I've heard he does."

"Hell, that damned Luis, backed by Anderson, told 'em they could join us," Brooks answered. "Wasn't much I can do. Even if you boys elected me captain, I don't have the right to turn down anyone who another member's brought in. I told them I was against the idea, but they both vouched for 'em. Besides, never enough hands to have if we encounter Bug's Boys."

Cooper had accepted it but was sure there was going to be trouble. Those suspicions grew over the past year, as Webster became more and more troublesome.

"Nothin' can be done about it now," Brooks said. He grimaced. "Damn, for certain I'm gettin' too old fer this foolishment," he mumbled. "That damned Taos Lightnin' likely'll be the end of me one of these days." Then he grinned. "But damn, these here was high doin's, now weren't they?"

"Shinin' times," Cooper said, life growing in him a little. He glanced back at Goes Far and managed a little smile.

"Ye got yourself a good 'un there, boy," Brooks said with a nod toward Goes Far. This chil'd do well to find one like her."

"Might be possible. Keep your eyes peeled on the

Nez Perce while we're travelin' with them. Maybe pick you out one who seems likely. When we stop and they put together their lodges, you can make your case with her pa."

"Bah. Ain't never worked in the time I've known the Nez Perce. Ain't gonna change now. Ye know this ol' coon ain't had a lick of luck when it comes to women. Remember that Crow gal? What'n hell was her name...?"

"One Eye."

"Yep, that were it. Damn she was a wretched critter. Don't know what I ever saw in that 'un." He allowed a chuckle.

"Me neither." Cooper laughed and realized that he was feeling a tad better.

"And then that damned Flathead. Gabby I called her. All she did was flap her gums. Never shut up fer a minute." He was laughing full now.

"Dammit, Elson, stop tryin' to make me laugh," Cooper said, holding his stomach. He wasn't that much better yet. "I'll get sick again you keep it up."

"It wasn't funny at the time," Brooks guffawed. "But the worst of the whole damned lot was..."

"No," Cooper gasped, "don't say it, El. Please. Don't talk about her..."

"Falls Back. Goddamn, she was..." He had to stop talking because he was laughing so hard that tears had formed. He groaned as his stomach lurched.

"Give it up, El. I'm gettin' sick again with all this shakin'."

But Brooks would not let up. He took a deep breath and settled himself. "Damn wolf bitch'd sleep with anything—man, woman, horses. I even thought I smelled goat on her once. And, I swear"—he doubled over with laughter—"I swear she was in love with that ol' silver-backed griz up on the Musselshell."

"They made a nice pair, them two." Cooper laughed, sucking in air to both calm himself and settle his stomach. "I even heard they had their own lodge."

"I ain't so sure I'll ever find me a good woman," Brooks said, finally managing to catch his breath.

"Don't you fret, El. We'll find you one. You just got to keep your pants on long enough once you see a woman to find out what she's like.

"Ain't likely." Brooks broke wind and moaned. "Ain't been able to do so in all the years I've know these people. Damn, that's the last time this chil's gonna partake of that gut-twistin' Taos Lightnin'." Then he grinned a bit. "But damn, these here was high doin's, now weren't they?"

"Shinin' times," Cooper said, life growing in him a little.

ONE

Late spring 1830

"THINK the mule's still there, Hawley?" Zeke Potts asked as he stuck another hunk of elk into his mouth.

Both men ignored the bodies of the Crow warriors they had just killed lying around the small campsite.

"Like as not he's long gone," Hawley Cooper responded, also gobbling down a piece of half-raw elk. "But knowin' how cantankerous that critter is, he might still be there just waitin' to give me more grief. If it ain't there, we'll figure something out. Maybe we can trade for a couple mules or horses."

"With who? Ain't no one around there but Crows and Blackfeet far as I know. And neither of 'em has any likin' for us—well, you at least."

Cooper just grunted, annoyed that there was no real answer, in part because the fact that he had gotten revenge for his wife's killing at the hands of these Crows had not quite settled on him yet.

ng that, Potts asked, "Want me to check on
tter?"

"Nah. I'll do so. If the beast is there, it's more used
to me. You see if you can rope a couple of these Crow
ponies. We might have need to use 'em when we find
my plunder. If the mule ain't where we left it, maybe
we can use the ponies."

"Crow horses ain't used to packin', Hawl."

"I know that, but they'll learn, dammit, should we
need 'em." Cooper finished chewing, then rose.
"Should've been horses stolen from other mountaineers." Cooper sighed. "Be back directly."

When he returned more than two hours later, with
the mule, Potts had three Crow ponies hobbled and
grazing nearby; two had basic Indian saddles, the other
a white man's saddle, stolen from some mountaineer,
the two mountain men figured. He had also dragged the
Crow bodies out of the immediate area lest the scavengers make an appearance.

"Looks like we both had some luck," Potts said. He
was back at the fire eating again but had slowed down
considerably.

Cooper just nodded, tied the mule to a tree, and sat.
"Have any trouble?"

"Nope. Surprised the hell out of me but those
ponies were easy to gather up. The other four got away,
though."

"Three'll be enough, I reckon. Dependin' on how
much of my plunder we find at the old camp, maybe we
can just use the mule and one pony. We can use the
others for tradin' should that become necessary, or even
possible."

"Ye know, Hawl, don't ye, that if we go straight to

where rendezvous is, we won't have nothin' to trade in. If we get your plunder first and then head to rendezvous, those festivities might well be over."

"Hadn't thought of that. My only concern's been for catchin' Black Moon's killers. Now that I think on it, though, I reckon you're right. Fetchin' my plews *is* a hell of a lot closer than rendezvous, but if that's over, we'll have wasted a heap of time."

"I figure it'd be best to go where ye left the plews and everything else and cache the furs, if there's enough to make it worthwhile. We'll take what supplies we can find and head into the Absarokas. Make our own fall hunt. Winter up that way. Come spring, we'll head to next year's rendezvous, stoppin' to pick up the cached plews along the way."

"Don't know where that rendezvous will be, Zeke."

"Ah, hell, Hawl, we're bound to run into some other mountain boys along the way who'll know."

"Likely," Cooper agreed. "Be short on supplies maybe. I ain't sure anything'll be left. Lots of mountaineers roaming these mountains as well as damn Injuns, especially Crows." A spark of anger kindled in his insides. "Critters likely got into any food that was left."

"Don't need much. Long as there's Galena and Dupont, we can fill our meatbags. Your traps'll need to be there, though, or it'll mean we need to try to find El. Havin' just mine will cut down on the furs we pull in."

"You maybe ain't so dumb for a youngster."

"Youngster? I ain't but a couple, three years younger than ye, ye old fart."

Cooper nodded but considered it. "Might make more sense to cache the plews, if they're still there, and then try to find El and the others rather than wait 'til next summer," Cooper said. "They should be well supplied after rendezvous. We can get what we need from them. Reckon we can catch 'em dependin' on where they're headed. Which is...?"

"Likely up toward Nez Perce country first, like usual, though it's a far piece. Good trappin' up there, and since a few of the boys' wives are Nez Perce, they can spend a bit more time with the people, let the young'uns live among the Nez Perce a little, absorbin' some of their ways."

"Where'll they go after that?"

"Head toward the Three Forks, I'm guessin'. It's what we did last year."

"Dangerous country up that way," Cooper said. "'Least that's what El said."

"Yep. It is, though we were lucky last year. Some of the other boys we talked to weren't so fortunate."

"Mayhap we can do both. Chase after El but do some trappin' as we go."

Potts grinned. "With us two bein' able to make beaver come with the best of the mountaineers, we'll likely pile up the pelts."

"Even with only your traps if we can't find mine?"

"Damn. Well, we'll both be runnin' the traps together anyway. We'll just split up those we find."

Cooper nodded.

"Another trouble is, like you said, the only animals to carry 'em are those Crow ponies, and there ain't enough of 'em. So, we could cache those plews too."

"Wouldn't work, Zeke. We'd have plews cached all over the mountains and spend more time pickin' 'em all up next summer we'd never get to rendezvous then either." He sighed. "I'm thinkin' your idea of makin' our own hunt after cachin' these plews—if they're still there and in tradeable shape—makes sense."

"One other thing, Hawl," Potts said quietly. When Cooper looked at him in question, he added, "Ye won't be able to see your Shoshoni friends."

Cooper stroked his long beard, then nodded. "Don't know if I could face 'em now anyway," he said softly.

———————

IT TOOK them more than two weeks to reach the spot along Clark Fork where Black Moon Woman had been taken, and the closer they got the more Cooper dallied.

"You've got to face this, Hawley," Potts finally said. "I know it ain't easy, but you're a tough ol' critter."

"Not for this, Zeke. I've faced all manner of hard times, things no chil' should go through, but this is one of the hardest, boy. Plumb hardest 'cept for tellin' the Shoshonis that Black Moon was gone."

"I know, Hawley, but this young snot knows ye can do it." He paused, then grinned. "Let's make tracks, ol' hoss. I want to see how many plews we—I mean ye—got and whatever other plunder ye left behind. Might be enough Lightnin' to have us a little spree."

Cooper looked at him as if he were insane, then sighed heavily and kicked his horse into motion. When he reached the old encampment, he sat on his horse and surveyed the site. No one seemed to have been there, which was good, but his mind drifted to his last time there. The gunfire, the shrieks of the orphaned baby Left Behind; dead, scalped Crows; an abandoned woman's saddle. He could see the enemy, smell them, even feel them, as it had been when he fought for his life and for Black Moon Woman's life as well as that of Left Behind. But it had been to no avail; he had been knocked down into the gully and could not get back up out of it in time to save them—the Crows were gone, not only taking the woman and child, but also the horses. Sickness, an acid roiling, grabbed his innards and twisted them mercilessly. He wanted to vomit out all the vileness, all the horror, all the loss and loneliness, all the despair and self-disgust. And hate. But he could not. The sickness sat inside him, evil, living, breathing.

He became aware of a faint voice calling his name over and over. Finally, he opened his eyes to see a worried Zeke Potts yelling at him to wake up out of his stupor.

Cooper shook his head to clear the webs of dread from his mind. "I'm all right now, boy," he growled in a soft voice.

"Ye sure?"

Cooper nodded, then managed a half grin. "As best I can expect, I reckon. Maybe I ain't a whole me yet, but I suppose I'll get there. Get a fire started while I tend the animals."

It took a bit to tend the animals, what with there being the men's two horses, a mule and the three Crow ponies.

"I RECKON IT'S TIME," Cooper said. They had eaten some elk that Potts had shot that morning, set up a small lean-to, and were sitting with another cup of coffee, the last they had. "There's still daylight left." His voice sounded far away to him.

"I can go take a look," Potts said. His face showed his concern for his friend and mentor.

"No. It's my plunder, and I best see to it."

"But I..."

"You can help get it all—whatever's left that's serviceable—back up here and then cache it."

"Old man like ye needs to be careful not to overdo things, ol' hoss," Potts said with a small grin.

"I ain't ever scalped me a snot-faced young white feller before, but there's always a first time." He tried a smile and almost succeeded. "Let's go."

"THERE'S a heap of plunder down there, Hawl," Potts said, looking down into the gully at the mess of equipment and packs of furs that Cooper had tossed down it when he had gone chasing after the Crows who had stolen his woman last winter.

"Yep. I just hope most of it's all right."

"Well, we best get to haulin' it up."

"Mornin's soon enough, Zeke," Cooper said.

Potts glanced at him in surprise but said nothing when he saw the look of sadness of his friend's face.

"HOW'S THINGS LOOK?" Potts questioned anxiously.

"Let me look, dammit," Cooper snapped. "Lord a'mighty if you ain't an impatient cuss."

"Well, if I was to wait for ye we might be here 'til Christmastime was upon us."

"Elson must be a saint," Cooper said as he started looking through all the things he had thrown down into the gully.

"Why's that?" a surprised Potts asked.

"For puttin' up with a devil like you he's got to be a saintly man. Now stop flappin' your gums and let me look."

"Well?" Potts called down after waiting all of ten minutes.

"Animals got to the saddles pretty much. Don't know why they didn't finish ' em completely. Maybe with winter comin' on they moved on lookin' for a place to hole up. Pemmican and jerky are gone, like we expected. Blankets are pretty well down to rags, what's left of 'em."

"We don't need blankets this time of year."

Cooper ignored him. "Somethin' good, a brace of horse pistols. And they did leave the coffee alone, lord knows why."

"Well, hallelujah on that at least. How about the plews?"

"They're still in the packs. They're half buried under rocks, dirt, tree branches and such brought down by floodin', and caked with old mud. The corner of one is torn open. The plews've been gnawed on some, but I don't think they're too far gone that I can't sell 'em." Suddenly he cursed.

"What is it?" Potts asked.

"The traps. They're here, but in the mud. The sack split and they're mighty rusted."

"Maybe you can fix 'em?"

"Hope so. There's some sperm oil down here that might help. Without 'em we're in for hard times." He searched some more. "Waugh! Found two extra pistols. They'll need some work, too. Also found Black Moon's rifle and pistol. Some tarps are muddy but seem all right. Best thing is, with most of the powder bein' in tin canisters, it should be fine. Unless some water seeped into the cans, which ain't likely seein' as how the caps on the tins are screwed down tight."

"We're in luck then. Reckon we ought to start haulin' things up?"

"Yep," Cooper said with a sigh that Potts could not hear.

Potts tossed a rawhide rope down.

It took much of the day, but they finally had hauled up much of everything Cooper thought was usable.

Cooper more closely examined the two packs of furs and determined that while some of those in one pack were indeed damaged, a portion of them severely, his early assessment of them being salable still held true. There were pots and pans that might be usable, though others were of iron and had rusted to the point of being unserviceable. What trade trinkets that hadn't become buried in the mud or swept downstream were mostly unscathed.

"I wonder why critters didn't get more of this plunder, Hawl," Potts said as they sat to supper. "Like ye said, the coffee was untouched, and that seems mighty odd. Should be good though if they haven't been leached out by the water. Sugar and salt are gone, as is the rest of the food. But why didn't they latch on to the plews?"

"Likely it was just luck. Best I can figure, it was

winter or nearly so, and the bears were hibernatin' or ready to. Don't know about wolves. Maybe they found better pickin's elsewhere. Plus they were covered with debris. Hell, I don't know." He shrugged. "Same thing when spring came. Bears and wolves wandered else-where 'cause they found good feedin' elsewhere. I just thank the Almighty that they're here and undamaged."

He shuddered, thinking back two years ago, when storms had sent his pack mutes fleeing, carrying all his and his woman's supplies and all the furs into the white blankness. He had recovered a few but not many. He had been mighty glad he found these intact.

That afternoon, they hung several tarps from trees and the next day they knocked the dried mud off with tree branches.

They spent two more days taking inventory, cleaning up what they could and casting aside what they couldn't use. Cooper made two more trips into the gully, checking more closely, trying to make sure he did not overlook something that could be of use. But there was little—a few more small trade items—that could be salvaged.

"We'll start the cache tomorrow?" Potts asked that night.

"Yep."

TWO

"I JUST THOUGHT OF SOMETHING, HAWL,"
Potts asked at the two men bedded down, "did ye see a
shovel down there? If there is, I missed it. Be damn difficult to cache a bunch of plews or anything else without
a shovel to dig the hole."

"There's a horn spoon in the plunder somewhere.
You should be able to use that to dig a big enough hole.
Might take you a spell, but a young feller like you can
do it."

"If I haven't told ye before, Hawley, go to hell."

Cooper grunted. "Been there, Zeke, twice, and it
ain't fire and brimstone like the preachers tell us. No,
sir, boy, it's cold, brutal goddamn cold. Cold that goes
right down into your bones and freezes the marrow.
Cold that puts icicles on your beard and mustache and
even your eyebrows. Makes your pizzle and stones try
to crawl up into your belly. Kills horses, too, leavin' a
man afoot. And wind, freezin', bitter goddamn wind
that batters you from side to side, knocks you down,
won't let you up as often as not. Snow that won't stop

for days 'til it gets to be chest deep in some places. Sleet, hail. Trees crackin' from the ice, makin' you think someone's shootin' at you. Wind, snow, and sleet make it damn hard to start a fire or keep one goin' if you do. No, boy, hell ain't fire. It's just the opposite."

"Jesus, Hawley, it was that bad what you went through? I heard stories but never knew whether to believe 'em."

"Yep, it was that bad." A shiver slithered through Cooper as he thought back to the past three winters, especially his first two in the mountains, times when the weather was infinitely more savage than any wild animal or Indian warrior.

"Lordy, Hawl, I hope if I ever encounter such troubles that I'll have your courage to face 'em."

"Doesn't take courage, Zeke. Just a will to live. And a feller doesn't know he has that will until it's put to the test. At least it was that way for me."

"You're one tough critter, Hawl, even if ye are a skinny old man." Before Cooper could say anything, Potts added, "It might not mean much comin' from me, Hawley, but I think you're a far braver and tougher man than ye might think ye are. And it's a damn fact ye got a strong will. Ye showed that by comin' here and doin' what needed doin'."

"You're a fool to believe such nonsense, boy."

"Like hell I am. What ye been through would've killed just about any feller I know."

"Just close your trap, boy, and go to sleep. And yes," he added as he rose, "I found a shovel when you were pilin' some things over there by that tree." He stretched out on his bedroll, but he had a tough time falling asleep, haunted as he was by the events that had happened here not so long ago.

COOPER SEARCHED AROUND a bit until he found a likely spot for a cache under some brush away from any aspens, whose roots ran long distances, tying together groves of the stark white trees.

Cooper handed Potts the shovel. "Here ya go, hoss. You seem strong, and you bein' so young and vigorous, and havin' all that energy you're not expendin' on women, you can do the diggin'."

Potts grumbled but attacked his work with a vengeance. He knew Cooper was still uncomfortable being here, that the place held haunting images for him, so he wanted to help his friend get away from here as soon as possible.

Cooper went back down into the gully and with his hands and much later with the shovel buried in the mud what was left that they couldn't use. Afterward, he did spell Potts at one point. Potts did not want to let him spend too much time digging until he realized that the work helped Cooper keep his mind off what had happened here.

It was done by early evening. And the two men took the time for a leisurely meal. But there was still daylight, so they lined the hole with canvas tarps, then deposited the two packs of plews as well as some powder and lead. With only one shovel, Potts piled the dirt back into the hole. It was dark when he finished, but Cooper spent time working to disguise the cache.

He finished that in the morning and was pleased with his work.

"Hell, we don't mark the spot," Potts said, "we won't be able to find it ourselves when the time comes."

"Hope you're right, boy. Hope you're right."

They relaxed as best they could, a difficult task for Cooper, for the rest of the day. As they sat gnawing on deer, Potts asked, "Whereaway now, Hawl?"

Cooper sat in thought for a spell. The Absarokas were close and there should be good trapping there, but they weren't far from here, where Black Moon Woman had been taken. The Bighorns and Powder River country were back the way they had just come, but those places held bad memories for him too. "Don't know, Zeke," he finally said. "I know the country 'round here pretty well, but not many other places."

"Like I said, best I can figure is that El and the others will be headin' to Nez Perce country at first, then move east. The Nez Perce are mighty friendly to us mountaineers."

"And that's where that woman you want is, ain't it?"

Potts grinned ruefully. "It is." He shifted a bit uncomfortably. "Still, we head northwest through the Absarokas, we might run into those boys somewhere. They won't stay with the Nez Perce long before headin' east."

"Sounds like a good way to go then."

"Trouble is, as best I can figure, it'll take us up near Three Forks, the heart of Blackfoot country."

"That might not be so good."

"No," Potts said dryly. "Reckon we can afford it if we're careful. Best trappin' grounds up that way, I hear.

'Course we might even run into El and the boys there since that's where they're likely headed."

"Then I reckon that's the way we'll go."

In the morning, while Potts packed up their few belongings, Cooper tore down their lean-to. They packed what they could use on the mule, then piled the scraps of what had been Cooper's gear when Black Moon Woman was taken onto a hastily made small travois. As they rode, they stopped periodically and tossed the debris into various spots along the gully, which stretched for some miles.

"Why're you doin' this, Hawl?" Potts asked as they stopped to do so for the third time.

"Anyone comes through that camp and sees these things layin' about in one spot, they'll figure folks have been here and might start lookin' for a cache. No need to take that chance when we can drop this plunder where it won't raise any suspicions."

AS THEY RODE side by side, Potts towing the mule and the three Crow ponies, after dumping all the debris, Cooper asked, "You said you went into Blackfoot country, you have any trouble with those devilish critters?"

"Not much. Just one battle that lasted less than half an hour before we sent 'em runnin' off like whipped dogs. 'Course there weren't but a dozen or so of 'em, and we surprised 'em, so it wasn't much of a battle. Met some other fellers who had a run-in with 'em and didn't come out nearly as well as we did. Lost several men, as well as horses, plews and such." He paused. "Ye ever fight 'em?"

"Twice, once when I was with the Shoshoni. We took care of 'em pretty well, too. Another time at rendezvous a year or so before I hooked up with El and the fellers. That was tougher, but we finally run 'em off. They were damn fools to go attackin' us, but you could tell they'd be real demons should they really put their minds to it or outnumber you by a heap."

"How'd the trouble with the Crows start? I always heard they were mostly friendly to us white men."

"I've heard the same. But you can't trust 'em, I've found. Not for a minute. Others've said the same. Those bastards'll act like they're your best friends, then run off with anything and everything they can get their hands on first chance they get, especially horses. Best damn horse thieves in the mountains. Our trouble with 'em just come on me and Black Moon. Several of 'em was headin' toward us lookin' like they were half froze to raise hair. Outnumbered by so much as we were, I figured that if they didn't kill us, they would've taken everything, including Black Moon. I couldn't allow that. So I put an end to that notion. Got 'em all but one. I don't think he saw me, but I can't be sure. Not long after, we found the baby."

"Left Behind?"

"Yep. His folks were Crows killed by the Blackfeet we figured. Reckon the Crows might've thought I did it. Later a couple of 'em came lookin' for presents, like our horses. Or so they said. Now that I think back on it, they might've been spyin' on us, seein' if they could find the baby. When I sent 'em on their way with a bit of tobacco, they left. They didn't see Left Behind, but like

I said, they might've figured I killed the family, so they chased after us. We fought 'em off a few days later, but I reckon the one that got away saw the baby and figured he was Crow. They seem to have wanted to get the child. So a couple months later they attacked and took Black Moon."

"And the baby?"

"Yep." The single word contained a world of hate.

"Well, it don't help much," Potts said softly, "and it won't bring Black Moon back, but we raised hair on the sumbitches who did you and her wrong."

"That we did, Zeke." It came out tired, almost forlorn.

Potts started to speak, then realized right away that no matter what he said would be wrong or useless.

THREE

AS WAS OFTEN THE CASE, the Blackfeet seemed to come out of nowhere. One moment there were trees and bushes whose leaves were blowing lazily in the breeze, and the next, eight screeching warriors were rushing at Cooper and Potts on foot from behind the foliage.

The two mountain men darted into the brush off the slim trail and slid out of their saddles, each leaving his rifle in the loop behind the saddle horn with no time to pull it free. They would be useless in the close confines of the small, foliage-heavy battleground anyway as would the Indian's bows.

Cooper managed to get one pistol out and blasted a Blackfoot who was within five feet of him. But he could not reach his other pistol before he had to duck the hard swing of a tomahawk in the hands of another warrior. He batted the weapon away, grabbed his knife from its beaded sheath and ripped it through the Indian's innards all in one swift move.

Potts also managed to shoot one of the warriors

before being overwhelmed by two Blackfeet bent on capturing him for their amusement while torturing him. He fought like a demon but was losing the battle when Cooper finally got his other pistol out and blasted one of those warriors.

Facing only one Indian now, Potts knocked him off, rose and kicked him in the face. He ducked just as another Blackfoot slashed at him. The knife's blade slid down Potts's back, and he fell forward, landing on top of the warrior he had kicked. He rolled to the side and came to his feet, pulling his own knife as he did. He feinted once, then shoved the point home into the warrior's heart.

The last two Blackfeet fled on foot, racing across the stream, not even bothering to try to grab ponies, which had wandered throughout the foliage.

Potts finished off the last of the Blackfeet lying there, then he and Cooper collected the scalps, cleaned their knives, and reloaded their weapons. Then they gathered the Blackfoot ponies, which took some time because the animals were so skittish, as well as the mule and the three Crow ponies. But finally the two mountain men had all eleven horses and the mule tied together.

"Best let me look at that wound, Zeke," Cooper said.

"Ain't nothin'."

Like you told me not so long ago, lettin' a wound sit untended is a good way to set it festerin', which won't be good, eh?"

"Reckon not. All right, take a look, but make it fast. Those two Bug's Boys who run off might come back with a passel of friends. Hell, we ain't even in Blackfoot country yet, and ye know those devils, they'll raid anyplace."

"Got scared all of a sudden?" Cooper asked with a grin.

"Not scared, ol' hoss. Just cautious. And sensible."

"Reckon that's true."

The wound turned out to be little more than a scratch. Cooper threw some water on it to remove the dirt and proclaimed Potts ready to go.

They rode off, Cooper in the lead, Potts behind with a string of Blackfoot and Crow ponies trailing him.

THEY ENTERED the Absarokas and wound their way deeper into those mountains. The two were wary, even a little concerned as they were in Crow country. Cooper had had more than enough trouble with those Indians, and really did not want more.

The going was rough and tiring. There often was no trail and the two mountain men had to hack their way up and down foliage-choked mountains; they had to avoid cliffs and steep canyons that sometimes offered no way out, so they had to backtrack. There were waterfalls to go around, and time spent trying to find a place to ford a river where the current was not rushing over rocks, spurring whitecaps. The ponies also were not happy with being tied together and often fussed at the ropes, making it difficult for Potts to keep hold of them. Cooper took his turn leading the animals on occasion, offering his younger companion some relief.

Not helping was the fact that they had to stand guard every night lest the Blackfeet or Crows come for scalps and the horses. With splitting the guard duty, the two never got enough sleep, so they were always tired, and both were growing cantankerous. Making matters worse, fall was just about on them.

Finally, Cooper said, "This is far enough. For now."

"We're stoppin'?"

"Yep. For a few days. We need rest, boy. We can recruit ourselves and let the horses do the same."

Potts nodded. "Give us time to get a little meat, too."

"Can't do too much. We don't need to attract the attention of Bug's Boys or any other hostile Injuns. I'll set to tendin' the horses and then makin' a fire whilst you go off to make neat. Just don't stray too far."

"I won't."

"And no more than one shot," Cooper yelled as his friend Potts disappeared into the forest.

Twenty minutes later, Cooper heard a gunshot, but it was another hour before Potts arrived back at the camp with a large selection of the best cuts of elk across his horse.

"You did well, boy," Cooper said. He was just getting the fire started after taking care of the animals and gathering a decent supply of firewood. They ate well that night and the next, but the day after, a storm swept over them with gradually increasing snow that as temperatures rose a little turned into pounding sheets of sleet, then rain, washing out the fire. Lightning sparked across the sky and thunder rumbled over the land, bouncing from one mountain to another, spooking the horses, who had to be calmed frequently.

The two men had seen it coming and had hastily

created a lean-to, but the crude shelter was far from waterproof.

"Damn if this don't beat all," Potts snarled. "Waugh! I was just startin' to relax and regain some energy."

"It don't shine, that's for certain." Cooper hunkered a little deeper into his buffalo robe. "And there ain't a damn thing we can do about it."

"Well, I can grouse about it." Suddenly Potts chuckled. "Of course, that won't do anything about the rain and it'll set ye to grumblin'.'"

"That's a fact," but Cooper also chuckled. "One good thing, though."

"What's that?" Potts asked.

"We don't have to worry about some Injuns tryim' to steal our horses."

The storm lasted two full days and part of a third before it finally drifted away, leaving behind broken branches and a mud lake. Cooper took the time to work on his traps.

Before the storm arrived, Cooper had had enough sense to cover their small supply of firewood with a tarp. When the rain stopped, he found enough dry twigs that starting a fire with the tinder he had saved was not that difficult. Before long, they were hungrily devouring large amounts of elk meat, not having really had anything to eat since the rain came.

"You stay and keep an eye on things, Zeke. I'll do the huntin' this time," Cooper said.

"Just mark your trail. With the ground dryin' and sendin' this mist up with it, you could get lost without payin' attention."

"I'll be mindful of that." He returned two hours

later with plenty of deer meat wrapped in the animal's hide.

There was more relief that evening when Cooper pronounced his traps back in working order.

"About time," Potts growled. But he grinned.

———————

"DAMN," Cooper said with a scowl.

"What is it, Hawl?" Potts asked, figuring he knew.

"More Injuns comin', dammit."

It was little more than a week since their battle with the Blackfeet. Cooper was tired of Indian trouble and strongly wanted nothing to do with more.

Four Crow warriors came wandering through the forest and stopped not far from Cooper. They were accompanied by three women, which meant they likely were not a war party. Potts tensed up more than Cooper and the latter almost smiled when he saw the hungry look on Potts's face when the younger man spotted one of the Crow women heading toward the stream. Cooper thought the woman cast an interested glance at the two mountain men.

"Let me have some of the jingly tin cones and a few beads, Hawl," Potts said urgently.

"Think that woman's gonna spread her legs for you?"

"I aim to find out. It's been far too long since I dipped my wick."

"You'll be lucky you don't lose your wick. Or maybe just your hair," Cooper said with a grin. "Go grab what you need, just don't get too greedy, we ain't got much."

"Thanks, Hawl." He handed the rope to all the

animals to Cooper and rushed to the mule to grab a few items. Minutes later, grunts and shrieks of pleasure came swarming over the others, who tried their best to ignore them, though chuckles rippled from both sides, which helped as they shared some lightness instead of trying to kill each other or the Crows demanding presents.

Still, it was a tense time before Potts and the woman popped out of the bushes, adjusting their clothing. Potts mounted his horse.

"Untie one of these ponies and hand it over to that Crow in the middle who looks like he's the leader."

Potts was surprised but did as he was told and received a nod from the warrior. Potts took the rope to the rest of the animals and he and Cooper saluted the Crows and rode off. Shortly down the trail, Cooper drifted back to make sure he and Potts were not being followed. They weren't.

"You satisfied now, Zeke?" Cooper asked when he returned to ride alongside his companion.

"For now." Potts grinned. "Won't be long though before I get the itch again."

FOUR

"HOW'D you get out here, Hawl?" Potts asked one night as they were sipping another coffee after filling themselves on a moose Potts had shot the day before.

They were taking a few days to trap some streams where they had found plenty of beaver sign.

"I was a damn fool, Zeke. Dumber than you even, I reckon. I sometimes ain't got the brains of a tree trunk. I was down and out in St. Louis when an old reprobate named Josiah Weeks hired me on as a camp helper with a promise of trainin' me to be a trapper. He had no such plan, I found out before long, but it was too late. He just wanted someone to do his foul work for him while he sat on his ass eatin', smokin' his pipe, and drinkin'. And," Cooper added angrily, "sportin' with an Injun woman he had picked up. A Pawnee named Tall Grass.

"Wasn't all bad, though, just ninety-five percent of the time. One of the good times was meetin' a Pawnee gal named Corn Flower. She introduced me to the ways a woman can please a man."

"First time?"

"Waugh! A wondrous day that was, I'm tellin' you."

"I can understand that, havin' had my first time with a gal lived a few houses down in St. Louis. Turned my head around for all time."

"Women'll do that for a man, yep. I also learned to fight Injuns. I don't know as if you could call that a good thing, but it's served me in good stead. Anyway, Weeks treated Tall Grass even more poorly than he did me. I protected her a time or two, and to show her thanks, she shared my robes a few times when Weeks was passed out drunk. He found out about it, though, banged me over the head and left me with nothin' in the heart of winter. Only thing I had was a few strips of jerky and a pocketknife I had hidden away. Other than that, nothin', no blanket, no coat, no gloves, no rifle, no pistol."

"Damn, that was evil."

Cooper grinned crookedly. "You could say that, yep. I started makin' my way to I knew not where. I just kept movin', fightin' animals, fightin' freezin' streams and rivers, fightin' snow and cold." He held up his hand showing the missing tip of the pinky. "Had to cut that off because it had frozen. I was fightin' a pack of wolves when I went down. I figured I was gone beaver for sure. Took me several of those critters with me, though."

"Well, it's sure a fact ye lived, as I can see with my own eyes."

"That I did. A Shoshoni war chief named Cheyenne Killer was out huntin' and found me. He brought me to his village. His wives and daughter nursed me back to health. He even adopted me. His daughter who cared for me, Pony Woman, was the most beautiful gal I'd ever seen. Good with carin', a good cook, funny. I fell in love with her right off. But since Cheyenne Killer adopted me, she was my sister, so I couldn't marry her."

"Then how'd ye and Black Moon..."

"She was Pony Woman's best friend, and Pony introduced us. Black Moon was every bit as beautiful as Pony, and her equal in all other ways that I could learn at the time. But she was betrothed to a young warrior about my age named Cuts Throat. One tough feller that one. In battle, he could live up to his name."

"I gotta ask again. How'd ye and Black Moon..."

"Like I said, sometimes I'm as dumb as a clump of dirt, and I foolishly challenged Cuts Throat to a fight over her hand. Lordy, I don't know how I beat that ol' hoss. Waugh! He's a strong one. But I managed somehow, and Black Moon became mine."

"And Pony Woman?"

Cooper grinned. "Well, she up and married Cuts Throat, who became my best friend among the Shoshoni."

"Damn, that's some tale." Seeing Cooper's face darken in anger, Potts quickly added, "Dammit, Hawley, ye know I don't mean a fanciful tale, I mean a story, a real story, like the knights of old I've heard about."

Cooper nodded. "I ain't so sure that's true, but it has been some life so far. Never thought I'd see such things or go through some of the things I have."

"Ye ever want to go back east to the States?"

"Why in the hell for?" Cooper asked with a laugh.

"Be some safer. No degenerate mountaineers, no

hostile Injuns, no smart-mouth young bucks who annoy ye all the time."

"True, I reckon. But, well, the first two don't bother me none, but that third one, lordy that might drive me out of the mountains."

"You seen Cuts Throat of late?"

"No. Haven't been back to Cheyenne Killer's village since I left when I took after the Crows who took Black Moon..." Cooper paused to let himself settle down a bit. "Might never go back. I reckon it'd be too hard."

"I think ye should. It always pays to have friends. Life's too precious to be without 'em. And Black Moon must've been a hell of a woman if she had two tough critters like ye and this Cuts Throat feller battling over her, and she was fool enough to marry a grumpy ol' critter like ye."

"You're pretty smart for a youngster."

"Bah. It's like as not none of my business, but I think ye should go back there for a visit. Or at least see them at rendezvous if they come."

"No, like I said, it'd be too painful."

"And ye don't think it's not painful for a friend to lose a friend? A woman to lose her brother? A father to lose his son? You're important to all those people, Hawley, and I bet ye have other friends there too. They'd know how painful it is for ye. It's painful for them too. Pony Woman's lost her best friend, Cuts Throat lost a sister-in-law, a woman he cared enough about to fight ye for her. I don't know about her parents or anything, but at least those two people miss her. I bet Cheyenne Killer does, too. She was his daughter-in-law."

"You keep flappin' your gums like this and you just might have me thinkin' that such might be a good idea."

"It is, Hawley. It might even bring a little peace to ye and the others despite the pain. Like I said many times in the short time we've known each other, you're about the toughest critter I ever met. Tougher than El or Two-Faces or Duncan or any of the others. Hell, there're times I think you're tougher than all them together."

"That's nonsense, boy. All of it's nonsense. Maybe you ain't as smart as I was thinkin' when you go spoutin' such foolishness. I reckon I'm tough enough, but no more than El or any of the fellers who ride with him."

"You're not only tougher'n all of 'em, but you're more stubborn than two mules pulling a rope in different directions if ye don't believe that."

"Waugh, you're a noise-makin' son of a bitch. Lots of sound but no sense in what comes out."

Potts considered getting angry, then grinned. "It takes a tough man to talk so poorly of himself when he has much to boast about. I'll say this though, ye may not think much of me but I'd never abandon friends or family that cared for me. My family doesn't give a damn about me, so I don't give a damn about them. But ye, after what I did to ye, have taken me under your care, I'd call ye my friend even if it's not reciprocated. And the way El talks about ye, even though he hasn't known ye long either, shows that he's a friend too. Are ye gonna abandon us too if times get hard?"

"Maybe I will, if ye and the others keep tossin' buffler droppin's at me like you've been doin'.'"

"Hell, Hawley, I give up. Ye ain't just stubborn, you're the most stubborn feller I ever met." Potts rose and headed off to his robes, for which he was grateful now that fall had firmly announced its arrival.

Cooper sat there for some time, thinking about what Potts had said. He came to no conclusion other than he would have to think about it all, and that maybe he could see his way to visiting Cheyenne Killer's camp at rendezvous. He missed his father and friend and sister, and as painful as it might be to see them, it would be a welcome thing, too.

AS WINTER ADVANCED, the two men made meat when they could, but mostly they spent their time trapping, then curing the plews they pulled in. The furs were thick and lush.

"Reckon we'll get us some prime dollars for these plews, Zeke," Cooper crowed more than once.

But finally, Cooper said, "It's about time we found us a place to be winterin'."

"Why don't we just stay here?" Potts asked. "We been here a while and got things set up with shelter and such. There's wood and fodder for the animals as well as water."

"'Cause snow's up to my horse's pizzle and more's on the way. 'Cause the cold and wind'll be freezin' *your* pizzle. It just ain't a good place for winterin'."

Potts nodded. "So we'll pull out soon's we get the last of these plews cured?"

"Yep."

But it was not as easy as they had hoped. Two evenings after Cooper had made his decision, Blackfeet suddenly swooped down on the horse herd.

"Waugh!" Cooper shouted. "No you don't, you red devils!" He snatched up his rifle and fired, killing one Blackfoot. He darted into the woods, heading for the two picket lines of animals. He spotted Potts also heading for the herd.

Cooper pulled a pistol and shot a warrior who was untying one end of the picket rope in the back. He grabbed the rope and quickly tried to tie it back to the tree.

Potts fired his rifle but missed. He tossed the weapon down and grabbed a pistol. He raced ahead. A warrior had cut the other line holding the horses and leaped on one animal's back. Potts shot him in the side, then managed to get the rope tied again.

But the Blackfeet were racing away through the trees. Both mountain men fired pistols. Cooper thought he might have hit one of the warriors, but he could not be sure. Finally, all was quiet.

"How bad was it?" Cooper asked.

"Lost four on my side."

"One on mine."

"Bastards," Potts muttered. "I was figurin' we'd sell those horses at rendezvous to help supplement what plews we've brought in."

"It could be worse. They could've gotten 'em all. We still have five left not countin' our own, of course. We'll do all right." Cooper grinned ruefully. "Unless, of course, some of 'em die over the winter."

"You're just a bushel basket of good news, ain't you?"

TO THE MEN'S RELIEF, fall lasted long, pushing winter back, and the trapping was good. By the time they were ready to find a wintering place, each had almost two packs of plews each. Figuring to get more, they traded their five remaining Indian ponies to a roving band of Shoshonis—one unknown to Cooper— for two mules the Snakes had gotten in trade with some other mountaineers when the mules were worn down.

They found a secluded little valley that they thought would be a good wintering spot, but there was a contingent of half a dozen free trappers there already.

"Name's Jim Thorne," one of the men said. "You're welcome to stay right alongside us. Seems we'll have enough water and forage. You look to be mighty scarce on meat, and we got none to spare, but doin' something about that's your concern."

"Reckon we'll move where there might be more game," Cooper said. What he didn't say is that he wasn't sure he could trust these men, not after last year.

"If that's where your stick floats."

"It does. Do you know where next year's rendezvous will be?"

"Place called Cache Valley, west of Bear Lake."

"That's a far piece."

"Reckon it is, but it's a good place. Good for winterin', too, but I reckon it's full up already."

Cooper nodded. "Be too far for us now anyway. Obliged."

He and Potts moved off. They found another valley two days' ride northwest and settled in. Winter was harsh, and they went hungry many days since there was little game in the area. When they were lucky enough to get some fresh meat, they ate their fill but also dried some as best they could for jerky. Neither one was good at it, but they managed.

As winter began to wane, they took up their trapping again, moving from stream to stream, ending up with just under three packs each. They combined some into one pack.

Even before spring fully arrived, they found a spot where they could cache those plews and made tracks to where they had cached their other furs back along the Shoshone River. Then they pushed hard to pick up the new plews and head toward rendezvous, their mules loaded down.

"INJUNS COMIN', Hawl," Potts, who was riding out in front this time, called.

"What kind?" Cooper asked as he pulled up alongside his partner sitting on a small bluff overlooking the prairie.

"Ain't sure."

"They're..."

"What's wrong, Hawley?" Potts asked worriedly when he looked at Cooper's face, which was pasty. "What is it, Hawley? They bad Injuns? They ain't Crows or Blackfeet."

"Shoshonis," Cooper responded in a strangled voice.

"But they're friendly, ain't they?"

Cooper said nothing. Instead, still looking stricken, he rode forward.

Potts followed, wondering, and saw a few warriors riding their way.

Cooper stopped, Potts halted next to him, and the Indians stopped a few feet in front of them. To Potts, Cooper seemed to relax quite a bit.

"How dare you show your face, white-eyed devil," one of the latter said.

FIVE

"OH, SHIT," a suddenly worried Potts mumbled.

"Just to annoy you, you red-skin skunk."

Cooper handed the rope to the pack mules to Potts, and he and the Shoshoni dismounted, grinned, and hugged. Cooper stepped back. "Zeke, meet Cuts Throat, the worst warrior the Shoshonis ever put on a horse."

"Worst white warrior—all are bad—I know is this pale-face." The Indian grew serious. "It's good to see you, Hawley. You've been gone long time. Your father misses you. Sister, too. Even I miss you but don't know why."

"You miss me because I'm the only friend you got."

"I think Flat Nose is a friend." He chucked a thumb over his shoulder.

A warrior who actually had a long, fleshy nose, grinned. "Sometime," he said, and the others laughed.

"Flat Nose, you and the others go tell White Wolf Killer's father he is here."

"No," Cooper said. "I'll ride on around the band. They can just keep movin'."

"But..."

"I ain't ready to see all of you, Cuts Throat. I just ain't."

"Don't be a damn fool, Hawley," Potts said in irritation. "I told ye before how important friends and family are. Now let's go. If ye don't want to go, I'll go in there, if Cuts Throat and the others'll have me. Ye'll have to take care of the mules, though."

"You're welcome in village. Well, will soon be village. Flat Nose, let's go tell the People we have a visitor." He looked at Cooper. "Maybe two." He swung onto his pony's back in a single fluid motion and raced off with the others.

Cooper sucked in a deep breath, then blew it out through puffed cheeks.

Minutes later, Cheyenne Killer galloped out from the travelers, who had stopped and were putting up lodges, and halted in front of Cooper, who was still standing in front of his horse.

The Shoshoni's face split into a grin that Potts thought would tear his face apart. "Welcome, my son," he said, holding out his arms.

Cooper did not move.

The warrior looked as if he had been kicked in the heart, and his face dropped. He nodded and went to jump on his pony.

"Wait, Father." When the Indian turned to face him, Cooper tentatively moved forward, uncertain, then embraced the Shoshoni. "I ain't worthy of you, Father. Not after..."

"I have spoken of this before. Things are as they

are. All die, some too soon, others later. Your woman died too soon. You did what you had to do for revenge, eh?"

"Yes, he did," Potts threw in just in case Cooper was going to deny it.

"Then all is well. Come, we will have a feast. We..." He stopped when a woman galloped up and jerked to a stop.

She threw herself off the horse and charged at Cooper, then skidded to a stop.

Cheyenne Killer smiled softly. "Act like white woman this time."

Pony Woman grinned widely and hugged Cooper, who tentatively put his arms around Pony Woman.

"I missed you, brother," Pony Woman said with a bright smile.

"You don't hate me?" Cooper asked.

She jerked back and stared into his eyes. "Why would I hate you?"

"Because of Black...your friend who is no more."

"I should hate you 'cause some stinkin' Crows," she spit the last word, "took and killed her?"

"But it was my fault she was taken."

"Hogwash, I think your people say," Pony Woman said. "You could not help it, could not defeat all those Crows."

"You sure?"

"Yes. No more argue with us," Pony Woman said.

"Yes, ma'am."

Mounted, they all rode slowly toward where the village was swiftly being erected half a mile away along the Salt River east of Bear Lake. The four men dismounted and sat by the water, ignoring the activity around them. Pony Woman dismounted too but stayed a discreet distance away.

"Tell of revenge," Cheyenne Killer said softly.

"Not much to tell," Cooper replied quietly. "Me and Zeke here followed the Crow village as it was headed to rendezvous. Took a spell before we got the bastards who did it away from the others. Killed the three plus several of their friends."

"You have their scalps?"

"Nope. I pissed on 'em and left 'em lyin' in the dirt where they belong."

The others nodded, accepting and agreeing with it.

"Where is daughter-in-law restin'?" Cheyenne Killer asked quietly.

"A Crow lad helped me on my quest," Cooper said with a wry smile. "Despite being a Crow, he was a good young feller. He was killed in a rockslide. I buried my wife in the same spot some days later. I reckon it wasn't in the way you would've done it, but it was the best I could do, and it was mostly the way my people do such things."

"You did right," Cuts Throat said, a statement to which Cheyenne Killer nodded.

There was silence for some minutes. Then, "Were we too late for the rendezvous?" Cooper asked, tossing a pebble in the water. "You wouldn't be heading home if it wasn't over."

"Supply train never come. All waited as long as they could. Finally, men began leavin'. Get ready for fall hunt."

"Even without supplies?"

"Nothin' they could do."

"Looks like we're in trouble, Zeke. Got all these

plews and nothin' to do with 'em. And no supplies. We already spent one season out there with no supplies. We'll have even less this season."

"We have things. Give to you," Cheyenne Killer said.

"I can't let you..." He shut up when his father glared at him.

"Tonight, we have feast and dance in your honor, *Too-Shah-Itsup-Mah-Washay*—He-Who-Is-the-White-Wolf-Killer," Cheyenne Killer said. "Welcome my son back to the People."

"That ain't necessary." Cooper was embarrassed.

"Yes, it is," Cuts Throat said. "I didn't want to but before your sister came to greet you, she said she'll not share the robes with me again if we don't do this."

Potts was shocked—until he saw the look of humor on both Cheyenne Killer's face and Cuts Throat's. Then he looked over and saw Pony Woman standing a few feet away, also grinning.

"Well, if I refuse, she'll probably thank me for saving her from sharing the robes with you ever again."

Everyone laughed.

SIX

Summer 1831

"HELLO, THE CAMP," Cooper called out. "Couple of mountain boys comin' in." It wasn't quite dusk, but it was getting there fast.

"That ye, Hawley?"

"El?"

"Sure enough. Come on ahead, already."

Cooper and Potts rode into the camp, the latter with the three empty mules in a string behind him.

"Well, look at that," Elson Brooks said, shaking his head, pointing to the unladen mules. "Looks like ye boys've been snookered in trappin'."

"Actually, we had us a good hunt. Two packs each and another to split. We left 'em with Cheyenne Killer's band."

"Well, that's better news," Brooks said. "George, Duncan, help Zeke set up a picket line near ours for them mules."

Duncan MacTavish and George Miles hurried up.

"Aye, Cap'n, but we'll do better than that. Give me the rope, Zeke, lad. We'll care for 'em."

Potts handed over the line stringing the three pack animals together and dismounted. "Much obliged," he said, grateful.

"Bill, Alistair, take Hawley's and Zeke's horses and tend to 'em, please." To the latter two, he said, "C'mon, boys, looks like ye two need to fill your meatbags and down some coffee."

"That shines," Cooper said as he handed the reins to his horse to Alistair Wentworth and Potts did the same to Bill White.

They took a seat next to Two-faces Beaubien at one of the fires, where Brooks directed them. Both sliced off a chunk of buffalo meat that had been hanging over the embers and stuffed it in his face.

And they did it several more times, before sipping some of the coffee that Little Fox, a Flathead who was one of Beaubien's two woman, had poured for them.

"How came ye to be here, Hawl?" Brooks asked.

"After takin' care of the Crows I was after, we headed to the place where Black Moon had been taken." His anger surged again, and he fought it back. "I had dumped all my plunder down a gully. Luckily no one had been by there to disturb things. Zeke and I cached the plews I had taken before the Crows attacked. About then, we figured it was too late to make rendezvous, so we thought we might catch up to you on the trail. Zeke figured you'd be headed to Nez Perce land. But with few supplies and winter comin' on, we did some trappin' and wintered up."

Cooper looked around. "We heard supplies never showed up at rendezvous, but looks like you boys're well supplied, and it looks like there ain't many packs of beaver here." Cooper waved a hand around.

"True to both." Brooks filled and lit his pipe. "We got to Cache Valley and with a heap of other mountaineers waited and waited. A couple fellers had a cask of whiskey, and we broke that open, but that was about all the merriment we had. Hell, there weren't even tobacco to be had. Ever'body had run out. Waugh! Those were some poor doin's." He puffed angrily at the remembrance for a minute, then continued. "Along about the beginning of August we figured supplies weren't comin' so ever'body moved off, headin' toward where they planned their fall hunt."

"So where'd your plews go? Did you cache 'em somewhere? And where'd all these supplies come from?"

"Damnedest thing," Brooks said with a grin that was real this time. "We were movin' north a couple weeks later when Henry Fraeb came on us. That was almost a week ago. He had the supplies we'd all been waitin' for and was tryin' to reach as many boys as he could to get 'em to the folks. We were lucky he came on us early because he had plenty of goods. We traded him all our furs for whatever supplies we needed. Got just about everything."

"You traded in my plews too?"

"Yep. Got five dollars a pound in trade. Kept all yours separate, though I had to use two of my mules," Brooks said apologetically.

"Seems fair. Take it out of the money you got for my plews. If that ain't enough, I'll make up the difference when I trade in this year's catch."

Brooks nodded. "Want to go check the supplies we traded your plews for, Hawl?"

"Mornin's soon enough. We're some tired."

"Where're the Nez Perce? And the Flatheads? Thought you'd be with 'em," Cooper asked as he stretched out his legs toward the fire. It wasn't that cool, but he enjoyed the heat anyway.

"They had more sense than us. They realized early on that supplies weren't comin' so they left long before we did,"

"How far to Nez Perce country, El?"

"Just a couple more days, I figure, if they put their village near where they usually do."

"Hope it's soon."

"Why?"

Cooper grinned widely. "Zeke here's been mighty patient with himself, keepin' quiet about wantin' a woman, but he's been fidgety of late. Even though he did meet a willin' Crow woman on the trail and had a roll in the robes with a Shoshoni. Still, I think he was fixin' to have a go at one of the ponies had we had taken from some Blackfeet if we were on the trail much longer."

"Dammit, Hawley, I never indicated no such thing. I..." The rest of what he had to say was drowned out by the burst of laughter from everyone within hearing distance. As things quieted down, he said adamantly, "Ye boys just wait. Soon's we get to the village, I'm gonna pay old Pale Thunder for Mornin' Song and make her my woman."

"How're you gonna do that, Zeke?"

"With some of my trade goods, which I expect are among the rest of the supplies."

"You don't have any trade goods, Zeke," Cooper said with a small grin. "No supplies either for that matter."

"But El traded my..."

"They weren't your plews, remember?"

Potts was about to retort but closed his mouth, stewing in his sudden burst of anger. "Damn ye, El," he finally snapped, "for givin' up all my hard-earned plews. And damn ye, Hawley, for takin' 'em."

"Just remember why I gave 'em to Hawley," Brooks growled. "Ye hadn't helped some scoundrel destroy his camp and steal his animals and such, I wouldn't have had to give 'em away. If I hadn't you'd be pushin' up wildflowers back along the Yellowstone."

Potts sat there torn between anger and despair.

"How's this, Zeke? I'll loan you some supplies against the plews you took this season when we trade 'em in."

"Will there be enough to pay Pale Thunder the bride price for Mornin' Song?"

"Depends on how much that ol' thief is askin'."

"Deal, Hawl."

There was silence for a little. Brooks puffed on his pipe and Cooper and Potts sipped coffee as night settled over the camp.

Brooks finally knocked the ashes out of his small clay pipe and said, "Time for this chil' to get some robe time. Ye boys are welcome to spread your bedrolls wherever it pleases ye. My boys'll keep watch as they have been. Tomorrow night ye can join in that duty."

"Expecting trouble?" Potts asked.

"Always, Zeke, always. It's why I've lasted so long out here when many others haven't."

FOUR DAYS LATER, they reached the village of which Red Leggings was civil chief. Though the tribe and Brooks's group of mountain men had been together only a month ago at rendezvous, the reunion was treated as a grand one. A feast was prepared and eaten; wives of the mountaineers visited their families; drumming and dancing were joyous and unrestrained.

Potts waited, though not happily, for two days before he went to visit Pale Thunder, whom he asked for his daughter in marriage. The Indian told what he wanted, and Potts haggled with him until Pale Thunder would lower his price no more.

Worried, Potts found Cooper and explained what Pale Thunder had asked for.

"That's mighty steep, boy," Cooper said. "You sure you want this woman that much? There's a heap of other maidens here won't cost you near so much. Maybe just a handful of beads for a roll in the robes."

"The Nez Perce ain't like the Crows or some other tribes. Their women are more chaste than other Injuns."

"If they're so pure, how do you know Mornin' Song is the right one to warm your robes?"

Potts grinned. "I didn't say they were completely innocent, just not the type to throw away their favors for a handful of foofaraw."

"And how did you learn that she was not one to warm the robes for just some geegaws?"

"My charm convinced her that she wanted to be my woman."

"And a handful of foofaraw was the way she found out?"

"Could be." Potts paused and grew serious. "It doesn't matter how, Hawl. It's just..."

"I might give you the goods, but where're you gonna get the horse or horses I expect Pale Thunder asked for?"

"Told him I'd get the two when I traded in my plews down to rendezvous."

"You'll be stretched mighty thin between payin' me for the trade goods I'll be givin' you and then the horses."

"I'll make do."

"If you say so. All right, I'll give you the goods. You'll have to find the horses yourself. Remember, though, if she tosses your possibles out of the lodge, you're not gettin' anything more out of me."

"Obliged, Hawl." Potts could not keep the excitement out of his voice.

Cooper shook his head as he went along with Potts to gather up whatever the younger man would need.

COOPER SAT at his fire with a bullet mold in one hand and an iron dipper in the other. An iron pot holding melted lead rested in the fire. As he poured some lead into the mold, a young Nez Perce woman strolled by. Cooper sucked in a breath and spilled the dipper of hot metal. For a moment he thought Black Moon Woman had come back to life as a Nez Perce woman.

The woman kept her eyes downcast, but glanced

over and smiled shyly at him, blushed and kept on walking.

Cooper shook his head and took a deep breath. He realized she looked little like his dead wife when Black Moon had married him, and he wondered why he had thought she did. "I miss you, Black Moon," he whispered.

He watched the woman walk off carrying a bucket of water from the nearby stream.

With a deep sense of sorrow, he went back to his work.

Elson Brooks plopped down across the small fire from Cooper. "You're lookin' a might peaked there, Hawl. Ye ailin'?"

Cooper shook his head.

"I think you're lyin' to me, hoss, but if that's the way ye want it, it ain't my business to interfere." But he followed Cooper's gaze. "You interested in Butterfly?" Brooks asked, surprised.

Cooper looked up from his task. "No. No, I just miss Black Moon, and for some reason that gal reminded me of her. Don't know why since she doesn't favor Black Moon all that much."

"Well, I nary encountered it, but I reckon the loss of a feller's woman must sit hard sometimes."

"That's a fact."

"Ye want me to see if I can get her pa to let ye meet her?"

"Reckon not." He sat staring a few more moments at the disappearing figure of Butterfly. He managed a sad grin. "Reckon you should meet her, El. Maybe you'll have luck with this one."

"Ain't likely. Ain't had such luck ever before. Best I

can do is a roll in the robes of a time. 'Sides, she's a wee bit young for this ol' feller," he said sadly.

"Like hell. She must be fifteen or so, of marriage-able age whether here or back in the flatlands."

"Well, then I'm too old for her." He grinned. "Doesn't matter. Reckon it ain't in the cards for this chil' to ever find himself a longtime woman. Likely just as well seein' as how some women can be troublesome." He grinned. "Hawk Flies is havin' a feast in his lodge tonight for some of us. Be best if ye come."

"Reckon I'll pass, El. I ain't of a mood to sit around jawin' with folks, even if some of 'em are friends."

"Ye don't show up, it'll be an insult to ol' Hawk."

Cooper looked at him, then sighed. "All right, come fetch me when it's time."

HAWK FLIES' lodge was large enough—barely—to accommodate all of Brooks's men as well as the war chief's two wives and two daughters.

"No other warriors comin'?" Cooper whispered to Brooks.

"Nope. This here is just Hawk Flies' way of honorin' his white friends."

"You must be big medicine to that ol' hoss."

"Reckon so. But I think he just wants to be on our good side 'cause it helps him in tradin' with other whites, especially down to rendezvous."

Cooper paid little mind to the conversation flowing around the circle of men. He tried not to look at her, but his vision kept returning to Butterfly. And to him, it seemed as if she had pushed her sister aside so she could be the one to feed Cooper and keep his mug filled with coffee. The mountain man was pleased but also unsettled. And while she kept her eyes averted, as a good Indian woman should, he occasionally caught her peeking at him.

He stayed throughout the feast but took little part in it other than eating. When he left, his mind was a jumble of emotions. He could not—would not—be untrue to the memory of Black Moon Woman. Yet this young Nez Perce, though she had done nothing more than smile at him a time or two, had wormed a small hole into his heart, and it confused and upset him.

Sleep did not come quickly, nor was it refreshing, and in the morning, he began saddling his horse.

"Aim to make meat?" Potts asked, walking up.

"Yep."

"Mind some company?" the young man asked cheerfully.

"Reckon not, Zeke."

"I do something to annoy ye, Hawl?" Potts asked, surprised.

"No, Zeke. I just need to be on my own for a spell, do a bit of thinkin'." He smiled just a little. "And that's hard to do with a jabber mouth like you."

"You sayin' I flap my gums too much?"

"No more'n bunch of gophers chatterin' because they suspect trouble's comin'."

"That hurts, Hawl," Potts said with a laugh. He grew serious. "Hope ye get your mind settled, my friend."

Cooper nodded and mounted and rode out of the village. Half an hour later, he heard something in the brush ahead of him. He dismounted and crept through the foliage, hoping to see an elk. What he saw instead was Pale Thunder taking aim at a deer bounding away in fright. And then he saw a foaming wolf headed toward Pale Thunder.

The two men had separated by just a few yards. The wolf was charging with a snarl. Pale Thunder managed to dodge out of the way, falling behind a tree.

The wolf skidded to a halt and spun, ready to attack again.

SEVEN

COOPER CHARGED FORWARD and went into a slide as the wolf leaped. He caught the animal's throat with the muzzle of his rifle and used the beast's momentum to flip it over his head, pulling the trigger as he did so. The lead ball and flash of powder blew a hole in the wolf's throat. The animal was dead when it hit the ground.

Pale Thunder helped Cooper up. "Very close, friend." He did not seem to be shaken at all.

"Too damn close. Reckon the son of a bitch was rabid."

"I owe you my life."

"Weren't nothin'. You would've done the same for me."

"Maybe not think fast enough."

THE MOUNTAIN MAN and war chief rode back into the village together, a deer draped over the back of the latter's horse. Cooper broke off from Pale Thunder and headed for his own camp. Along the way, he spotted Butterfly and thought he saw her glance at him. He gritted his teeth, upset at himself for his feelings. He rode off. Not only had his hunt not settled his mind, but the sight of Butterfly had also increased his inner turmoil.

He sighed as he tended his horse. Finished, he hunted for Brooks and found the older mountain man playing hand with a couple of warriors. Brooks took a break when he saw Cooper and stood. "What can I do for ye, hoss?"

'When're we leavin'?"

"Figured day after tomorrow, maybe day after that. Why?"

"Seems we've spent more'n enough time here already. Time's a wastin' and if we want to get to good trappin' grounds before others, we best be on the move."

"Something sittin' in your craw, Hawl?"

"Nope."

"Second time of late ye've given me a story that ain't exactly the truth. It don't shine to be lied to by one of the men who ride with me. Ye got something to say, say it. Or take your leave if that's where your stick floats."

Cooper sucked in a deep breath and let it out slowly. He was ashamed to admit to Brooks what he was thinking and feeling, but he wasn't sure he could spend a couple more days here with such emotions roiling his brain.

Brooks seemed to catch on. "Butterfly's gotten inside ye, eh? That it?"

Cooper nodded glumly.

Brooks stood in thought for a bit, then said, "We'll

be headin' east toward the Bitterroots. Why don't ye head off without us. We'll catch up on the trail."

"Tryin' to get rid of me? I been that much of a pest?"

"If ye wasn't a friend and a valued member of my little troupe, I'd smack ye down, boy. I said we'd catch up to ye on the trail. To think that ain't true is callin' me a liar, and this chil' won't stand for bein' called a liar agin. Your choice, hoss, ye either leave with the agreement that we'll catch up to ye on the trail, or ye leave on your own hook."

Anger flashed in Cooper's eyes, then he let out his breath, deflated. "Sorry, El. I don't know what's come over me. That damn woman ain't done a damn thing, yet she's burned a hole in me somehow."

"Women can do that to a man," Brooks said. Then he grinned. "So I've been told. I ain't ever experienced it myself bein' so unfortunate with woman as I am, ye know."

"Reckon I'll pull out in the mornin', then. I'll move slow so we'll meet up soon."

"That shines. Leave your supplies and such with us. No need for ye to be haulin' them things around by your lonesome when the bunch of us can do it."

"You sure?"

"Callin' me a liar again?" Brooks's voice had turned hard.

"Christ, El, leave off with the liar nonsense. I just don't want you haulin' my plunder around if it'll be a burden."

Brooks nodded. "I said we'll do so, and we'll do so. Just take enough to tide ye over a few days."

"If you weren't such a good friend as you've been, you'd be a pain in my rump." He smiled. "Obliged, El."

COOPER PULLED out the next morning trailing a mule with some supplies. Though he took his time, it was still a little over a week before Brooks and the others caught up with Cooper. He had begun to worry if the men had indeed taken his supplies and headed off in a different direction. He didn't really believe that, but the possibility did cross his mind more than once.

But one afternoon, he heard a group of animals behind him, and he cached into the trees along what some might humorously call a trail. He fought his way in through the brush and trees until he was in a spot where he would be hidden but still see the trail. He waited, sweat trickling down from under his hat, hoping that these were not Crows or Blackfeet.

After ten tense minutes, Elson Brooks rode into view, followed by the others and the herd of horses and mules being driven by Sam Bacon and Alistair Wentworth. Cooper breathed a sigh of relief and began to push his way out of the foliage. "Ho, Elson," he called.

Brooks stopped and grinned when he saw Cooper. "Waugh! Thought ye'd gone under, hoss, when we didn't see ye after a few days."

"Well, if you boys knew how to ride at more'n a snail's pace, you would've caught up to me days ago."

"Ah, *M'sieur* Coopair, we would 'ave caught you a day after you left if *M'sieur* Brooks hadn't called for camps an 'our after we left every morning," Jacques Dubois said.

"Ah, laddie, if ye knew how to saddle yer steed, we would've been able to ride longer," Duncan MacTavish said. "But yer cinch kept coming loose and ye kept fallin' off yer horse, slowing us doon considerably, ye *clatty dafty*. Och! Ye were troublesome, as always."

"Y'all weren't much better, ya drunken Scottie," Bill White tossed in. "Staggerin' through the camp all the time, too full of Lightnin' to help us with camp duties."

By now everyone, including Cooper was laughing. Finally, Brooks managed, "All right, boys, ye've had your fun, time to move on."

"See, *m'sieurs*," Two-Faces Beaubien said, "Ze leader 'e is a short-tempered critter, always taking ze fun out of life for us 'ard-working 'ommes. It is lucky all of us don't die from working so 'ard."

Everyone, including Brooks, continued to laugh, but they were moving up the trail at a more than leisurely pace. Cooper fell in alongside Potts.

"Ye doin' better, hoss?" the latter asked.

"Some. How's doin's with Mornin' Song?"

Potts glanced behind him at his woman and grinned. "Shinin', Hawl. Plumb shinin'."

If his friend wasn't so happy, Cooper might have felt poorly about not having Black Moon Woman at his side. But Potts's joy made up a little for the loss.

EIGHT

Late Fall 1831—Early Summer 1832

THE TRAPPING WAS GOOD, and it looked as if they would weather the winter well as they set up winter quarters in a small valley along Rock Creek in the Bitterroot Mountains.

As winter began moving in, Cooper, while trapping with his usual efficiency, had become quieter, less likely to join in the banter around the fire at night. Some of the men, especially those he was closest to, noticed.

"Somethin' plaguin' ye, Hawl?" Brooks asked one afternoon as they sat in the hastily built cabin that was their winter home.

"Nah. Just moody."

Brooks was quiet for a bit, then said, "It's Butterfly, ain't it?"

Cooper hesitated, then nodded. "I don't know what the hell it is, El, but that damn woman's got a hold of me. I hardly met her. Hell, haven't even really met her."

"Sometimes they can get to ye, I've heard," Brooks

said with a smile. "Ain't a one ary got her hooks in me like that. Reckon that's why I nary found me a woman for keeps."

"You can't find a woman 'cause you're an ugly, incorrigible codger with nothin' to offer a woman." Cooper managed a small laugh.

"Well, there ain't much can be done about it now."

Cooper nodded glumly, his little bit of humor gone.

Two days later, Cooper dropped an armful of wood next to the fire, then turned and said, "I'm headin' out, El."

"What?" Brooks stuttered. "Where the hell are ye plannin' to go?"

Cooper jerked his head toward the west.

"Nez Perce country?"

"Yep."

"For Butterfly?" Brooks asked, incredulous.

"Yep."

"Ye're loco, Hawl."

"Mayhap, but it don't change anything."

His friend shook his head in disbelief. "Ye got enough horses and such to pay Hawk Flies her bride price?"

"If it don't take more'n three. I got that many. I ain't aimin' to give over any of my horses, but I figured I can use those Crow ponies I got when we stopped that little Crow horse stealin' raid a couple months ago."

"Forgot about those." Brooks paused. "I still think ye're crazy, but if that's where your stick floats I ain't about to be the one who says nay to ye. But I got to ask ye, though—are ye sure she wants ye?"

"Nope," Cooper said with a wry grin. "But I'll find out right soon."

"Ye want some company in case ye run into some Blackfeet?"

"You're needed here, El. I'd ask Zeke, but then we'd have to drag along Mornin' Sun. Not that she'd be any hindrance, but I'll be damned if I'm gonna listen to his ruttin' every night on the trail."

Brooks laughed. "There is that." He paused, then, "Ye sure ye want to face another winter out here alone? Ye ain't had a good time of it the past few years."

"I don't look favorably on it for certain, El but I reckon it's necessary."

"That woman certainly does have her hooks in ye, boy, if ye can't wait 'til rendezvous."

"Like you said, I've lost my sense, I reckon."

LESS THAN TWO DAYS OUT, Cooper began to regret his decision. Fighting the snowstorm that had swept down on him that morning, adding to the foot or more on the ground was bad enough. Doing it while trailing four horses and a mule was far worse. But he persevered despite the horrors of the past few winters rummaging through his brain. And with that, the more he thought of what he was doing had him half convinced that he really was insane. Here he was braving another hellacious winter to fetch a woman he didn't even know, one he had not spoken even half a dozen words too.

"Yep, ol' hoss, you're one foolish feller, dumb as a tree root," he muttered with regularity. "Maybe the most foolish hoss ever to walk the earth."

He finally reached Red Leggings' village, much to

the surprise of the residents. He paid his respects to the civil chief, then tended to his animals. Grateful for the lodge the Nez Perce provided, he stored the supplies and trade goods he had brought.

He sucked in a breath when Butterfly entered the tipi, carrying a pot, coffeepot, cup, bowl and fire making tools. She offered a small, shy smile and began laying a fire. Soon she had food and coffee being readied over the flames.

"You eat when done," she said as she headed for the flap.

"Wait, please," Cooper said through constricted throat.

She stopped, turned, smiled nervously again, and took a seat across the fire from him. Neither said anything.

Before long, Butterfly served him a bowl of boiled buffalo and a tin mug of coffee.

"Thank you," Copper said softly, staring nervously at her. She refused to look into his eyes, sitting with head downcast. He ate in silence, then gently put down the bowl and cup. He cleared his throat, then asked, "Do you have a husband?"

"No." It was said confidently.

"Would you take me as your man if your father agrees?"

"Yes." Said more firmly.

Cooper smiled. "I'll talk to Hawk Flies tomorrow."

A smile also bloomed on Butterfly's beautiful bronze face. She rose and said, "I must go now."

Cooper nodded and leaned back a little when she had left. *Maybe I ain't so mad after all*, he thought.

In the morning, Cooper went to visit Hawk Flies.

The mountain man expected the bride price to be high, but he managed to whittle the price down a little. Still, it cost him two horses—one of his and one of the Crow ponies—a trade rifle with powder and ball, and two Hudson Bay blankets.

That night, Butterfly, with what possessions she owned, moved into the lodge Cooper was using.

With a sudden case of trepidation, Cooper took her hand and led to the robes. The young woman nervously disrobed and lay on the robes. Moments later, his nervousness fading, Cooper joined her.

In the dim light cast by the fire's embers, Cooper thought at times that he was with Black Moon Woman again. It was an eerie feeling. But while his eyes might deceive him, his hands and lips and more did not. Except for her work-callused hands, her skin was soft and smooth, her body shapely. It was not long before he lost himself in her.

That led to feelings of guilt in the morning. As he went about preparing to leave, he felt remorseful, as if he had betrayed Black Moon. Butterfly, sensing something wrong, said nothing and crept around him, fearful that she had offended him and would be cast aside. She was relieved somewhat when he nodded and smiled at the fine job she had done packing the mule. She felt even better when he made sure she was well covered in a buffalo robe when she mounted her pony on the woman's saddle her mother gave her.

They rode off into the bright, dazzling sunshine that did nothing to ease the bitter coldness of the day. Again, Cooper had flashbacks to his past winters, particularly the one where he and Black Moon had almost perished. *You're doin' too much thinkin' about*

Black Moon, he thought numerous times during their journey through snow choked passes and across glimmering meadows where the sun reflecting off the snow was almost blinding. They wore pieces of buckskin with slits cut in them for their eyes for protection against the glare. It wasn't perfect, but it helped.

The weather was not as bad as he thought it would be—they only had to stop twice because of snowstorms, once for two days, the other for three but it was still almost three weeks before they arrived at their destination.

COOPER SAT astride his horse at the edge of the trees looking out over the meadow. All that was left of the camp was detritus—a trio of mostly collapsed cabins, stacks of firewood, some piles of cottonwood bark, the picked-over remains of two dead horses.

Butterfly moved up beside him, yet still a little behind. "Were they attacked?" she asked.

Cooper shook his head. "Don't think so. Any Indians attacked, there'd be cut-up bodies all around. Crows or Blackfeet wouldn't take bodies with them. Prisoners maybe, but not bodies. And they wouldn't have captured all the boys. Still, why they pulled up stakes is concerning. Maybe they saw sign that Blackfeet were about and moved off. Maybe they just decided they didn't like the camp here. Don't know when they pulled out, though. Could've been yesterday, could've been soon after I left a month and a half ago." He sighed. "Well, no matter."

"You find?"

Cooper looked at the woman, ready to retort at her insult to his abilities, then realized she hardly knew him, did not know his skills. He nodded. "I find. But the search can start tomorrow." He headed into the meadow and toward the cabin that looked minutely more substantial than the others. By the time Cooper had tended the horses, Butterfly had a fire going and a hunk of moose cooking.

Soon, Butterfly served Cooper, who was sitting on a log near the fire, a good-size chunk of meat on one of the two tin plates he had brought along. She got a small portion for herself and then sat next to him on the log a couple feet away. The woman was still tentative around Cooper, having known him really for less than a month, but she was beginning to think he would be a fine husband. She edged closer to him, then more, then still more, until her side was pressed lightly against his. Making a daring move, she rested her head on the top of his arm.

Cooper stiffened at the move, then relaxed. They were still getting used to one another. While the intimacy in the robes was comfortable and pleasing, the relationship outside the robes was still very new and would take some time getting used to. "You warm enough?" he asked.

"Yes, my husband."

He shook his head a tiny bit. He was still unused to hearing that as she was in saying it. "This cabin ought to be sturdy enough for the night," he said.

"I think yes."

COOPER STOPPED in the center of a long, narrow meadow and watched. He saw curls of smoke on the horizon, seeming to come from beyond the thickly treed forest before him. He was fairly certain this was Brooks's new winter camp, but he had to proceed cautiously. It could very well be the camp of a Blackfoot war party.

He edged his way into the trees, weaving among the pines. Butterfly followed, towing the pack mule. Suddenly he stopped, bringing his rifle up, thumb on the hammer, ready to cock the weapon when he heard someone coming.

Then a voice slid between the trees, "Whoevair you are, show yourselves to me before I shoot you dead."

"Two-Faces?" Cooper responded. "That you?"

"'Awley?"

"One and the same."

A mounted Two-Faces Beaubien came out from behind a cluster of tall brush. *"Bonjour, mon ami."* He grinned. "I see you 'ave brought a *mam'selle* with you."

"That I have. Her name's Butterfly."

Beaubien removed his badger fur hat and waved it around grandiosely. "Welcome, *Mam'selle Papillon.*"

*"Katsee yow yow—*Thank you," the woman answered shyly. She did not know how to react to him. She had seen him around the village when Cooper and the others were there, but she had never interacted with him. But she looked forward to seeing Morning Song, a friend from the village who was now married to Zeke Potts. She also knew that Beaubien had a Nez Perce wife, named Dancing Water, she thought, though she had never met her.

COOPER'S RETURN brought a small celebration as he rejoined his companions after sending Butterfly toward the other women. Morning Song hurried over to greet her. Cooper was glad his new wife would have other Nez Perce women to be with.

"Why'd you leave the other place, El?" Cooper asked as he and the others crowded near the poorly made stone fireplace in one of the cabins.

"Game got scarce right quick."

"Luis' pepper farts scared all the buffler away," Potts said innocently.

Luis Gamez scowled and let out a string of Spanish that no one could understand, but they all laughed at the Mexican's outrage.

"Forage was gettin' to be a mite scarce too," Brooks continued.

"I figured it might be one or both of those."

"Turned out to not be a very hospitable place with the weather, too."

"Never figured on that. Everything better here?"

"So far. There were a few buffler a few miles northeast, but we picked off one now and again. If there's any left it's only one or two and they've drifted on. Plenty of sweet cottonwood bark. Ought to last 'til spring if we keep a watch on it."

"Weather?"

"Better'n it was at the other place." Brooks grinned. "But there ain't no place out here that's exactly comfortin' weather."

"That's certain," Cooper agreed, thinking with a

shudder his experiences in fighting winter weather in the mountains.

THE WEATHER WAS MILDER than expected, and the group rode it out with a minimum of trouble—a lack of game since the buffalo had moved on; little forage near the end; the occasional fury of a snowstorm. George Miles lost two mules and Duncan MacTavish a horse to the weather.

Despite the relative ease of the weather, the men were mighty glad when spring arrived. They renewed their trapping with a vengeance, pulling in prime plews by the dozens.

They were happy too that there were only two skirmishes with Blackfeet, both with little more than a couple of flesh wounds among the mountain men.

As spring began easing into summer, Brooks and his men headed toward rendezvous.

NINE

Summer 1832

THEY RODE into Pierre's Hole on July fifth. There was a heap of mountain men there already, including a number from the American Fur Company.

Cooper and Brooks grabbed one of the passing mountain men. "The supplies ain't here yet?" the former asked.

"Be poor bull they don't arrive again," Brooks added.

"That it would," the man agreed, looking a little worried. "Word is, Sublette's on his way, but Fontenelle is too." The man spit. "I heard Broken Hand's out tryin' to find Sublette now, see if he can hurry him along some. Fontenelle gets here first with the supplies, all us free trappers are gonna sell our plews to him. We do that, the Rocky Mountain boys'll be in deep debt, I figure."

"You'd go against Sublette and the others?" Cooper asked.

The man shrugged his broad shoulders. "Can't be helped. After last year, we'll sell to whoever gets here first. Can't go worryin' about gettin' supplies from Sublette when there'd be plenty already here."

"We'll stick with Sublette, hoss," Cooper said, and Brooks nodded assent. "Even if the Company supplies arrive first, we'll hold on for s spell anyway."

"You'd be damned fools to do so," the man said, stalking away.

Brooks's men and all the others waited anxiously. But three days later there was a whoop and a holler and gunfire exploded. Word raced through the camps: "Sublette's almost here!"

There were high doin's for sure when the supplies arrived. As soon as business was mostly done, the festivities began. Whiskey flowed like the Teton River nearby, and the men were drunk constantly. The men danced with each other and with Indian women— Shoshonis, Nez Perce, Flatheads, even Crows—who came by the hundreds. They fought and caroused, gambled and told tales, they threw tomahawks and knives; they shot rifles and pistols; they sang and had tobacco-spitting contests. Then they drank some more.

Cooper got his older plews from Cheyenne Killer.

Cooper made more than two thousand dollars for his catch, and the first thing he did was to pay for next season's supplies. That done, he bought a heap of foofaraw so he could deck Butterfly out proper as befitting the woman of a free trapper at rendezvous— vermilion to paint circles on her cheeks and the center part in her glossy black hair; bright cloth to make clothes; beads, shells and metal to decorate her creamy white elkskin dress; new beaded moccasins, bought with great reluctance from the Crow, who made the finest on the Plains; small bells to trim the hem of the dress; earrings; necklaces, bracelets, and more. Until the woman was weighed down with glittering baubles.

"You sure do look fine," Cooper whispered softly as they retired to their lodge, set up among the Nez Perce camp. Cooper had restrained himself mightily that day, taking care of business first, and then keeping his intake of the fiery whiskey to a few toasts. Tonight would be hers. and tomorrow night. After that...

"I glad," Butterfly happily said.

He smiled and pulled her to him...

TO BUTTERFLY'S SURPRISE, Cooper did not begin his spree right then. He instead spent time in the Shoshoni camp, talking with Cuts Throat. By late afternoon, he was back in his own lodge, much to Butterfly's relief.

In the morning she fed him and watched sadly as he strode off, decked out in his own finery, bought from a Flathead woman, a gleam of anticipation in his bright gray eyes. She had been warned by Beaubien's and White's Nez Perce women that she would hardly see him for the next two weeks or so. He would be almost constantly drunk, stumbling back to their lodge occasionally, if he had not fallen asleep in a stupor somewhere. She would be safe here in the lodge, pitched among her father's band's tipis along a creek. And she would be protected by her father—and by everyone's knowledge that she was now Hawley Cooper's woman.

So she put her worries aside as best she could and

spent time with the other Nez Perce women. She worried about him, though—anything could happen at a rendezvous, and often did. Men were killed by stampeding buffalo that occasionally roared through the miles-long camp; or horses ridden madly in a race; guns were fired indiscriminately; and there was a fight it seemed every minute of the day between at least two men but usually a group.

She was also worried for herself. As a new wife, she did not know where she really stood in Cooper's life. She had heard stories of how white men treated their Indian wives, and she worried that he would be one of them. She had seen no evidence of that in the short time she had known him, but still, the thought lingered uncomfortably in her mind.

Cooper and his friends Brooks and Potts caroused for two solid weeks and then some. They bet heavily on horse races, card games, hand games, tomahawk throwing, knife throwing, shooting, foot races or anything else they could lay a wager on. This year they were lucky, winning more often than they lost, and by the time they were ready to ride out, had asked some of the boys heading back to St. Louis to bank a little of their money.

Weary, sick, hungover, and aching from the last brawl he had found himself in, Cooper dragged himself into the saddle and, with the sixty plus other men, rode out of rendezvous with guns blazing, and head held high. It was only after they had ridden a mile or so, until they were away from the eyes of those still at rendezvous, could he and the others slump and allow their misery to shine through. And they gratefully made a small camp after making about eight miles.

TEN

August 1832

AS THE MEN of Brooks's little group, other free trappers and a relatively small Rocky Mountain brigade were starting to break their sparse camps the next morning, a shout suddenly went up. Everyone looked around and saw a man pointing. A long line of people was starting across the valley a mile or so away.

Nathaniel Wyeth pulled out his telescope and scanned the distance. "Indians," he muttered nervously.

"Gimme that," Joe Meek, one of the leaders of the Rocky Mountain brigade, said, grabbing the looking glass. He peered through it. "Damn it all," he muttered. He tossed the telescope back to Wyeth and ran. "Blackfeet!" he shouted. "Blackfeet comin'!"

Some of the men hastily started throwing up a barricade with whatever was handy. Others gathered horses and mules, driving them into something of a box in the trees along the river where they could be protected.

Cooper and Brooks rushed to get their own men ready, and their women and children safe back in the trees. Then they watched the Blackfeet head toward a thicket-filled swamp across the valley.

A half-breed named Godin and a Flathead warrior rode out to meet the Blackfeet. A war chief broke from the slowing group and moved forward by himself.

"Parley?" Brooks asked, surprised.

"Reckon it's supposed to be," Milt Sublette, another leader of the Rocky Mountain brigade, said. "But I have my doubts. Sons a bitches probably just want to get forted up, and that ol' chief's out there to buy 'em some time."

"You look worried," Cooper said.

"I am," Sublette said bluntly. "Them goddamn Gros Ventres never took to whites, which ye should know havin' encountered 'em before. And, hell, you seen what they did to Broken Hand."

Cooper nodded. Everyone at the rendezvous had.

"That ol' coon had him some poor times, that's certain," Cooper said, remembering the sight of Fitzpatrick being brought into camp barely a skeleton with his hair gone white seemingly overnight and a tale of escape from the Blackfeet that was harrowing. A tinge of worry grew in Cooper, his hangover lessening a little as adrenaline began pumping.

"I don't expect them boys yonder to be of a peaceable frame of mind," Sublette said. "So I sent one of the boys headin' back to rendezvous to get us some help, should that need arise."

"Anyone left, you reckon?"

"Certain. By brother's still there with his men and a heap of the free trappers ain't left yet."

"What about the Company?"

"I expect they'll be sendin' some folks," Sublette said, though he did not sound entirely sure. "We might be enemies in the trade, but they won't like the Blackfeet bein' on the warpath no more'n we do. 'Specially if they're plannin' to follow us as we trap Blackfoot country."

There was a gunshot and a shout, making the three men look up. The half-breed had killed the Blackfoot chief and he and the Flathead was racing back toward their group, waving the scarlet blanket Godin had grabbed from the dying Blackfoot. Bullets flew, but none touched them.

"Goddammit, no!" Sublette bellowed, swinging his horse around and racing off, shouting orders.

Zeke Potts rode up, his face pasty from a hangover. "What the hell happened?" he asked, not sounding at all nervous.

"Damn fool half-breed just killed that Blackfoot war chief," Brooks said. "This here is poor bull for goddamn certain."

They quickly took cover in a shallow buffalo wallow and were joined by the rest of their group.

Scattered fire came from the Blackfeet, with the trappers sporadically returning it. Most did not want to waste powder and ball on an enemy this distance away and well hidden. Then word filtered around the large group: "Help's comin'!"

A few minutes later, Bill Sublette, Robert Campbell, and several dozen trappers, along with a mass of blood-lusting Flatheads and Nez Perce came riding up.

"Well, lookee who's here," Potts said, sarcasm heavy in his voice. He pointed.

Cooper and Brooks looked to where the newcomers sat on horses blowing from the hard run. Cooper grinned. Showing up at the end on a flea-bitten, slouch-backed, splay-footed old appaloosa was a warrior named Sits Down, not so resplendent in smeared paint. He carried a lance with a dull iron point, a quiver with five poorly made arrows, a bow with a flayed drawstring and a pistol that likely would explode if he fired it.

"Goddamn, look at that miserable sack of buffler dung," Potts said in undisguised contempt.

Sits Down was the brother of Potts's wife, Morning Song. With the woman whom he called Betsy, he had "inherited" her family. Most of them were all right but Sits Down got his name from his chief occupation.

"Looks ready for war, you ask me," Brooks said with a snicker.

Potts spit. "Reckon it's about time for his nap," Potts said, still disgusted. "Look at him, fer chrissakes. "Fat, stupid, lazy sumbitch." He turned away.

"I reckon we can rest easy," Cooper said, jabbing Potts in the side with an elbow. "Now Sits Down's here, we don't need to do a damn thing 'cept sit back and let him raise hair on them Blackfeet." He laughed as Brooks snickered again.

"Goddammit, boys," Potts said in exasperation, "I didn't ask fer that useless, fat fool to be part of my family."

"You ought to be more careful when you go pickin' out a woman next time," Cooper said, laughing.

Potts's face reddened, making him even angrier. "Dammit," he shouted, much to the amusement of all the men within earshot. "I love that damned Nez Perce woman and I'll take whatever family she's got just to keep her." He puffed out his cheeks and set his eyes straight ahead, across the valley to the Blackfoot camp.

"Mite touchy this mornin', ain't we?" Brooks asked in mock innocence.

Potts turned toward him, anger blazing in his eyes. "Why you rotten-bellied..."

"Not now, boy," Cooper interjected.

Firing was sporadic from both sides, as the Blackfeet aim was poor, and the mountain men could see little to shoot at inside the Indians' "fort." Quickly they retreated.

"Come on, boys," Bill Sublette yelled. "There's Blackfeet there to raise hair on. Come on, I'm sayin'. Let's go get them red critters?"

"I'm with you," Campbell shouted. Several others took up the chorus.

"Me, too," Cooper offered. He wasn't sure why he was so itching to fight these Blackfeet, but he was. It was almost as if he had never faced any before and wanted to see what it was like.

"And me," Brooks threw in. When Potts gave him a strange look, he added, "Somebody's got to look after ol' Hawley here."

"Well, then, me too," Potts said in resignation. "You sumbitches are gonna get me killed sure as hell."

"I go, too," Two-Faces Beaubien said, moving up alongside the three men.

Sublette jumped up, Campbell at his side, and roared, "Let's go!"

Nearly sixty men, including Cooper and his friends, headed out on the run, racing for the cottonwood and willow-choked thicket. Balls whistled by as they ran. But they all made the trees.

"Now what?" Potts asked sarcastically.

"Hell if I know," Cooper said.

"We wait," Beaubien said.

"For what?" Potts asked.

Beaubien shrugged.

Cooper cleared his throat, then said softly, "I'd like to make my will with you, El. Just in case."

"No need."

"I'm hopin' not. But I'd feel a heap better. When Brooks nodded, Cooper said, "Well, as you boys know, I ain't got much, but what I got, I'd like you boys to have if I go under. Two-Faces, you can have my string of horses and mules, 'cept Sally's." Soon after their joining, Cooper had begun to call Butterfly Sally.

Looking solemn, Beaubien nodded.

"Zeke, you bein' one of the best shots I know, I leave to you my fine rifle here. You can have the pistols, too, less'n someone else wants to lay claim to 'em."

"I'll use 'em well, Hawl. I just might," he added with a fierce grin, "use 'em to make wolf bait out of the sumbitch what gets you."

"It's a comfort," Cooper said dryly. "And, El, you get the best. But you get more to worry over. I'm leavin' you my woman."

"What?" Brooks exclaimed. "I don't want..."

"Don't try'n play the innocent with us, El," Potts said. "You've had your eye on that little gal ever since Hawl there took her to his bed six, seven months ago."

"I..." Brooks protested.

But Potts would not relent, though he winked at Cooper, who grinned. "You ain't foolin' nobody, I tell ya. Nope. I've even seen you sharpenin' that ol' Green River of yours, drawin' the steel over the stone nice and slow, lickin' your chops and castin' an evil eye on poor ol' Hawl there, just wantin' to take that ol' knife and..."

"I never done such a thing," Brooks exploded. He turned to Cooper, the battle forgotten for the moment. "I swear, Hawl, I never done such. Never would think of it."

"I know, El," Cooper said, laughing. All the others save Brooks joined in. "He was just funnin' you." He turned serious. "But was I to go under, I want you to take care of Butterfly fer me. If she don't want you, just make sure she gets back to her people all right."

"I'll do so, certain, Hawl." Brooks's tone let Cooper know that Brooks would cross the Wind River Range naked in the dead of winter to help Butterfly if it was called for.

"You can have the specie I just give over to Sublette to bank for me in St. Louis, too, El. There ain't much, but what's there is yours. As fer the rest, my traps and other truck, divide it up as you will amongst the boys. It'd be..."

A rifle ball thudded into a tree trunk inches from Beaubien's head, and the four men sprawled in the damp dirt.

"I make a will too," Two-Faces said, and did so. The others followed suit.

With the serious business out of the way, they looked to the fight. They crawled forward through the muck and underbrush, firing occasionally if they saw a Blackfoot rise for a quick shot. It was hot and close and dank and dim in the tangled mass of brush and trees, and the Blackfeet were well forted up.

"Damn, this ain't gettin' us nowhere," Potts grumbled.

"Look," Beaubien said, pointing with his rifle.

Nathaniel Wyeth and his New Englanders had gotten lost in the thicket and had stumbled around until they wound up on the side opposite the rest of the mountain men, behind the Indians' barricade. Several trappers had been shot, as had some Nez Perce and Flatheads, and Cooper began to suspect that some of them had been hurt by their allies as Wyeth's men fired back toward the rest of their comrades.

Then came word that Bill Sublette had been wounded.

"Time to skedaddle," Potts said. "I ain't amin' to get shot, especially by one of our own."

They worked their way back until they were at the edge of the trees. They could see their fellows and plunder across what now seemed like a vast expanse of empty.

"No use settin' here," Cooper said. "Them Black-feet'll find us soon enough." With that, he sucked in his breath and ran, shoulders hunched, expecting at any second to feel a rifle ball or arrowhead tear into his back. He heard a shout behind him and cranked his head around in time to see Brooks fall and bounce, his lanky body kicking up small dust clouds.

He jerked to a stop and hurried back. Brooks was getting up, blood oozing down one leg. Cooper grabbed him by one arm, and Potts the other. The three ran, Beaubien behind them, almost making himself a target so the men, slowed by the wounded Brooks, would have a better chance of getting to safety.

They stumbled and almost fell into the wallow. They climbed back out the other side and made it to where the other men from their party, and the women with them, waited. They slumped.

Beaubien left and returned a few minutes later with one of his two wives, a Nez Perce named Dancing Water. Brooks had pulled the arrow from his left leg. Dancing Water slit open his wool pants and studied the wound, clicking her tongue and muttering something only she and Two-Faces could understand.

She set down a sack and took some small buckskin pouches out, then a small dish carved from a gourd. She poured a little water from another small gourd into the dish and then various things from the pouches. She quickly layered it over the wound.

Brooks sat tensely, expecting it to hurt. But to the contrary, it cooled the fire that had been there. "What is it?" he asked.

Beaubien grinned and said, "Better not to ask."

Brooks nodded. Dancing Water wrapped the leg in some clean calico and left. Brooks pulled a twist of tobacco from his possible sack and tore off a chunk with his stained teeth. He leaned back against a tree and closed his eyes, chewing slowly, working the tobacco to the right consistency.

Butterfly and Morning Song came up. The former carried a small black kettle of steaming stew, which had still been on the fire as they had prepared to leave earlier. The latter had wood bowls and horn spoons. The women served each of the men, then sat near their husbands, quiet. From a pouch she wore across her shoulders, Butterfly took out a moccasin she was making and worked on it. Morning Song's fingers were busy beading a rosette on a dress.

"I say we ought to make tracks out of 'ere," Jacques Dubois said.

"You ain't..." Potts started, then broke off when he heard a commotion a ways off.

"Let's go see what the fuss is about," Brooks said, pushing himself up, favoring the wounded leg.

He and several companions strolled to where the Sublette brothers, Bill with his shoulder bandaged up good, his face grimacing with pain, backed by Henry Fraeb and Joe Meek, were arguing with several Nez Perce and Flathead war chiefs.

"What's doin'?" Brooks asked Meek.

"Bill and I decided we ought to burn those red devils out of their hole."

"Good idea," Paddy Murphy said.

"So we thought."

"What's the problem, then?" Cooper asked.

"Flatheads and Nez Percy don't want us to do it. Say it won't leave any plunder when them Blackfeet are done in."

"Them doin's don't shine with this chil'," Fraeb growled. "Not one damned bit. I've had truck with them devilish critters afore, and they ain't deservin' of no consideration, I'm sayin'."

"They're mean ones, that's certain," Cooper said. "But burnin' 'em out?" He shook his head. "I ain't so certain of that."

"Why not?"

"There's a mess of women and young'uns in there. It's against my nature to fry women and kids, even if they are Blackfeet."

"Goddamned   lily-livered..."   Fraeb   muttered,

trailing off when he saw Cooper's eyes darken with anger.

The argument with the friendly Indians broke off, and the Nez Perce and Flatheads moved off to make yet another attack on the Blackfoot. They had been doing it all day, off and on.

Robert Campbell came stomping over to the small group, muttering darkly. "Damned stupid Injuns. Goddamn. Gonna risk gettin' everybody killed so they can grab some plunder when it's all over. Damn. Well, I ain't listenin' to 'em. Some of you men start pilin' some wood up against that thicket."

Some men began doing so, while the others watched the Nez Perce and Flatheads attack again and then retreat to safety.

Then a Blackfoot stood and yelled across the meadow.

"What'n hell's he sayin'?" Campbell asked.

The others shrugged, and Cooper and his friends drifted back to their camp.

A Flathead who knew the Blackfoot language was summoned.

Soon after, Fraeb came running up to where Cooper and the others were resting. "Come on, boys!" he roared.

"What's doin'?" Brooks asked.

"We finally learned what that damned Blackfoot was sayin'."

"And?"

"And there's six hundred, maybe eight hundred Blackfoot warriors about to attack the folks left at rendezvous. Now get in the saddle and move."

Brooks and his men broke for their animals. In minutes, Cooper and most of the others were saddled, mounted, and had joined the mad rush of trappers heading hell for leather back to the rendezvous site. A few of the mountain men stayed behind, scattered through the thickets to make sure the Blackfeet there didn't try to join their friends.

But there was no sign of Blackfeet at the rendezvous site, eliciting a chorus of curses from the trappers.

"Well, hell, I'm headin' back," Cooper said, annoyed.

"Me, too," Potts agreed.

They had left their women back at their camp and neither was eager to let them stay there without protection. Their protection.

"It's nigh onto dark, boys," Brooks said. "Your women'll keep. Ain't no one gonna bother 'em."

"Sorry, El," Cooper said. "But I ain't leavin' 'em there with a pisspot full of Blackfeet still roamin' around." He pulled himself onto his horse. "You can stay here, if there's where your stick floats, but mine don't."

Brooks, Potts and the others of their group who had women—Jacques Dubois and Bill White—trotted off.

ELEVEN

BUTTERFLY AND MORNING Song were wailing in grief, their voices strange. The ululating sounds bounced back off the mountains and rattled around the wide, grassy valley.

Hawley Cooper and Zeke Potts had not found their women in the small camp they had left behind. "Zey are in Pale Thunder's camp," Two-Faces Beaubien, one of the few who had stayed behind, said, pointing.

Cooper and Potts, joined by Beaubien, hurried there to find their women, several others, and a few men howling in their grief.

"Bad medicine," Beaubien said. They were prepared to agree.

"I don't like the looks of this," Cooper said.

"Me, neither." Potts looked more than a little worried.

They found the women together, slumped in mourning. Their hair was hacked short.

"Least they didn't cut themselves," Cooper said, "something I've heard many tribes do."

Cooper kneeled next to Butterfly, stroking her shaggy hair. "Who was it?" he finally asked, ice drilling a hole in his belly. He had not seen Pale Thunder or Hawk Flies.

She quieted. Then, reluctant to use the dead's name said, "The one who was my father."

Cooper shook his head. "Damn. I'm sorry, Sally." He had liked Hawk Flies, the proud war chief of his Nez Perce band. It would be as hard for the tribe to lose him as it would be for his family. Cooper had liked the short, bow-legged Hawk Flies, had enjoyed his stories of war, and his joyful, lusty humor.

He waited a bit, then asked, "Why's Mornin' Song grievin'? She's mournin' too much for it to be just 'cause she's your friend and is grievin'."

"Those who were her sisters' husbands and..." She paused to draw in a ragged breath. "One who was her brother."

"Not Sits Down?"

"No."

Cooper shook his head, pained anew. Though Two Clouds was not regarded as highly as Hawk Flies, he was, however, expected to be so in the not-so-distant future. Still, he was an esteemed warrior, and his death would be hurtful to the band.

Cooper rose. "Come on, Sally," he said gently. "Let's get back to our own camp. Get you away from here."

"No."

"Yes." He took her hand and pulled her up. He looked over at Potts and Morning Song. The young man's face was stained with tears, as was his woman's. He looked up forlornly at Cooper, who said, "You two come along, too. Back to our camp. We'll be with our own people there."

Potts nodded and murmured in Nez Perce to Morning Song, who stood shakily. The four walked, leading their horses the short distance to their camp.

The women automatically began gathering firewood and then put some meat to cooking, though they did so in a daze. Cooper and Potts sat, not knowing what else to do with themselves.

"Why, dammit?" Potts said, spitting the foul taste of the day out of his mouth.

"Why what?" Brooks asked, plopping down next to them.

Not being beholden to Nez Perce tradition even though Morning Song and Butterfly were right there, Potts said, "Two Clouds has gone under."

"Ever'body's time comes, Zeke," Brooks said.

"Hell, I know that, El," Potts said. "I sure do. But, dammit, why couldn't it have been that fat, lazy, good-fer-nothin' brother of hers instead of that fine ol' hoss. Huh, can ya tell me that?"

"Can't say for certain, of course, Zeke," Brooks said easily, though not lightly. "It were his time, I reckon. Good Lord don't make sense sometimes. Leastways to folks like us. But I reckon he's got his reasons. Two Clouds is probably happier'n a pig in swill where he is now."

"How can you say somethin' like that, El?" Potts demanded angrily.

"Don't go lettin' your grief do your thinkin' for you, boy. He went out like a warrior, just like he wanted to. He didn't go under from old age, with creakin' bones and no teeth. He went out fightin', and I figure he took one or two Bug's Boys with him when he passed over. I reckon that had you asked him, he would've told you he would be proud to go that way."

"Damn, I know," Potts muttered. "Just don't seem fair is all. Not when he's got a brother that ain't worth snake shit."

"There's no explainin' such mysteries. Your time'll come soon enough. And when that time comes, mayhap you'll cross over whilst you're raisin' hair on some Blackfeet."

"Reckon I will, El." Potts managed a weak grin. "It'll sure as hell beat dyin' in some stinkhole of a cabin back in the settlements."

The two women picked up their howling again and sat under a tree to grieve alone now that they were in their own camp.

"Me, neither, El," Cooper said firmly. "No, sir. I aim to go under with a Blackfoot arrow or a Crow rifle ball in me. Just like Hawk Flies."

"Hawk Flies was rubbed out?" Brooks asked in surprise.

"Why didn't ye say anything before this?" Potts demanded.

"You were expounding on Two Clouds."

"But Christ, Hawley, Hawk Flies is one of the most important men in the village."

"That he was."

"Lordy, that'll be hard on the Nez Perce."

"Yeah, it will. There weren't no warrior in that band as important to the people than Hawk Flies."

Brooks and Potts nodded silently in agreement.

They quieted and sat back. "Most of the Rocky Mountain boys're ready to move on," Brooks said quietly. "The free boys, too. Wyeth's goin' with Fraeb, Milt and Meek, headin' toward the Snake. Bonneville'll be pullin' out soon. I'd be plenty surprised if that dumb little Frenchman lives out the winter. Sinclair's ready to move. Onliest ones that'll be left come mornin', afternoon at most, are Campbell and Bill Sublette."

"How's Bill doin'?" Cooper asked.

"That shoulder wound is pretty bad, but it ain't likely to hold him up long."

"Speakin' of the tiniest wounds, how's your leg, El?"

"Hardly know it was hit. Now, as I were sayin'..."

"You tryin' to say you want us to be movin' on right off?" Cooper asked.

"Reckon, I am."

"Where away?" Potts asked.

Brooks pulled off his fox-fur hat off and scratched his unruly flaxen hair. "Well..."

"I thought we was goin' with Fraeb and his boys," Cooper said.

"Only fer a ways. I was thinkin' we'd head..."

"I'm goin' to Nez Perce country," Potts said, as if suddenly making up his mind.

"...thinkin' we'd head for Nez Perce country like we always do. This time you and Hawley'll be along so that when they bury Hawk Flies and Two Clouds along the trail, you'll be there for Butterfly and Mornin' Song."

"You think they'll bury Hawk Flies, as important as he is, on the trail somewhere 'stead of bringing him back to their own land?" Potts was surprised.

"Of course. For one thing, it's their way to bury their dead a day or not much longer than that. And it'd be ridiculous to take the bodies all the way up there, Zeke. It's summer, and Ol' Hawk Flies and Two Clouds

will be mighty ripe long before they get to their homeland. They'll bury em along the way and do it soon, lest
their spirits be restless. We can ride along with the Nez
Perce 'til we hit their land and do some trappin', or we
can go our own way once they see to Hawk Flies and
Two Clouds."

THE NEXT MORNING, to everyone's surprise, the
Blackfoot were gone, having slipped away during the
night. With relief, Brooks and his group set off, riding to
the side of the Nez Perce, but not actually with them.
Because of the slowness of the Nez Perce caravan, the
men were fidgety about taking the time. They liked the
Nez Perce but traveling with all the women and children was too much. And there would be time spent on
Hawk Flies' funeral.

Still, the men were happy with going to the Nez
Perce village. Bill White and Jacques Dubois had Nez
Perce wives and one of Two-Faces Beaubien's wives
was of the tribe. It would give the women a little more
time with their families, plus the trapping was good.

The night before they left, Fraeb and Milt Sublette
had tried to talk them out of it and to stick with them.
"We need as many hands as we can get," Sublette told
them.

"We'll be fine on our own."

"Where ye headed?" Sublette asked.

"Up to the Nez Perce country, then head toward
Three Forks."

"You'll be headin' into the heart of Blackfoot country," Fraeb threw in. "You know them red devils ain't gonna take a shine to that. Not after this."

"Been there before. Maybe it'll keep the company off our tails," Brooks said with a laugh. "And I'm figuring you're figuring to do your trappin' up there too and don't want the competition."

"We got nothin' to worry about from them Blackfeet," Cooper said. "They were bloodied right well here. They'll not be lookin' to cause a ruckus, especially in winter."

"You're damn fools," Sublette said. "They've sure as hell've been known to raid in the winter. You know that. Those boys are plumb *loco*."

"We'll take our chances," Potts said. "You boys can run from the Blackfoot if that's where your stick floats. We ain't afeared of 'em."

"Bah," Fraeb growled, waving a hand at them in disgust as he and the others turned and stomped off.

Brooks's party and the Nez Perce moved west out of the big valley, reaching the Teton River before noon. The tribe set up camp and before dusk, in a pleasant spot along the river, laid Hawk Flies and Two Clouds to rest in the forks of two cottonwoods.

The groups continued moving slowly northwest, crossing Henry's Fork and picking up Birch Creek, skirting the Lemhi Range to their left. They soon picked up the Lemhi River and followed it to the Salmon River and west to its confluence with the Salmon's North Fork.

Cooper, Brooks, and the others rode a quarter mile or so west of the Indian caravan to avoid at least most of the thick cloud of dust kicked up by the dozens of horses as they trod across the brown seer grass. The whites chafed at the slowness, though the Nez Perce were traveling faster than usual. But within two weeks they had reached the site where the Nez Perce would put their village. Brooks's men placed their camp just outside it.

TWELVE

Fall 1832—Spring 1833

"WHERE AWAY NOW, EL?" Cooper asked as they sat at a fire in Red Leggings' village a few days after arriving.

"Ain't we goin' to Three Forks country again?" Potts asked.

"Ain't so sure, Zeke. I was talkin' to some of the other boys on the way here and word is that the Blackfeet ain't too happy about that little fracas down to rendezvous, havin' lost a heap of warriors, and they're fixin' to raise hair." He pulled off his hat and scratched his long, greasy hair. "So I was figurin' to try Maybe the Absarokas."

"Crow country," Cooper said.

"Yep."

"That suits, I reckon," Cooper said.

"You do realize, don't ye that the Blackfeet have been known to attack anywhere anytime. Won't make no difference where we'd be," Potts said.

"Reckon that's right," Cooper said. "But with the thirteen of us, we'll be all right."

"Then it's settled?" Brooks asked.

"Why're you askin' us? You was elected captain long before I showed up," Cooper said.

"Well, don't let it go to your head, but I've come to see ye as my second in command."

Cooper looked at him in surprise. "You've lost your reason."

"No he ain't," Potts threw in. "Other than El, you're the toughest and..."

"That don't matter none. I..."

"And even though that don't mean much," Potts said, cutting him off, "you're the most level-headed fellow besides El that's with us."

"You've both gone loco."

"Just clamp your pie hole shut, Hawl. I need your help."

"I'll give my help when needed, but I ain't about to go bossin' around the boys. And you best clamp your pie hole shut about this." Cooper glared at Potts. "And you, too, you jabberin' jay bird."

"Damn, Hawl, ye sure know how to take the joy out of a feller's life."

"Hell, if you're relyin' on me bossin' the boys to get your joy, you're in sad shape, boy," Cooper said with a laugh. "I reckon I just might tell Mornin' Song, she ain't givin' you enough joy in life. Maybe she'll go off and find someone else she can make happy."

"Don't ye dare, Hawl," Potts snapped. Then he too laughed.

"When are we leavin'?" Cooper asked.

"Few more days."

"I say we best be gone soon. There's a heap of travelin' to be done, and we've got to be trappin' along the way," Cooper said.

"We can move pretty fast, Hawl," Potts said. "Even with the women and young'uns. Ye know that."

"Yep, I do. But we also have to make meat, and that takes a spell. *You* know *that*."

"You're right, Hawl," Brooks said. He grinned. "It's why I made you my second in command."

"Don't start with that nonsense again, El."

Still grinning, Brooks nodded and said, "We'll leave day after tomorrow, maybe day after that."

"Day after tomorrow is best."

Brooks nodded again. "That suits."

PLANS WERE MADE and before dawn on the second day they were pulling out of the Nez Perce village, heading northeast. They moved fast for three days, and on the fourth they made their way through Lost Trail Pass and continued on for three more days, turning south along the Big Hole River, where they made a camp.

They started setting their traps in the river and the streams that fed into it the next morning, but they found their take was rather poor.

"A bit too early yet," Brooks said that night. "Judgin' by what we found, though, it won't be long before we start pullin' in prime plews."

"Since we're here and set up for a spell, how's about we start makin' meat?" Bill White asked.

"You see any buffler about?" Potts asked.

"No, but there's plenty of elk, and while that don't make as good jerky as buffler, it'll do."

"Bill's right," Brooks said. "Hawl, ye and Zeke go out huntin' tomorrow. The rest of ye can trap if that's where your stick floats, but we'll all have to help with the butcherin' and such, as usual."

"If Duncan 'elps with the butcherin', I ain't doin' so," Two-Faces Beaubien said. "Ze fool, 'e is so bad 'e makes blood and meat go flyin' all about, makin' a mess of my fine clothes." The beginnings of a grin crept onto his face.

"Hell, lad, ye've nae had clean 'skins since the day after ye come out of your mam's womb," MacTavish retorted with a chuckle. "Ye e'er wonder why we ne'er have trouble with bears? It's 'cause ye smell so high, those poor critters are afraid to come around us."

"For which you should thank me, m'sieur."

Laughter slid through the camp.

TWO DAYS WAS enough time to realize that the trapping was getting no better here, nor was making meat. So they pushed on, catching the Beaverhead River and following it northeast toward the Jefferson, trapping the streams clean along the way. Three months later, as winter began pressing its heavy hand on the land, they moved into the Tobacco Root Mountains, where they found a large valley surrounded by pine- and aspen-studded hills. There was plenty of beaver sign and there were a large herd of buffalo. They settled in for the winter. trapping and making meat. Both went well.

As spring edged into the glen, and the men set about their trapping again, Cooper, Brooks, and Potts set off on a trading trip to a Flathead village they had found before winter had set in a day and a half ride northwest of them.

"SOMETHING AIN'T RIGHT HERE," Cooper said when he and the two other mountain men were less than half a mile along the well-worn path to where the men had made their winter camp among the widely spaced trees.

"I was thinkin' the same," Brooks said. "Too damn quiet. The boys ought to be makin' some noise. At least we should hear the horses and mules."

"Maybe we just can't hear anything with the stream so close," Potts offered.

"Ain't no stream runnin' hard enough to mask the sound of a herd the size we got, nor the sound of young'uns playin'," Cooper responded.

Potts tied the three pack animals to a tree, and then, without needing instructions, the trappers began to spread out a little as they rode slowly forward. And they stopped as one, firearms ready, behind trees and peered out at the camp. Cooper, in the center, looked at Brooks to his left, then Potts to his right, their eyes wide. Where there should have been sixty or so horses and mules, there were four of the former.

Teeth clenched in anger and concern, Brooks led the way into the camp. He and the others were greeted by a dejected batch of mountain men, none of whom was inclined to look at the three returnees. The women and children were behind them, scared and worried looking.

"Ain't even a one of ye got the stones to greet your three compadres returned from their long trip?" Brooks asked harshly.

When he got no response, he roared, "What the hell happened here?"

The men in camp shuffled their feet but no one said anything.

Brooks spat. "Duncan? Two-Faces?"

The two named, and all the others, hung their heads, not wanting to look at their leader.

"Somebody doesn't answer me right quick," Brooks snapped, "me and Hawley will commence to whalin' the tar out of each and every one of ye 'til somebody tells us what went on here."

"White men," said Little Fox, one of Two-Faces' two wives.

Brooks stopped halfway off his horse, glared at the assembled men, then finished dismounting. "White men?? Mountaineers?"

"*Oui, Capitaine*," Beaubien said softly, not raising his head. "Zey take us by surprise."

"Anyone hurt?" Brooks asked, puzzled.

"*Mais non.*"

"No one was hurt in an attack?" There was disbelief in the captain's voice.

"There weren't no attack, El," Paddy Murphy said, looking as if he were trying to crawl into a hole.

"Someone best tell me what's gone on here," Brooks barked, anger flaring uncontrolled.

"Alistair," Cooper said, "our pack animals are a

couple hundred yards back the way we came. Go fetch 'em."

Alistair Wentworth hurried off, face showing his great relief.

"Well?" Brooks demanded.

Beaubien took a deep breath and let it out. "Three trappairs came into camp. We welcome zem like we ze good 'ommes we are. We all sat, ate food, and talked a little. Everything seemed all right, so we relaxed. Zen more zan a dozen others came out from behind ze trees, weapons cocked and ready."

"They have plews with 'em?" Brooks asked. "If they didn't, ye should have been suspicious."

"*Oui.* Three mules *with* packs."

"Zey caught us flat-footed. When ze others come out, some hold us under ze threat of guns while ze others took all ze plews, then zen all left with all ze 'horses and mules."

"We lost a horse and beaver? Everything?" Brooks exploded.

"*Oui.*"

"How could ye let this happen, Two-Faces? You're too experienced to let your guard down when a batch of anyone comes into camp that you don't know."

"I was not thinking, El. I..."

"Och, tell him the truth, lad," MacTavish said, lifting his head and gritting his teeth against the truth he was about to provide.

"*Mais non, mon ami.* I..."

"Och, shut yer mouth wi' such nonsense. Two-Faces, Grady, and Alastair were nae here in camp, El. They were out huntin'. The rest, it happened the way Two-Faces said. Aye. By the time he got back here, the bastards were gone. What we did nae tell him, he could puzzle out."

"I would 'ave maybe done ze same, *capitaine*," Beaubien added.

"Ye should always be wary around folks ye don't know, even if they are in the same trade as us. 'Least 'til ye get to know 'em and know their intentions. Ye should know that, Duncan."

"Aye, 'tis certain. I was too trustin' because there was only three of 'em, and seven of us in camp here." He sighed. "I allowed meself to be made a fool of. It cost all of us dearly." He sighed again. "'Twas me who's responsible. I let those buggers into camp and treated the malicious bastards like the friends they claimed to be. Och, I was a damn bloody fool."

"Mayhap," Cooper said. "Ye said there were more than a dozen?"

"Aye."

"With Two-Faces, Grady, and Alastair out of camp, that was strong odds in their favor. Two to one or so."

"Does nae matter," MacTavish said. "'Twas my doin' that caused all the trouble. Ye should punish me, El, not Two-Faces or the others, who only followed me." His back straightened, and he stared at Brooks, ready to take his penalty.

"I'll deal with ye later, Duncan. But I reckon it won't go bad for ye. There were five or six of ye in camp and only three of them devils. Ye couldn't know there was a dozen in hidin'." He paused, then, "Paddy, go help Alistair with the pack animals and our horses." He stood, thinking, as Murphy gathered up the three horses and moved away.

Cooper smiled wanly at his woman, who had

quietly approached him. "Goes Far, get food for me and El and Zeke," he said softly. He watched her walk away, thinking about how long he had taken to get used to her new name. At the last rendezvous, she had told some of the other Nez Perce women of her travels far and wide, and they had given her the new name to reflect that.

When they had eaten, drunk coffee, and lighted pipes, Potts asked, "What're we gonna do, El?"

The rest of the men in camp began quietly gathering, sitting on the ground near enough to hear but not so close as to draw attention.

"Hell if I know. This here's poor bull and there ain't no use in denyin' it." He looked at MacTavish. "When did this happen?"

"Yesterday afternoon."

"They've had a hell of a start on us then," Potts said.

Brooks glared at him for a moment, letting the younger man know just how stupid and unnecessary the statement had been.

"Well, I'm goin' after 'em," Cooper said with finality. When the others looked at him, he shrugged. "I ain't about to let these shit piles get away with stealin' my horses and plews, if I can help it. I got my horse and my rifle. And I got a heart full of hate for those pusillanimous snake humpers. I don't take kindly to such vermin stealin' my animals and the rest of my hard-won plunder. No, sirree, I sure as hell don't. And I aim to get my things back even if it takes me the rest of my life."

"It might take your life, Hawl," Brooks said.

"Ain't much of a life when all I've worked for is taken by a bunch of thievin' bastards."

THIRTEEN

Spring 1833

"HOW'RE y'all gonna find 'em?" White asked.

Cooper cast a gimlet eye on him. "You tellin' me I can't follow a trail left by more than a dozen mountaineers, sixty or more animals, some of 'em loaded with plews?"

"Foolish question," White said. "Sorry, Hawl."

"What about the rest of us?" George Miles asked. "What're we supposed to be doin' while you're off chasin' those thievin' sons a bitches?"

"Ain't my concern, George. You others can stay here 'til I get back with all our plunder or you can follow along on foot and what animals are left. With the few horses left and the three pack mules we just come in with, you can make do. Some of you ride—maybe takin' turns—while the others walk."

"That's not good, *señors*," Luis Gamez said. "Why should we take turns riding when you and the others go off on your own horses?"

"Then stay here, Luis," Brooks snapped.

"We don' care for your woman," Jacques Dubois rasped.

"Ain't askin' you to, nor do I expect it," Cooper said, "especially from a weak-kneed useless ol' critter like you. I'll either leave her in someone's care or take her with me."

"I'll be comin' with ye, lad," MacTavish said. "That is, if ye'll have me."

Cooper gave it a little thought, then asked, "One of those horses yours?"

"Aye."

"You got a rifle?"

"Aye."

Cooper thought a bit more, then nodded.

"I come too, eh?" Beaubien said. It was not a question. "I 'ave my 'orse and rifle because like Duncan says, I was out 'unting."

"What about your women?" Cooper asked.

"Zey can take care of zemselves and our children."

"I'll watch over 'em, Two-Faces," Bill White said. "Goes Far, too, Hawl, if y'all want."

"Ye'll watch Mornin' Song, Bill?" Potts asked.

"Sure enough."

"Then I'm goin' too."

"And me," Brooks added.

"No, El, you're not goin'," Cooper said. When Brooks looked at him in surprise, he added, "You're needed here. You're still the captain of this outfit, and everyone'll be countin' on you to make sure they're all safe."

"But..."

"He's right, El," Grady Murphy said. "Those who

ain't with Hawley and the others will need a steady hand to guide 'em whether they stay here or follow along."

"I ain't happy about this, ye know."

"Didn't expect you to be," Cooper said.

"We best get a move on then," the ever-impetuous Potts said.

"Mornin' Song won't like it," Cooper said, though there was no laughter from him or anyone else.

Potts's retort froze before it could escape his lips when he realized the truth of it.

"They've got enough of a start on is that another night ain't gonna make a difference, I reckon," Cooper said. "Besides, there's work to be done here maybe."

"Like what?" Wentworth asked.

"Depends on what the others plan on doin'. If they plan to come traispsin' after us, they'll need to cache what we got—the plews we just brought in, anything left that might be usable later. Elsewise, like the rest of us, they best get some rest—" He glared at Potts. "We'll be leavin' before first light."

AS COOPER WAS SADDLING his horse in the still-dark morning, MacTavish walked up, towing his horse. "Ye know I made a hash of things, Hawl," the Scotsman said. "But I..."

"That you did, Duncan. You was made a damn fool of." Cooper clapped him on the shoulder. "Just remember you ain't the first one who's been made a fool of." He remembered the time, not so long ago, really, when he had been hornswoggled by Josiah Weeks.

After all this time, and having gotten his revenge, it still sickened him. "And you won't be the last. Now let's get movin'."

The four men moved northeast as fast as they dared while keeping up a constant vigilance. They moved out of the Tobacco Roots and onto the Jefferson River then turned north along Whitetail Deer Creek before the trail led them into the Elkhorn Mountains. Two weeks into their quest, the track led them to Beaver Creek, which they followed northeast where they closed in on the renegade mountain men.

Leaving their horses well back in the trees, the men crept forward to reconnoiter. To their surprise, they saw a well-appointed camp that included two tipis and three tents. The men figured they were for some of the thieves with Indian wives. More than seventy horses and mules, as best they could see from where they were grazed just to the west under the watchful eyes of three guards. Cooper and his companions crept back to where their animals were.

"What in hell are those lads doin' sittin' here with all the animals? And the plews?" MacTavish said.

"Hell if I know," Cooper responded. "Maybe they're waitin' for others of their ilk to show up to help move everything. Maybe they're just restin' before they move on to wherever they plan to sell everything.

Maybe Fort Union or one of the Hudson's Bay houses. Likely they're dealin' with The Company. Don't matter none to me."

"It's a good spot for them, maybe," Beaubien said. "Zey are well protected here, out of ze way but only ten, maybe fifteen miles to ze Missouri, I t'ink."

"Like Hawley said, it don't matter," Potts said. "What does matter is now that we found 'em, what're we gonna do?" Potts asked.

"Maybe we wait 'til just before dawn, eh. Zen one or two of us sneak down zere, and run off with ze animals, while ze others shoot any damn mountaineers except us, of course, eh, who come after us."

"Just like that, eh, Two-Faces?" Potts said with an annoyed grin.

"*Mais oui*."

"Are all half breeds as crazy as you, Two-Faces?"

"*Mais oui!*" Beaubien grinned.

"That might work," Cooper said quietly, "but it ain't likely."

"We could use the other lads," MacTavish said almost forlornly.

"That we could, Duncan," Cooper said.

They fell silent.

"Maybe we can," Cooper finally said in a voice that was both wistful and calculating.

"How do ye figure that, lad?" MacTavish asked.

"Well, they had just about enough horses and mules to mount everyone, even if a few of the women had to double up."

"So?"

"So if they've been moving with any alacrity, they might not be too far behind us."

"Don't see why they should, lad."

"With few guns and with women and children along, they might be concerned about an attack by Crows or Blackfeet so are movin' as fast as they can to not fall too far behind us."

"Again, so?"

"Well," Cooper said thoughtfully, with just the barest hint of a smile in his voice. "If a certain smart-mouth young critter was to ride hard along the back trail, he might just find the others and hurry 'em up to get here."

"Ye best not be talkin' about me, Hawley Cooper," Potts snapped.

"Who else?"

"But..."

"It'd give you a chance to see Mornin' Song."

Potts's eyes widened. "Maybe that ain't such a bad idea," he said, more excitedly than thoughtfully.

"That'd mean thirteen of us—if every lad has a firearm—to raise bloody hell on those schemin' devils that took our plunder," MacTavish said thoughtfully.

"Yep. Even the odds up a heap. 'Course Zeke might not be able to run the others down, or some red devils might arrive.

"Or they might move the camp," MacTavish said.

"I don' t'ink zey do zat at last for a spell," Beaubien said. "Zey 'ave plenty of wood, water, and forage."

"It was nae reasonable for them to stop here and put up a camp that looks to be here a while longer either," MacTavish said.

Beaubien nodded, thinking that over. "I t'ink now you say it, you maybe are right. Maybe zey wait for others to 'elp drive all ze horses and take ze plews to a trading post to see zem. Or maybe zey 'ave sent a couple men to Fort Union or whatever place zey are dealing with to bring back buyers along with 'elp."

"Or," MacTavish added thoughtfully, "maybe there's other of these bloody vermin out there preyin' on other mountaineers and will be bringin' that plunder here."

"Damn," Cooper muttered. "If any of that's true, others might be here at any time. That don't help matters any."

"Nae it dunna," MacTavish said. "But maybe those nasty lads'll stay here without help for a spell."

"Long enough for us to get reinforcements," Cooper said with a nod.

"Aye."

"There's still some daylight left, Zeke. You want to leave right off?" It was an order rather than a suggestion.

Potts nodded and stood.

Before the young man headed for his horse, Cooper said, "I don't need to tell you not to dally..."

"Then don't."

Cooper nodded. "Don't keep on the search too long. Day and a half, two days maybe at most, then head back here. If the others aren't with you, we'll figure out something to do."

Once more, Potts nodded and hurried off to saddle his horse.

FOURTEEN

COOPER and the others were beginning to despair that Potts would return, concerned that he had met a sorrowful fate at the hands of some Indians. But five days later, Potts led a bedraggled group of trappers, women and children into the sparse camp.

"About time you showed up, Zeke," Cooper said as his friend dismounted. But he smiled. The smile grew when Goes Far rushed to him and hugged him tightly.

"Have any trouble?"

"Nothin' we needed to be concerned about," Brooks said.

"Took you long enough."

Potts's eyes blazed for a moment, but it was Brooks who said, "We were doin' all right. Not really kickin' up dust but movin' steadily. Good thing we cached those plews back where this happened."

"Ye moved our camp up some, I see," Potts said as he started to unsaddle his horse, as did the others.

"Yep. Put a good ten miles or so between us and those sons a bitches."

"They still there then?" Potts asked.

"Yep. I get the feelin' they won't be much longer. I sense they're ready to head wherever it is they're headin'. Been so ever since another feller come ridin' in day before yesterday."

Potts and Brooks nodded. "Any food to be had?" the latter asked.

"Ain't much. Two-Faces has brought in a couple deer, using his bow."

"Good thinkin'," Brooks commented.

"We've been wary about fire, though. We've only had one, that's all the three of us have needed. We stoke it up once come night, in a deep fire pit surrounded by rocks. I reckon you can start a couple others come dark, just bein' mindful like the three of us have been. There's a supply of good dry wood over there," he said, pointing.

The women needed no instruction on what to do and by the time the men had unsaddled the horses and mules, four fires were laid in rock-surrounded fire pits ready to be lit.

In the meantime, the men sat under the shade of trees.

"Ye've had a heap of time to think, Hawl," Brooks said. "Ye made any plans on how we're gonna get our plunder back?"

"Well, I was waitin' for Zeke to get back. He's such a polite, level-headed ol' hoss, I figure we just send him over to that camp and have him ask them real nice to return out horses and plews."

Everyone looked at his as if he were insane.

"Ye must be joshin', Hawl," Potts sputtered. "I...we..."

Suddenly Brooks began to laugh. "Might be best to send Al. He's got that kindly face, lookin' like an angel or a saint or something and..."

The others joined in the laughter, even Potts, who realized he was the butt of the joke.

The sound died down, and Brooks asked, "Any plan for real, hoss?"

"Maybe. It ain't much of one, but it might be the only one." He paused, then said , "All you boys have guns?"

"I got two but they're only pistols," Paddy Murphy said.

"Same here," White tossed in.

"That'll have to do."

I figure to send Bill, Two-Faces, and Paddy to get the animals. They're used to dealin' with the fractious beasts. Two-Faces, think you can take out the horse guards quietly?" Cooper said with a smile, knowing the answer.

Beaubien offered a malicious grin. "*Mais oui, m'sieur!*"

"Good. I reckon Bill's mare'll lead the way for the most part once they get to runnin'. If the animals scatter, we can gather 'em up after we take care of those bastards down there."

"You mean *if* we take care of zose 'ommes," Jacques Dubois said.

"No," Potts answered for Cooper, "he means after we dispose of those critters. I ain't about to lose, and I reckon everyone else feels the same. Except maybe ye."

"*Mais no,*" Dubois protested, though he didn't sound all that convincing.

"You endanger these doin's, Jacques," Cooper growled, "and you'll pay dearly for it. You understand?"

"*Oui*," the older man said sullenly.

"Gettin' the animals movin' will draw those fellers out from wherever they are," Cooper said.

"And we shoot those sumbitches down," Potts added.

"Aye," MacTavish interjected.

"Might not be that easy," Potts said. "There's a hell of a lot open ground once we leave the trees, and we'll have to do that because some of the men only have pistols."

Cooper nodded. "Could be risky, that's certain. But those boys'll be exposed too. Those of us with rifles can down several of 'em straight off, then those with pistols can close in on 'em."

"We're still outnumbered," Murphy said. "Especially with three of us off dealin' with the animals."

"We ain't outnumbered that much now with all of us here, and our plews and animals are worth the risk, don't ye boys think?" Brooks asked. When no one said anything, he added, "Any of ye don't want to join in, ye can stay here with the women and children."

There was silence for a bit before Cooper asked, "Two-Faces, can either of your women handle horses?"

"*Oui*. Both of zem. Why?"

"If they help with the horses, we can keep another man with us. That's if you don't mind them riskin' their necks." He raised his eyes in question.

"*Mais non, m'sieur* Coopair. Zey are not as valuable to me as my plews and ze 'orses," he said. But he winked.

Cooper and the others chuckled a little.

"Then it's done," Cooper said. "Paddy, you'll stand with the rest of us. Two-Faces, go tell your women. Jacques, since you don't seem to be eager to join the battle, you'll stay behind to watch over the other women and children."

"I am not a nanny, *m'sieur*," Dubois said indignantly. "I am..."

"What ye are is a dried-up old man who'd only put the rest of us in danger if we let ye come along," Potts snapped.

Before Dubois could respond, Cooper said, "There's seven, maybe eight women with 'em down there, and a bunch of young'uns. Unless they put up a fight, leave 'em be."

"If they are wi' these skunks, lad, they dunna deserve consideration."

"I ain't a woman killer, nor a baby killer, Duncan," Cooper said. "If they cause too much of a fuss, I'll make gone beaver of 'em without worryin' about it. But I don't aim to kill any women and kids just because they're with these miscreants. Might be that they're not with them of their own accord. We get done with this, we can give each of 'em a horse, maybe some meat if it's available and send 'em on their way."

MacTavish thought that over a moment, then nodded. "Aye."

"When do we do this?" White asked,

"I can't see no point in dawdlin'," Brooks said. "First light. We'll move up right to their camp just before dawn and be ready."

LEAVING BEHIND MOST of the women and all the children under the protection of Jacques Dubois, the other men and Beaubien's two Indian wives, carefully made their way through the woods, Beaubien, White and the two women on horseback. It was tricky going in the dark with the light of the full moon partially blocked by the canopy of trees, but Cooper and MacTavish had carved out something of a trail to follow.

Before leaving, Cooper had sketched out in the dirt where the camp's layout. "From the east there's a tent, then a lodge, two more tents, one of which is where it seems the plews are bein' kept, and another lodge. A stream runs roughly east and west, maybe twenty yards behind the lodges and tents. It curls sharply south a quarter mile or so from the last lodge. The herd is kept on the west side of that beyond a small, thin stretch of cottonwoods along the stream. The tree line across from us is thirty or so yards north of the stream behind the lodges."

"How far from the tree line where we are to the tents?" McTavish asked.

"Sixty, seventy yards. It's why I think they set the camp where it is. The stream is between them and the thinner timber over that way and a longer spell of empty space to the heavier woods on this side."

"Tougher to cover the distance from better cover on this side," Brooks said.

"Yep."

Minutes later, Beaubien, his two wives, and Bill White made their way toward the herd. The rest of the men took their positions to await the dawn.

As the sky was just beginning to lighten, several

women came out of the lodges and went to the creek with buckets. Moments later, Cooper smiled when he heard a rumble and figured Beaubien and the others had gotten horses and mules to start flowing away from the camp. His smile deepened when Beaubien let loose with a war cry learned from his mother's people.

FIFTEEN

MEN BOILED out of the tents and lodges, several of them slipping suspenders over shoulders with one hanmd while holding a rifle in the other.

"Now!" Brooks said.

Five rifles roared and five men in the camp went down. Brooks and his men swiftly reloaded and let fire another volley. Three more of the thieving mountain men in the camp went down. Confused and with nothing to shoot at, the rest scattered, seeking refuge behind the tents or tipis.

"Be good to know for sure how many of 'em were in that camp," Cooper said as he reloaded his rifle.

"Can't be too many left," Brooks responded. "There's eight of 'em down in the camp, plus two or three who were watching the horses."

"That's ten or eleven. Duncan said there were more than a dozen, so there could be five or six, maybe more if others joined 'em in the past couple weeks."

"And they're pretty well hidden," Potts said.

"So are we."

"Seems a standoff, then, lads," MacTavish said.

"What'll we do now, El?" Potts asked.

"I ain't sure. Hawley?"

Cooper was silent for a little, then yelled, "You boys down there in the camp. Come on out and surrender, turn over all the plews you stole from us, and you might live to see the sunset today."

"Go to hell," a voice drifted up from the camp.

"Come on down and get us," another shouted.

"We will, boys, no fear."

"Did ye think that'd work, Hawl?" Alistair Wentworth asked.

"Nope, but I thought I'd try it before another idea I had."

"Which is?" Potts asked.

Cooper drew in a breath and let it slowly out. "Ain't sure it'll work, but I figure Two-Faces and the others ain't too far off with the animals. Likely just drove 'em out a mile or so down the valley to wait for us to finish our work here rather run 'em into the trees where they'd be harder to control."

"So?"

"Paddy," Cooper said, "mount up and ride down the valley a ways, see if you can find Two-Faces and the others."

"Then what?"

"Tell 'em to stampede the animals back this way."

"What?" Murphy, Potts, and Brooks said in unison, startled.

"Run 'em right through the damn camp. That ought to send those bastards down there scatterin'. Before the dust settles, we move in and finish those boys off."

"Waugh!" Murphy said with a grin. "That shines with this boy-o. Aye, it does."

"Good. Don't spend too much time on it. If they ain't within a couple miles or so, or if they've moved out of the valley, it might not be worth our while to keep searchin' for 'em and we'll try to think of somethin' else."

"Aye," Murphy said, and then he was gone.

"Rest of you boys keep your eyes on those tents," Cooper said. "Any of 'em tries to move, we fire at him, in this order: me, Zeke, Duncan, El."

There were murmurs of acknowledgment.

The minutes crawled along like hours as Brooks's men waited amid the trees in the growing heat, sweating. Their only solace was that the men in the camp had no protection however meager, offered by trees.

They were quiet but nervous, the tension increased by the faint report of a gunshot from far to the west.

"Damn, I hope that don't mean trouble for Two-Faces and the others," Brooks muttered.

No one bothered to respond.

Then came a deep low rumble from the west.

"Reckon, Paddy found Two-Faces," Cooper said with a relieved grin. The smile turned to shock, and his eyes widened as a herd of a hundred or more buffalo came thundering through the trees at the curve of the stream, cross the creek, and into the camp.

"Jumpin' sweet lord almighty," Potts said in awe.

"Waugh! If that ain't the damnedest thing I ever seen," Brooks muttered.

Several other men expressed their surprise with various exclamations of awe and wonder.

Out in the flat, one of the women stuck her head

out of the farthest lodge, spun, spoke hurriedly to those inside, and moments later, they were fleeing toward the trees on the north side of the creek barely beating out the rushing herd.

At the same time, the men there fired several rounds at the rushing beasts, hoping to turn the stampede. Then they were scrambling for safety, if they could find it, as the animals, not slowing, roared along, taking down the lodges and tents, scattering all manner of gear as well as packs of plews in their headlong rush.

Three of the thieving trappers were mashed under the hooves of the thundering rush of the massive animals. A few of the others raced after the women; two more headed toward Brooks and his men around the end of the charging buffalo, tossing down their rifles as they went.

"Surrendering now won't save your bloody hair, mate," Alistair Wentworth snarled as he shot down one of the pair.

The other trapper yelled over the din of the stampede, "Don't shoot me, boys! I..."

A lead ball from Luis Gamez's pistol stopped the man in midsentence. "Steal my plews, you think, señor? Not with this hombre, you hijo de una puta."

"Time to end this, boys," Brooks said after the buffalo had moved on in a rush, leaving behind a lingering cloud of dust.

"Shouldn't be hard," Potts said. "I think I only saw three of them fellers reach the trees."

"They're still armed," Cooper cautioned as he rose.

The men moved out of the trees and into the screen of dust. As they came out of it, two shots rang out from the trees. The mountain men dropped down flat, most of them letting loose a string of curses.

"Everyone all right?" Brooks called.

Six men responded.

"Mulligan?" the leader called. But he got no answer. "Damn," he muttered. "Any of ye see where those shots come from?"

"One of 'em come from about five yards to the left of where that one woman and child are tryin' to hide behind that pine and not doin' a very good job of it," Potts said.

Moments later, a flash of red was seen slipping through the trees away from them. Potts fired but missed, letting out a string of oaths.

"I'll take that son of a bitch," George Miles said. He leaped up and charged into the trees.

Moments later, there were three shots from within the trees.

"Come on ahead, boys," Paddy Murphy's voice suddenly came strongly from the trees. "Ain't but one of these boy-os left and he's got an achin' head."

"You seen George?" Brooks called as he rose.

"Gone under. One of these boys got him but he got that son of a bitch."

"Damn," Brooks muttered again. He and the others walked toward the voice and found Murphy standing over a dazed trapper.

"Why ain't you with Two-Faces?" Cooper asked, not entirely friendly sounding.

Murphy's eyes raised. "Him and Bill didn't need me, so sent me off to come up on this side of the stream to get behind these bastards."

"He still got the horses?"

"Of course." The Irishman grinned. "He's just waitin' for one of us to tell him it's all right to bring 'em back here."

"Whose idea was it to run the buffler through here?" Potts asked.

"I must confess, lads, that it was me," he said with a wide grin. "We saw that herd out there grazing nice and peacefully. Then the idea hit me. Me, Two-Faces and Bill talked it over, and we all agreed it'd be a good idea if we could get it to work. We moved the horses and mules off a little way so they wouldn't be spooked, then me and Bill got them shaggies movin' with a gunshot and some blanket wavin'. Didn't take much to get 'em riled up and movin'. Seems to have worked, eh?"

"Aye, lad," MacTavish said with a laugh.

Brooks nodded and smiled, but then grew serious. "Al, ye and Luis, go get our men's bodies and set 'em next to where that one lodge was. We'll see to 'em shortly. Duncan, get those women and children. Let's see if we can do anything with 'em. Paddy, head on back and tell Two-Faces to bring the horses in."

"What about Jacques and the women and children?" Murphy asked.

"I'll send one of Two-Faces' wives after 'em once he and the animals are back."

Murphy nodded and headed off, as did the others with their missions.

"What about him?" Potts asked, pointing to the captured mountain man.

"Maybe he'll talk to us," Cooper said.

"Like hell I will."

"Then you're in for a bad time, hoss."

"Tie him to that limb there," Brooks said, pointing.

"Stretch him so he's barely on his toes. Don't hang him —at least not yet." When that had been done, Brooks stood in front of the trapper. "What's your name, boy?"

"I ain't tellin' ye nothin'."

"Things'll get painful for you," Cooper said.

The man shrugged as best he could. "Ye boys are gonna make wolf bait out of me anyway, so I can't see any reason to talk to ye."

"Ye think it's a good thing to steal horse and beaver from feller mountaineers?" Cooper asked.

Another shrug.

Cooper slammed as butt of his rifle into the man's side, snapping several ribs. The man sagged a little but was caught up by the rope around his neck.

"Such doin's don't shine with me. Nor any of the others."

"Wouldn't with me either," the man gasped.

"Then you shouldn't have done it," Cooper responded.

Horses, pushed slowly by Beaubien and his two wives ambled back into the ravaged camp.

"Nice work, Two-Faces," Brooks said. "Send one of your women back to get our own women and kids." When Beaubien went off to talk to his wives, Brooks said, "Well, this feller needs to fill his meatbag," Brooks said. "We can take up the chat with this feller again later. Let him think about things for a spell."

Followed by the others, he plopped down at what was the remains of a fire in the jumbled mess left by the stampede. "Somebody go get these boys' women here and have 'em start fixin' us some food."

"Whatever possessed ye to do such a thing as

stealin' our horses and plews, hoss?" Brooks asked the man tied to the tree.

"Easier than trappin' 'em."

"What were ye gonna do with 'em?" Potts asked.

"Told ye, I ain't sayin' anything."

"I can get him to talk," Potts said.

Brooks considered that for a moment, then shook his head. "No. He may be a fool and a reprehensible ol' bastard, but I reckon he's a tough ol' critter."

"So what do we do with him?"

"Leave him."

"For how long?"

"For as long as it takes whatever critters are around to find him," Brooks said flatly. He turned and went back to the fire. "Dan, you and Al take over watchin' the animals, let Two-Faces come fill his meatbag."

The thieves' women, after having served Brooks and the others, sat nearby, huddled together in fear. Brooks, Cooper and the others paid them little heed until Dancing Water and Little Fox arrived with the other women and children.

When the two had eaten some, Brooks said, "See if ye can find out from these men's women why they stole all our plews and horses. Indians'll do that, but I never heard of white men doin' so to another, at least not in such a manner or scale." He hesitated, and before the two women moved, he said, "First ask 'em how many men were here."

Dancing Water nodded and sat with the thieves' women and chatted with them in several languages. Within moments, she called to Brooks, "Eighteen men. Two gone from here."

Brooks counted in his head, then nodded. "All're accounted for, if those numbers are right."

After a tense twenty minutes, Dancing Water took a seat near Brooks, Cooper and the others. "Like all women," she began matter-of-factly, "these women know little. We not told much. But they overhear the men talkin' when they think their women not listenin'. They say something about Crows and American Company..."

"American Fur?" Cooper asked sourly.

Dancing Water nodded. "Also say Crows help 'em sell plews at Fort Union."

"It don't surprise me," Cooper said, "that the Crows and the American Fur bastards are behind this. I'm surprise we ain't heard similar from others."

Brooks said. "Maybe we're the first and if they could get away with it, they'd take on others."

"So what do we do now?" Pott asked.

"We take our plews and our animals and get back to trappin'."

"What about these fellers?" Potts waved his arm around, taking in the bodies scattered around the camp.

"Ye concerned?"

"Nope, just wonderin'."

"To hell with 'em. We leave 'em here for the scavengers. Ye want to scalp 'em, go on ahead. Ain't no one gonna stop ye."

"Much as I despise these boys for what they done, it don't seem right to take their hair."

Brooks nodded. "Get a couple of the boys to help dig some graves for George and Grady. We'll hold whatever kind of service we can figure out over their bodies before buryin' 'em. A few of ye others, drag these dead bastards off near their amigo tied to the tree so the scavengers can feed on all of 'em. We'll spend the night here and pull out in the mornin'.'"

But it was not a peaceful night with the thieving mountain man's screams and the growling of the wolves and coyotes in their feeding frenzy.

THE NEXT MORNING, Duncan MacTavish set down his bowl after finishing his breakfast. He sat up a little straighter. "'Tis time, El."

"For what?" Brooks looked surprised.

"For passin' judgment on me for bein' responsible for all these doin's."

Brooks sat thinking about it, then turned to Cooper. "What do ye think, Hawl?"

It was Cooper's turn to sit and think that through. Then he shrugged. "Like I told him as we were leavin' to chase down these wretched miscreants, he ain't the only one who's ever been hornswoggled, and he won't be the last."

Brooks nodded thoughtfully. "Reckon it's all turned out all right," he said. "I can't see no reason to levy some sort of punishment. It's..."

"No, no, Señor Brooks," Luis Gamez said. "It ees not all right."

"I agree," Jacques Dubois said. "'E cost us much time lost in trapping and troubles."

"And the loss of two men," Sam Bacon added.

Brooks considered that, then said evenly, "Ye others didn't do much to help him, boys."

"But we..." Dan Anderson started.

"No one elected Duncan as leader. Any one of ye could have seen through the plot maybe."

Tension built as Brooks pondered the situation. Finally, he nodded and said, "How's about this, boys? We take all of George's and Grady's possibles and divide 'em amongst us. Equal share of the plews. We keep the horses and mules separate 'til rendezvous, sell 'em and split the money. Take whatever else is theirs and divide it amongst us or sell it at rendezvous. Neither man has kin that I know of that we can send the money to."

"That don't shine," Wentworth said. "It's rewardin' him for bringin' these troubles on us."

He held up his hand to forestall any more protest. "Ye didn't let me finish. As his punishment, Duncan gets no share of any of it. No plews, horses, mules or specie."

After some argument, through which MacTavish stayed silent, Two-Faces Beaubien nodded. "*Bon, Capitaine.* Jacques and Luis disagree, but all ze others think it's fair."

Brooks gave MacTavish no chance to speak. "It's done then," he said with finality.

SIXTEEN

Summer 1833

"LOOKS LIKE YOU DID ALL RIGHT," William Sublette said as he toted up what Cooper was due for his three packs of plews. "Have any trouble? Outside the usual, I mean."

Cooper cast a sharp glance at him, but decided Sublette meant nothing accusatory or disdainful. "Nothin' I'd want to tell of," Cooper said noncommittally. None of the other of Brooks's men standing nearby said anything.

"Good thing," the trader said. "Some of the fellers said the Crows as well as the Blackfeet were on the prowl."

"You don't say. We had a run-in with both but nothin' worth talkin' about."

Sublette nodded. "Looks like you're due about twelve hundred at four dollars a pound, Mr. Cooper."

"That's a mite light, Mr. Sublette. "Got almost six dollars last year."

"Things change, boy," the trader said, nonplussed. "But I'll tell you what, Since I'm takin' you at your word that these packs are a hundred pounds each and not five or ten pounds less, I'll spring for four dollars and a quarter a pound," he added magnanimously.

"Obliged," Coper said through clenched teeth. He figured that even if things had changed, the plews should be worth at least five dollars a pound. Or so he had been told by others that that is what they had gotten from some other traders on the way to rendezvous. But there was nothing he could do about it. "Like as not you'll be chargin' a heap for supplies too."

"Like I've told you and others, a man's got to pay his way through life, and he needs money to do that."

"A man ought to be able to be paid decent money for his labors, too,"

"You can take your plews elsewhere and sell 'em," Sublette said arrogantly.

"The Company's offerin' more I hear, but we don't want much to do with them boys if we don't have to, Rather stick with you as you've been fair in the past." Cooper responded, barely holding back his anger. After what he and the others had gone through, this galled him.

Sublette stood in thought for a moment. "Tell you what, son, I'll go four and a half, though it breaks my heart to part with so much. But that's the best I'm gonna do."

Now it was Cooper's turn to think things over. He knew he could get at least five dollars a pound from whoever was trading for the Company this year, but it stuck in his craw to have to deal with them even though it would cost him some money. Still, the Company seemed responsible for the theft of his group's horses and plews. He sighed and said, "Keep the money with you for now, Mr. Sublette, if you're willin'. I'll be back for my supplies on the morrow when you ain't as busy what with all my friends here waitin' on you."

"It'll be here." Sublette's face grew stony. "And so will your money."

"Never said it wouldn't be." Cooper turned and stomped out. He climbed on his horse and with his empty mules trailing behind, headed for the small camp he and the others had put up. Goes Far came out of the lodge to meet him and smiled up at him. Some of his anger faded. They hobbled the mules and let them out to graze. He was a little uncertain about it. After the spring's events, he wasn't too sure he wanted to leave any property lying around to be taken.

Goes Far hopped on her pony bareback and the two rode off, the Nez Perce woman looking a little nervous.

They found Cheyenne Killer's camp several miles up the river. Cooper dismounted and hugged Cheyenne Killer and Cuts Throat, both of whom were standing in front of the former's lodge.

His sister, who had been standing out of the way, moved up with a grin. "Good to see you, brother," she said. She looked up at the still mounted Goes Far and asked, "So who's this?"

"My wife, Goes Far. A Nez Perce."

"She pretty. Too pretty for you," Pony Woman said with another grin. "As pretty as my friend who is no more."

Cooper's face clouded in sadness at the mention of his former woman, slain by the Crows.

"Is good you found another woman."

Pony Woman looked up at Goes Far and smiled. She indicated that the Nez Perce should dismount.

Goes Far looked at Cooper, trying to fight back her worry.

"It's all right," Cooper said with a soft smile. "She is my sister. She'll treat you well."

With some trepidation, Goes Far dismounted. Her eyes widened in surprise when Pony Woman hugged her and said, "Welcome" in her own language, even though the visitor likely did not understand her.

Still smiling, Pony Woman took the rope to Goes Far's pony in one hand and placed the other arm through her visitor's. Goes Far looked fearfully over her shoulder. Cooper nodded and smiled. The two women walked off, one chattering, the other silent, still nervous.

"They will be like sisters by night," Cuts Throat. "No tellin' how women do it."

"Come," Cheyenne Killer said, leading the way into the lodge.

Soon after filling their bellies, the men sat back with pipes. "Was good season?" Cheyenne Killer asked.

"Mostly." He smiled ruefully and then explained the theft and recovery.

"White men did that to others?" Cuts Throat asked, not too surprised.

"Ain't heard of such before, at least like this. But it's true. They won't be causin' no more trouble though."

After some talk of no consequence, Cheyenne Killer said, "We will have a lodge set up for you before tonight's celebration."

Cooper shook his head. "No, I won't be stayin' here, Father."

Cheyenne Killer looked hurt.

Cooper grinned a little. "Last thing you need is a drunken mountaineer staggerin' through the village causin' trouble."

"But..."

"He's right, Cheyenne Killer," Cuts Throat said. He grinned. "He's enough trouble when he's not full of firewater."

The chief nodded, sad but acknowledging the smartness of it. "You will stay the night, after the celebration," he said more than asked.

"I don't think that'll..." Cooper grinned. "Yep."

BROOKS'S GROUP left the '33 rendezvous the way they usually did—hungover and noisily. Until they got a mile or so away, when they slowed and just plodded along. Cooper and Brooks rode in silence for a while. There was no more need for them to talk just now, especially the way they were feeling.

The day was hot and muggy as they rode, and both men went to their gourd canteens frequently. But the water helped only to cut the dust in their throats; it did nothing to quench the fires in their bellies. Cooper cranked around to smile at his woman, who smiled back. It was a pleasant sight, comforting.

"What do ye think of the two new men?" Brooks finally asked.

"Don't like 'em, especially Webster. Wheeler ain't much better, I reckon seein' as how he's partnered up with Webster. Can't say why, but I figure they're gonna be trouble."

"I don't much like 'em either. Like ye, I can't say

why exactly. There's stories about 'em, Webster particular, of him causin' trouble on the Mississippi. Or maybe the Missouri. Lookin' at Webster, I can believe the stories." Brooks sighed. "But Luis and Dan vouched for 'em."

"Don't much care for those two either."

Brooks nodded. "Ain't much we can do about any of it now, though I figure I'm gonna regret takin' 'em on. We'll keep any eye on 'em. They start causin' trouble, we'll figure out what to do then." He cast a look back at the brutish Malachi Webster and the sycophantic Dave Wheeler and a shook his head.

They followed their usual route to the Nez Perce land, and then east and southeast until they reached the Big Hole River, which they followed north. Along Clark Fork, they set up a semi-permanent camp and swarmed the many creeks and streams that fed into the river. Before winter, they headed southeast and into the Boulder Mountains.

"THESE DOIN'S HERE SHINE," Zeke Potts said, stretching out his legs before the fire. "Plews are plentiful, ain't but a couple inches of snow on the ground, no Injun troubles to speak of. Seems Two-Faces has found us a good winterin' spot not too far off. Ain't had no trouble, really. Can't ask for much more."

"I told you before, Zeke," Cooper said in all seriousness, "not to go sayin' such things."

"And I told ye you're nothin' but a superstitious old coot worse'n any Injun I ever knew of."

"You're temptin' the Good Lord to send some deviltry at us."

"Bah," Potts said with a grin. "Ye just can't stand good fortune."

On the other side of the fire, Elson Brooks shook his head. "I hope you're right, Zeke," he said. "Be nice to get through a winter with no Indian trouble and with good trappin'."

Cooper had to agree after another couple of weeks at the spot they had found a day's ride from the place they planned to winter. But the trapping was too good here to move on just yet, especially with the weather mostly cooperating. They had had some snow, but little accumulated and the cold was still bitter, it not as intense as it could get.

As was usual, Cooper and Potts, who worked trap lines together, and Brooks and Beaubien, who part-nered on the trap lines, gathered every day to relax by the fire after the day's work had been accomplished.

And each day, to Cooper's annoyance, they would gleefully recount the day's success and then harangue each other.

"Ye seem a mite cheerful, Zeke, seein' as how Mornin' Song is havin' that time again and won't have nothin' to do with ye," Brooks said with a grin.

"Trappin's been too good to worry about such a thing," Potts responded, surprising everyone, including himself. "I..."

He stopped when Murphy came running into the camp bellowing, "Indians! Blackfeet!"

SEVENTEEN

Spring 1834—Fall 1834

THE MEN BURST INTO ACTIVITY. "Paddy! Bill!"
Brooks roared. "The women and children!"

Almost everyone else, not needing direction,
headed for the herd of horses and mules.

Cooper and Potts stayed behind in the open area of
the camp and dropped down two of the Blackfeet, then
ran toward the woods, reloading as they did.

Gunfire popped from inside the woods as the two
raced into the trees. The other men were surrounding
the horses and mules. Along with the women who
weren't playing mother hen to the children, the men
were fighting to calm the animals while fending off the
warriors.

Cooper fired again, hitting one Blackfoot, then
slinging the rifle over his back by the buckskin strap. He
grabbed out a pistol.

Potts dropped another warrior, as did several of the
other men.

MacTavish's voice rose above the noise, bellowing, "Shoot me, ye damn, festerin' bastard? Take this, laddie."

Cooper fired both pistols, hitting one Blackfoot but not killing him. Potts was better, taking down two warriors with pistol shots at close range. Cooper dropped one pistol as he started reloading the other.

"You had to go mouthin' off about how good things were, didn't you, Zeke, you damned fool," Cooper said as he hurried reloaded his pistols.

"Ye can chastise me later, Hawl. Right now, we're a bit busy," Potts responded as he did the same.

Before Cooper could finish reloading, a Blackfoot came rushing through the trees at him, lance in hand. Cooper darted behind a thick oak trunk and walloped the warrior on the back of the head with a pistol as the warrior slid by trying to stop. He quickly slipped a cap on and shot the Blackfoot in the back of the head. He began loading the pistol again. It took only moments, and then he reloaded the second before charging off through the trees, heading toward the other end of the animal herd.

He suddenly dropped to a knee at the side of a body, swung his rifle off his back and fired at a fleeing Blackfoot. The heavy lead ball caught the warrior in the back propelling him forward a few steps before he sprawled face first in the pine needles.

Cooper glanced at the body at his side and growled softly. Sam Bacon had not only been killed, he had been scalped. The mountain man headed to where the dead Indian lay, loading his rifle as he went. He rolled the Indian over and found the bloody scalp stuck through

the buckskin thong through which his buckskin breech-
cloth hung.

"Son of a bitch," Cooper muttered. He picked up
the scalp, kicked the dead warrior in the face and
turned to head back to Bacon's body. But he stopped,
turned back and scalped the Blackfoot. Moments later,
he gently lay Bacon's scalp on the man's body. He was
less gentle when he flung the dead warrior's scalp into
the dirt beside his friend's corpse. He rose. "Your spirit
ain't gonna wander with no way to get to the Hereafter,
ol' hoss," he said quietly. "But that bastard's will."

He spotted another Blackfoot. Trees were in the
way, so Cooper could not get a shot off. He slung the
rifle on his back and charged after the warrior. The
Indian seemed to sense someone coming and turned
just in time to have Cooper slam a shoulder into his
midsection and drive his back into a tree truck. The
warrior grunted and almost collapsed. Seeing no reason
to waste powder and ball, Cooper grabbed the warrior's
own knife and split him open.

Sporadic gunfire still popped, as did white men's
curses and Blackfoot war whoops. But all were fading,
and Cooper figured the warriors were running off. He
spotted one dashing through the woods and brought his
rifle up but a rifle cracked off to his left, and the Blackfoot went down, dead.

Potts came walking out of the trees. "Didn't know
ye had a bead on him, Hawl."

"Don't mind. Long as the son of a bitch is dead."

Brooks's voice called out, "Hawley! Hawley, you all
right?"

"Yep," Cooper yelled back. "Zeke too."

Other voices came drifting though reporting that they were alive. Then Brooks called, "Sam? Sam?"

"He's gone under," Cooper said.

The usual cavvy handlers, Dan Anderson and Paddy Murphy, along with Jacques Dubois and Alistair Wentworth, were already moving among the horses and mules calming them. The women tentatively came out of the thicket in which they had been hiding.

Dancing Water, one of Two-Faces Beaubien's wives, and White's Nez Perce woman, Bloody Hair, whom he called Martha, were treating Duncan MacTavish and Bill White, who had suffered mild wounds.

"Hawley, ye, Zeke and Two-Faces scout the area," Brooks said. "Make sure none of these savages are lurkin' about."

The three men nodded and headed off in separate direction. By the time they returned, having made a thorough search, the other men were sitting around the fire, boasting of their prowess, their crowing tempered only by Bacon's body resting under a blanket nearby.

"None of 'em out there," Cooper said.

"'Least none of 'em alive," Potts added. "I found six of them wretched critters. Made sure none of 'em'll get to the Happy Huntin' Grounds."

"Same with the eight I found," Cooper said.

"And I do ze same with ze five I find."

"Damn," Murphy crowed, "nineteen of these bastards gone under at our hands. Should teach 'em to keep away from us boys."

The others hooted and yelled their agreement.

"How'd the new boys do, El?" Cooper asked while watching the others celebrate.

"Best I can tell, Webster did all right. Wheeler seemed to be tryin' to hide when I saw him."

They buried Bacon with little ceremony later that afternoon other than a few prayers and a grave covered heavily with rocks to keep the scavengers out. That night they rested to the rousing chorus of yips and howls of wolves and coyotes gorging on the remains of the Blackfeet.

They moved the few miles to the valley Beaubien had picked for their winter camp. Trapping, which was good, continued for another month before the creeks and streams iced over. They had no more trouble.

They made a triumphant entry into the rendezvous at Ham's Fork that summer. To their surprise, they learned that William Sublette and his partner, Robert Campbell, had sold their company to the American Fur Company.

"I would've never thought you'd do such a thing, Bill," Cooper said as he traded in his furs.

"A man's got to be concerned with his business interests," Sublette responded without embarrassment. "The trade is changin', boy. You'd best be aware of that."

"I'll do so." He grinned ruefully. "It'll be some strange, though, to be trading in my plews to the Company. Those boys've been something of an enemy all along."

Sublette shrugged. "Like I said, Hawley, things change, and men have to change with 'em."

Cooper nodded. "What're you payin' for plews this year?" Cooper asked, figuring the answer would not be pleasing. With Sublette selling out to American Fur, there was little competition for the men's trade.

"Four dollars," Sublette was said evenly.

It wasn't as bad as Cooper had feared. "You can't go four and a half like last year?" Cooper was only a little hopeful.

"Not even four and a quarter. Four is the best I can do."

"Well, tote it up then," Copper said, discouragement sitting on his shoulders.

Business concluded, Cooper got Goes Far and rode off, looking for the Nez Perce camp. To his surprise, he found only a small one.

"Where're all the others?" he asked Buffalo Horn, a minor chief among the People.

"Come only part way. Say to come here was too far."

"Then why're you here?"

"Me and the others, we come to meet missionaries. Want to ask if they or others like them will come to our land, bring us their religion."

Cooper didn't want to tell the Nez Perce that he thought the idea foolish, that the Indians had a good religion, but it was not his place to say. Besides, he thought, he could very well be wrong.

"Did the others stay in your homeland?"

"No. Come part way. Wait for us in land of the shooting water."

Cooper nodded. "Well, then,. good luck with your quest."

From there, he and Goes Far rode to Cheyenne Killer's camp where his father held a celebration for Cooper and most of his friends that night.

The next day, Cooper and the others started their

spree. It was a muted affair at first, but as they filled up with *aguardiente*, they began crowing about their victory over the Blackfeet. The approbation they eared from everyone who heard, dulled the discouragement of the news about the Company, and their festivities grew wilder.

And as usual, they were a miserable looking—and feeling—bunch of men when they pulled out more than two weeks later.

They headed north along the Green River, then moved onto the Gros Ventre River. As they neared the confluence with the Snake River, Brooks sent Cooper, Potts and Beaubien scouting. Cooper crossed the Snake and followed its northeast path. Beaubien turned southward along the Snake, while Potts followed the east bank.

Cooper was the one who found the Nez Perce village set up along a creek that ran into the Snake. He rode in and was greeted enthusiastically.

"If you come this far, why didn't you just go the rest of the way to rendezvous?" Cooper asked as he and some warriors sat around a fire, eating, drinking coffee and smoking.

"Too far," Pale Thunder said. "This far enough. We wait for word from others about missionaries."

"You really want missionaries?"

Pale Thunder nodded. "They have powerful medicine, we have heard. We will learn of it," he said seriously.

In the morning he headed back toward where the rest of his companions would be following the Snake. Along the way, Beaubien showed up. Late in the afternoon, they found the others slowly making their way northeast up the Snake. A camp was quickly thrown up.

"Best go lookin' for Zeke tomorrow, Hawl," Brooks said.

Cooper grinned. "I'm surprised he's stayed out this long. I'd have expected him to spend no more than half a day out there before he started missin' Mornin'' Song."

"She won't have anything to do with him." Brooks chuckled.

"That time, eh?"

"Indeed."

IT WAS BARELY NOON when Cooper came across a dejected-looking Zeke Potts. "You look some melancholy," Cooper said.

"Couldn't find Red Leggin's camp, and I miss Mornin' Song."

"Reckon you do. I found the village. West side of the Snake about half a day's ride from here."

EIGHTEEN

Fall 1834

"WHERE'S ZEKE?" Brooks asked as he walked up to where Cooper was sitting with Pale Thunder in the temporary village along the Snake River. Though the Nez Perce was Morning Song's father, the war chief and Cooper had become close since Cooper had saved the warrior from the rabid wolf and the two often spent time talking.

"Where do you think he is?"

"Again? Damn. That boy'll wear himself down this way to where he'll be an old man come rendezvous." Brooks sighed. "Go find him. We need to get on the trail."

"You go find him. I ain't his wet nurse."

"Dammit, Hawl. I got to round up everyone else, and you're his friend."

"So're you." Cooper rose. "But since you're my friend, too, I'll go fetch him. Don't think I'll do this regular, though."

Brooks just grunted and stalked away.

Cooper headed to Potts's lodge and popped inside without announcing himself. He found the startled young mountain man rolling in the buffalo robes with Morning Song. "Time to go, boy," Cooper said with dash of amusement.

"Already? It ain't hardly dawn."

"Dawn was an hour ago. The rest of the boys are gettin' their plunder together and will be pullin' out soon."

"Hell, I ain't done here."

Get done or get left behind. I doubt El will be happy with you slowin' everyone else down. We'll be pullin' out within an hour, so you best be puttin' your pizzle back in your trousers and get movin'."

"Maybe I'll just stay a while, catch up to ye and the others in a day or two," Potts said, stroking Morning Song's bared breast from where it rose from under the buffalo robe. She showed little embarrassment.

"Just remember, boy," Cooper said with a wicked grin, "that if you stay here, you'll have to deal with her family, includin' Sits Down, not just her."

"Oh, Lord A'mighty," Potts snapped. "Get out of here, Hawley, whilst I get ready."

Chuckling, Cooper left and went back to Pale Thunder's lodge, and retook his seat. Goes Far had shown up when he was gone and sat working quietly with Morning Song's mother and another woman Cooper did not know.

"You have everything ready?" Cooper asked his wife.

"Yes." She did not bother looking up from her work.

Cooper just nodded.

A shadow suddenly blocked the sun and Cooper looked up to see Sits Down standing there, waiting to address him. The huge, fat, filthy, unkempt warrior had his poor bow and quiver of few arrows. In his right hand was the stone-headed lance that would double as a coup stick—if he ever dared to try to count coup. On his left arm was a bull-hide war shield. It was poorly painted and showed signs of neglect.

"I come with you," Sits Down said in his firm bass voice.

"No, Sits Down, we ain't takin' you along."

"I come. Fight Blackfoot."

"We ain't gonna be fightin' no Blackfoot if we can help it. All we're gonna do is trap beaver and hunt buffler when we have a mind to."

"I'm good beaver trapper."

"I doubt that," Cooper muttered. Aloud he asked, "You ever really trapped beaver?"

"Many times. Trade at fort." He waved a hand vaguely toward the east.

Cooper looked at Pale Thunder for help.

The chief shrugged and tried to hide his grin—or was it a grimace? Cooper wondered. *His people do not want him*, Cooper thought. *He has no wife and is of little use on the hunt. All he does is eat. His family wants to get rid of him.*

Cooper looked at the slovenly younger man. The mountain man thought he caught a glimpse of sadness flicker across Sits Down's face before settling on stoicism.

Cooper hated doing it, but he addressed Pale Thunder, speaking as if Sits Down was not there. "Is he of any use?"

Pale Thunder laughed. "Will you have eatin' test? He's good at that. He can do nothing else."

Cooper looked at Sits Down and asked in Nez Perce, "Do you have horses?"

"Two. Good ones."

Cooper looked at Pale Thunder again as the renowned warrior snorted. Cooper raised his eyebrows in query.

"If I had horses like his," Pale Thunder said in Nez Perce, "I'd feed them to my dogs. It is all they are fit for."

Cooper looked up at Sits Down again and saw a man who had come to a juncture in life. One who had gotten by with little effort but had done nothing more. Now he had to prove himself or die, or so it seemed. Cooper was sure Sits Down would not succeed. He shook his head. He knew he shouldn't do this, especially because of Potts, but he said, "All right, Sits Down, you can come. But the first sign of slackin' off and we'll kick ye out of camp."

"I work hard," Sits Down said, joy now stamped on his face.

"You'd best, boy." He stared at the broad, flabby warrior for a few moments, then asked. "You got any supplies? Pemmican or jerky for travelin'? Sleepin' robe? Blankets to keep you warm come the winter nights? Extra pair of mocs or two? Anything?"

"My two horses, one blanket, my weapons. Is enough."

"What're ye gonna do for feed, boy?"

"I hunt. Have plenty buffalo to eat."

Cooper was already regretting his decision, but it

had been made and he would stick with it. Making it all the worse was that Pale Thunder was laughing.

"Only way he'll kill buffalo," the older warrior said in his language, "is if one breaks its legs and falls at his feet so he can stab it with his lance, and I don't think that will do it."

Cooper sat it out for a bit. When Pale Thunder's chuckling had faded, the white man said, "How's about you trade ol' Sits Down a couple good horses for his two. And maybe give him some supplies?"

"Trade horses to him? His would endanger my good horses." Pale Thunder grunted in annoyance. "His horses are the worst my people have ever seen. Too poor to even drag a travois any farther than I can shoot an arrow. Worthless. Just like him."

"If they're that bad, they won't be able to carry Sits Down, that's fer certain. So tradin' with him would be doin' me a favor."

"The Nez Perce snorted. "What would I do with such poor animals but feed them to my dogs like I said??"

Cooper looked up at Sits Down, whose face had gone blank again. He looked back to Pale Thunder. "Gettin' tight-fisted in your ol' age, Thunder?" Cooper said sarcastically. "I thought you was a big chief, proud warrior, mighty hunter."

Pale Thunder stiffened some, but Cooper went on. "Far as I've seen, the Nez Pere have generous chiefs, who help those in need when they had more'n they could use for themselves. Reckon you ain't quite so high and mighty as you'd like folks to think. Maybe your people'd like to hear what a miserly ol' bastard you're gettin' to be."

Goes Far looked at her husband in horror. She could not believe anyone could or would speak to a chief in such a manner, and she was afraid there would be dire consequences.

"And just remember, Thunder, who it was saved your ass from that sick wolf."

Pale Thunder clenched his teeth and his face burned with rage, the coal-black eyes smoldering. Cooper stared back.

Time seemed to hang suspended before Cooper smiled a little. "Look at it this way, Thunder, I'll be takin' this big, ugly lump of wolf bait off your hands for you. Ain't that worth a couple horses to you?"

Pale Thunder stewed for a few more moments, then said tightly, "He shall have horses, My two finest war ponies. And two others I choose."

"Why, that's mighty generous of you, Thunder," Cooper said with a disarming smile, watching the war chief. "Now, what say you throw in some supplies?"

Goes Far, who had started to relax, tightened up in fear again. He would get them both killed, she feared. But she was surprised to see a small smile build on the war chief's face.

"He shall have two blankets," Pale Thunder said in Nez Perce. "And my buffalo robe for sleeping. No moccasins. I'll give enough hide to make some. He can do it himself," the chief added with a snort of derision, "or have daughter do it."

Pale Thunder grinned some more. "I will let him fill a parfleche with pemmican and jerky."

"Damn," Cooper said magnanimously. "You are a givin' ol' boy, you are, I'd be sayin'. Now, how's about some..."

"No. I have given enough," Pale Thunder said sternly, though with a smile.

"Well, I reckon that'll have to do." He pulled out a small pouch of tobacco and tossed it to Pale Thunder. "We will smoke."

Pale Thunder nodded. Doing so would solemnize it. As Cooper watched him filling his special pipe, taken carefully from the beaded buckskin pouch his wife had brought to him, Cooper relaxed. He knew he had pushed the Nez Perce mighty far and was relieved to see that it all had worked out.

Pale Thunder handed him the pipe. He took it, offered it to the four directions—north, south, east and west—then upward to the Sky Father and downward toward the Earth Mother before puffing several times. He handed it to Sits Down, who went through the ritual before smoking. The pipe was passed around more comfortably after that.

Potts strolled up with Morning Song. He looked even more disheveled than usual. As Potts sat, Cooper said with a grin, "Couldn't hold off, could you?"

"There's just some things a man's got no control over," he said, smiling. He took the pipe, offered it, then smoked. "What in hell's he doin' here'?" Potts asked, jerking his head toward Sits Down.

There was no better time than the present, Cooper thought. "He's comin' with us," he said without preliminary.

"Have you gone plumb *loco*?" Potts exploded, passing the pipe to Pale Thunder. "Why?"

"He asked, and I agreed." He still didn't know why, so could not offer an explanation even if he had been so inclined, which he wasn't. He couldn't quite figure it out, but there was something about the big warrior, something not quite meeting the eye.

"Dammit, Hawley, ye can't do that. El would have to decide. He's the captain of us boys."

"He don't like it, I'll go my own way."

"Dammit, Hawley, this is the most god-awful, stupidest thing I've ever known ye to do." He did not see Cooper's face start to darken with anger. "Ye know how lazy that sumbitch is. And how much he eats. He could more'n likely put away a whole buffler calf all to himself. Ye know who's gonna get stuck with feedin' him all winter, don't ye?"

"Me, I reckon. I'll see to it."

But Potts was on a roll and ignored him. "No, it ain't ye, dammit. It's me. And why? I'll tell ye why, goddammit. Because that fat, high-stinkin' sumbitch is family, that's why. He..."

Cooper's anger was fading fast as he smiled at Potts's vehemence.

"Yes, dammit, family. I don't like acknowledgin' that, but it's the truth and I'm stuck with it. But I got to do it, so much as I hate it—and him—I'll be seein' to it he gets fed all the damned long winter, 'cause I know my responsibilities, and I ain't one to shirk 'em. Not like some others I know of." He stared at Sits Down, eyes agog, while the Nez Perce looked back impassively.

"I've done it before, ye damned well know, and I'll do it again, if I'm forced into it..."

Notwithstanding his disdain for his brother-in-law, Potts had, Cooper knew, helped Sits Down more than once in small ways. The reason he hated the obese Nez Perce was the Indian's innate laziness, which indeed, was legendary. Despite all Potts's faults, he was a hard and tireless worker, and he had little compassion for those who were not like-minded.

"...But that don't mean I got to like it none. No sirree, I most purely don't, I'll tell ye that straight. It don't shine with me one bit, and I don't give a hoot if the whole goddammed world knows it, neither."

Cooper and Pale Thunder were laughing at the ranting, and the women, now including Morning Song, working nearby over a stretched-out buffalo robe were giggling.

"But he ain't stayin' in my lodge, that's fer goddamn certain, I'm tellin' ye. No, sir, dammit, he..."

"Would you just shut your goddamn trap fer a minute," Cooper said, laughing. "Lord a'mighty, you're blatherin' on more'n a whole lodge full of squaws gettin' ready for a feast."

"Well, I'm just tellin' ye...he...dammit all..."

"If you'd just shut that gapin' hole in your face long enough to draw a breath you might hear somethin'. I said I'll see to it. It ain't none of your consarn."

"Oh, no ye don't, Hawley Cooper. Ye ain't gonna be a martyr to save my hide from doin' what's needed. Nope. I'll be seein' to it, that's certain."

Cooper grinned. Potts would be true to his word; he would take as good a care of Sits Down as he could, but it wouldn't stop him from insulting his brother-in-law at every turn.

"If you're through jabberin', boy, I say it was time we see to things. The boys'll be waitin' fer us."

Potts nodded and stood. He knew it was time and knowing that, he was about ready to drop his foolishness. But he did get in one last shot. "Speakin' of the boys, El and the others ain't gonna be happy about this neither." He smirked a little. "Come on, Betsy," he said to the short, slim, beautiful Nez Perce woman, without waiting for a response from Cooper.

The two walked off as did Pale Thunder and Sits Down, who went to choose the horses the war chief was going to give to the large sorry excuse for a warrior. Cooper and Goes Far wandered over to where their things were. He was packed and near ready to go but he and his woman would leisurely finish their preparations, saddling their horses and loading the packed panniers on the mules and they would be on their way.

Brooks indeed was not happy with this new development, insisting that it was his right as captain to make such decisions. "So he stays behind," Brooks concluded.

"Then so do I," Cooper said with a shrug.

"And me," Potts proclaimed.

"I thought ye hated the lazy bastard," Brooks said, shocked.

"I do, but my friend Hawley said he could come along, so I accept that, and I'll stick by him and his decision."

The other men grumbled, but Potts said. "He won't be a burden to any of ye. Just to me. I'll see to it he's fed and such, but I won't neglect my work. And if ye boys don't like it, then, I'll be headin' off on my own. Be happy to have Hawley with me if he so chooses."

"I would." Cooper was beginning, though, to wonder if he made a mistake. He didn't need to cause dissention among the men, who always got along, except for the relative newcomers, Malachi Webster and Dave Wheeler.

"Besides," Cooper added after a few moments.

"Luis and Dan brought in Webster and Wheeler without askin'."

"Damn, well all right, though he better not become troublesome."

"He won't."

NINETEEN

A FEW DAYS LATER, Brooks's men and the Nez Perce parted ways, the Indians heading northwest, the mountain men following the Yellowstone north for a spell.

Though it was still August, it fell below freezing the first night and by morning a light blanket of snow covered the ground. It cleared quickly, making travel a muddy experience as the day wore on. But with the warmer daytime temperatures came an unexpected rainstorm—great slashing sheets of water, punctuated by long, ground-shaking thunder, and darting, dazzling tongues of lightning.

With the difficulty in traveling through the storm, they made a short day of it. It was a miserable camp, with much grumbling. There was the cover of cotton-woods and willows, but their leaves were turning and falling, providing little protection from the pummeling of the rain.

"I plumb hate this," Potts griped as he hunkered

under the hood of his thick capote, sipping a cup of quickly gone cold coffee.

"Weren't for spendin' so much time with the damn Nez Perce, we wouldn't be settin' out here in this goddamn storm," Webster snapped.

"It don't rain elsewhere?" Potts countered angrily.

"Not like this it don't."

"You're full of buffler shit," Cooper shot at him.

"You callin' me a liar, Cooper?" Webster asked, voice full of anger.

"Yep."

"That don't shine with this chil' none so ever," Webster said tightly.

"What shines with you, boy, don't concern me the least little bit."

"Mayhap this'll concern ye," Webster said, rising in a fluid motion. He shrugged off his capote and drew his Green River. He stood waiting, knife in hand, calm.

A stone-faced Cooper rose. Webster had been a thorn in his side since joining the group just a few months ago and Cooper had known this would happen sooner or later. This was as good a time as any to settle it. He stood, letting his own cream-colored capote with the three broad bands of color slide to the ground. He pulled his own big knife and took a step forward.

"No knives, boys," Brooks said sharply. "I ain't fixin' to bury anybody this day."

Both men hesitated, waiting for the other.

"Put 'em away, boys," Brooks said a little harder. He pulled his .54-caliber mountain pistol from his belt and held it loosely under the hem of a capote sleeve to keep the lock dry, muzzle between the two men. "If there's to be killin' today, I'll be the one to do it."

Cooper shrugged and slid his knife back into the hard leather sheath at the small of his back.

Webster grinned evilly, showing a few missing teeth. He hefted the knife a few times. Then he glanced around and realized several guns were cocked and pointed at him. Quickly, without changing his expression, he returned his Green River to the beaded sheath at his side.

The two men circled each other warily as the other men gathered in a tight circle, shouting encouragement or taunts. Suddenly Webster charged, head down, arms in a semicircle in front of him. Cooper had nowhere to go and Webster plowed into him as the other men scattered out of the way, sweeping his arms around Cooper's middle in a crushing bear hug. He straightened, looking with an evil glint in Cooper's eyes. He laughed harshly. He reared back his head, then snapped it forward, his forehead slamming into Cooper's face.

Cooper's nose snapped, squirting both men with blood that quickly disappeared in the sheets of rain. He grunted with the shock of it, and involuntary tears broke from his eyes.

"Does that concern you, boy?" Webster asked with a hoarse laugh.

Cooper spit at him, spraying his face with spittle and blood. Then he latched his teeth on Webster's nose and chewed mightily at the tip.

Webster roared with pain but would not release the bear hug. Cooper chewed for all his worth, working his jaws furiously, still trying to breathe through his own shattered nostrils. Webster howled more, and suddenly Cooper pulled his head back. He spit the small tip of Webster's nose into his foe's face.

"Damn!" Webster bellowed, releasing Cooper and reaching up for his nose with both hands. They came away covered with blood that swiftly drained away in the storm. "You son of a bitch," he hissed. He snatched out his knife, but the blood on his hands made his grip precarious, and Cooper quickly kicked the blade from his hand.

Webster charged again, but Cooper had more maneuvering room now. He sidestepped the rushing enemy and hit him with both hands locked together on the side of Webster's head.

Webster grunted and fell sideways, sliding in the mud out of the way as Cooper tried to kick his face. He scrambled up, breathing heavily, anger flushing his face. He circled, moving ever closer to Cooper, who watched warily. Suddenly Webster launched a foot at Cooper's groin, but it was easily blocked.

But it gave Webster an opening and he grabbed Cooper by the throat and squeezed. Cooper choked but did not panic. He jammed his thumbs into Webster's eyes as hard as he could. Webster gasped with pain but would not release his grip. Cooper brought his arms to his sides and then jerked them upward, his balled fists smashing into Webster's forearms from below, knocking them free of his throat.

Gasping for air, Cooper slammed a right fist into Webster's face, staggering him. Before Webster could recover, Cooper pounded him three more times in the face, shattering Webster's nose and knocking out a tooth. But Cooper had to slow down and catch his breath. He stood, hands on his knees, sucking in air. Watered-down blood still dripped from his own broken nose. Webster stood a few feet away, weaving, eyes clouded in pain and rage.

"You boys had enough fun for this day?" Brooks asked with a chuckle. The other men laughed.

"Not just yet," Cooper said, straightening. He moved forward, as the other men watched with interest, quickly increasing their bets.

Webster was too weak to do more than feebly struggle as Cooper wrapped a hand around the back of Webster's head. With a good grip on Webster's long, greasy hair, Cooper reached far back with his right hand, then whipped it forward. The heel of his hand crashed into Webster's head just above the nose.

Webster's eyes crossed as his head snapped back despite Cooper's grip. Then his eyes rolled up and his mouth fell open, allowing a thick line of drool to snake out the corner and into the tangle of beard, and then wash into the mud.

Cooper started to fall, but Potts and Alistair Wentworth, who happened to be closest of the others, caught him and helped him over to sit back against a tree. Brooks kept an eye on Dave Wheeler and Luis Gamez, who were pulling Webster up and dragging him off.

It was still raining when they pulled out the next morning, but it had tapered off to an annoying drizzle. To the west, over the mountains, they could see scattered patches of blue.

Hawley Cooper and Malachi Webster were something to behold. Both had their noses bandaged, and both had beautifully colored mottled faces, especially around the eyes, where the black, blue, purple, and sickly yellow colors fought each other for supremacy.

Cooper's knuckles were split open on his right hand and his whole face hurt.

But he was in better shape than Webster, who suffered a massive headache from the pounding he had taken. His eyes were puffed nearly shut and his tipless nose throbbed. He was still groggy and could barely hold himself in the saddle once he was helped up. But the pain and dizziness could not dampen the hate that burned inside him.

Cooper took some good-natured joshing about the fight and worried looks from Goes Far. Brooks had seen fit to warn him that morning. "Ye'd best watch your back permanent, Hawley. Malachi ain't gonna forgive ye fer this."

"I ain't worried," Cooper said quietly.

"Ye should be. From what I've seen, he's a sneaky bastard and ain't likely to come at ye from the front again."

Cooper nodded. "I'll be more watchful than usual."

On the move again, they picked up the Gallatin, crossed the Yellowstone and moved north, following the Missouri, and moving into the Big Belt Mountains, trapping all the while after the first couple of weeks. Then it was time to make meat for the winter.

Before long, they found a large valley along a good-sized stream none of them knew the name of in the heart of the mountains, and Brooks called for a stop. And here they made their camp.

Buffalo were plentiful enough, and among the trees that lined the valley there were copious growths of chokecherry and thimbleberry bushes amid the pines, firs, aspens and cottonwoods. There was plenty of wood and forage for the animals; the water was cold and sweet tasting. With the weather looking a bit sketchy, they set their tents and a couple of lodges in the clusters of trees. It started snowing the afternoon they arrived, but there was little accumulation, and the following day broke warm and sunny.

"Who're you gonna have fer your hunters?" Potts asked.

"You and Hawley, of course, as if ye didn't know," Brooks said. "You're the two best shots we got. As ye damn well know."

"Best shots in the mountains," Cooper corrected with a grin.

"The two of you will be enough, I figure?"

"Sure," Cooper said. "It ain't like we'll be shooting down the whole herd. 'Sides, who else we gonna get," he added with a chuckle. "Next two best shots we got are Duncan and Two-Faces, and they're about useless."

The chuckle turned into a laugh, and it flickered around the fire.

"That hard-headed Scotsman is reliable enough, but he ain't as good as two-Faces. But as ye know, Two-Faces is excitable and has that habit of shouting a war cry every time he downs a buffler, making them critters skittish."

"You're just jealous, *mon ami*, that you can't come up a proper victory cry," Beaubien said to laughter.

The next morning the two hunters crept up on a herd grazing contentedly. Cooper stretched out on his belly, picked out a fat cow, took careful aim and fired his heavy, powerful Dickert rifle. The sound rolled across the prairie for an instant. The cow immediately dropped, legs kicking for a few moments. The other buffalo continued grazing, unperturbed.

He and Potts fired slowly, carefully, at regular intervals, always taking out the buffalo that seemed to be most nervous. If one anxious buffalo took off, the whole herd would blindly follow.

The other men sat behind them, quietly cheering them on or giving them a hard time in the rare case of when they missed a shot. Finally, Brooks said, "That's enough, boys."

Cooper nodded and fired once more, purposely nicking a skittery cow. The buffalo snorted and shook her great head, then took off at a run, heading north away from the men. The rest of the herd flowed unhesitatingly after her.

The two hunters had killed ten buffalo. It left the rest of the men and the women plenty of work, since they would be doing the butchering.

"Let's get to carvin' them critters up, boys," Brooks said.

"Ain't they goin' to help?" Luis Gamez asked, jerking a thumb at the two hunters. He knew the answer, but this was just his way.

"They done their work," Brooks said. "Just like always. And we're gonna do the same, just like always."

Gamez grumbled as usual but went with the others as Cooper and Potts sat, cleaning their rifles. They watched silently as the other men and the women peeled off the great hides to save them and then butchered out the meat. The poorer cuts, mixed with berries and fat, would make good pemmican; the rest— what they didn't eat fresh now—would be dried in the sun or smoked slowly over fires to make jerky.

TWENTY

"I NARY WOULD'VE BELIEVED it, Hawl," Brooks said the next day, pointing at Sits Down, who was butchering the last of the buffalo.

"What?" Cooper looked up from the meat he was slicing.

"Sits Down. He's been workin' like hell all the while we been here."

Cooper glanced over at the big Nez Perce, who was covered with blood, and laughed. "'Course he's workin' hard. As long he's butcherin' he kin get his fill of fresh livers, hearts and such. I reckon you keep an eye on him fer a spell and he'll be swallerin' fresh boudins, too."

Brooks laughed. "That shines with me, I reckon. Long as he keeps workin' hard."

They had argued about the Nez Perce on the trail. Sits Down seemed to be doing little as they traveled. "I thought you said he'd be doin' his part, Hawl," Brooks said one evening around the fire chucking a thumb at the warrior. "Damn it, Hawley. We got enough troubles tryin' to feed ourselves without bringin' him along."

"He ain't no trouble," Cooper said tightly.

"Certain he is," Malachi Webster said. He stood, legs a little apart, thumbs hooked into the hard leather belt studded with brass tacks.

"Your face might be all healed up, Malachi," Cooper said flatly. "But I'd be happy to color it up for you again."

Webster stared at him but said nothing.

"We don't need trouble, nor no slackers," Brooks said. "Why'd you go'n bring him anyway? Ye got no likin' fer him."

Potts started to retort, but Copper cut him off with a chopping motion of his right hand. "It ain't really any of your concern, El," Cooper said, his face hard. "But if you're bent on pryin', I'll say this—his people don't want him no more."

"Hell it ain't no mystery they don't want him," Bill White said. "He ain't good fer anythin'."

Cooper stared from one man to the next, and each fidgeted under his gaze, as if they knew what he was thinking: How could such a bunch of outcasts and misfits reject a man who was not wanted even by his own people? And this bunch truly was a collection of misfits: Brooks, who had killed a man for insulting his mother; Potts, whose father sent him packing from St. Louis on a rendezvous supply train because he was "a troublemakin' little snot," as he himself put it; White, who fled the plantation where he had been born a slave, child of the plantation owner's son and one of their slave girls; whiny Jacques Dubois, slowed now by age and rheumatism, a voyageur before some of these other men had been born; Two-Faces Beaubien, half white, half red, at home in neither world; Luis

Gamez, up from Taos and not entirely trusted by many because he might be too close to the despised Mexican authorities; Duncan MacTavish, the disgraced refugee from the old Northwest Company; Dave Wheeler, reportedly fleeing the law back on the flats; Paddy Murphy, who left a pregnant girl in his native Ireland; Alistair Wentworth, an Englishman who arrived in the States after what he called a misunderstanding with a neighbor; the late Grady Mulligan, accused of stealing horses back in Missouri; the late Sam Bacon, who was said to have knifed to death the son of a plantation owner; the late Georges Miles, who fled a posse after him for stealing a horse; Dan Anderson, a weak-willed fellow who followed Malachi Webster and Dave Wheeler most of the time; Wheeler, also reportedly fleeing the law back on the flats, a sycophant of Webster; and Webster himself, with his badly scarred face and reputation as a dirty fighter on the riverfronts of the Mississippi and Missouri. Even Cooper himself, a young man hornswoggled by a disreputable mountain man and the adopted son of a Shoshoni war chief, did not have the most glorious reputation.

Cooper glared, rose, and headed toward his lodge, a simple lean-to on the trail. Goes Far had heard the exchange and was already bringing the mules up. The two of them began packing.

Potts followed, giving the others a withering glance as he strolled off to do the same. Sits Down, whose face had not changed since they rode into the camp followed.

Heavy, dark clouds were growing when Brooks wandered over to Cooper's makeshift lodge. "I didn't mean nothin', Hawley," he said, looking the least little bit pained.

"Then you should've kept your mouth shut," Cooper retorted, still angry.

"I reckon. I feel plumb foolish."

"You ought to. You..."

Goes Far said something in a low voice to him. He snapped at her in return, his Nez Perce punctuated sharply in his anger. Again she said something. Cooper nodded and turned back toward Brooks. He smiled wanly. "Sometimes we don't give our women much thought, but more often than not they're right as rain when they say something."

"I ain't never had one like that," Brooks said with a grimace. "What'd she say?"

"That you'n me been friends fer a spell, and she can't see no reason fer us to be carryin' on such."

"You're right, she's a smart one."

"You gonna give me more trouble over Sits Down?"

"Reckon not, less'n he stirs up trouble. Can't say as I'm happy with it, though. Neither are the others."

"I ain't worried about them others. If you ain't gonna give me grief about him bein' here, I can't see no reason fer us to be feudin'." He held out his hand.

Brooks smiled in relief and grabbed it.

The following days were the same as the previous few, with Cooper and Potts each downing an animal or two in the morning, and all the men and the women, spending the day peeling hides and butchering. Once the meat began coming in, the two hunters joined the other men in setting it to drying while the Indian woman began tanning the hides. It was hard work, scraping, drying, working a compound of mashed brains into the skins, stretching.

By the fifth day, the camp was a mass of meat-drying racks and stretched out buffalo skins. The men had to be on guard all night, in shifts, to keep the wolves, coyotes, and other scavengers from meat and hides. The men were thankful, though, that they had had no rain, allowing the bright sun and dry air to cure the meat.

That afternoon, a party of Bannocks arrived and set up camp nearby. That night there was some feasting and talking.

A FEW DAYS LATER, Cooper saddled his bay for the short ride to where the herd had regathered. Potts did the same with his pinto pony. They were considering maybe taking one or two more of the animals but had not decided. MacTavish rode along just to skip out on the work around camp for a bit.

There were nearing the herd, from downwind, when they spotted a dozen Bannock warriors riding toward them and the buffalo. They stopped and waited.

"Wonder what they want," Potts said.

Cooper shrugged. "Maybe just to thank us fer visitin' them the other night," he said sarcastically. "Or maybe...." He let it go.

The warriors halted not far from the mountain men. A warrior of maybe forty, wrapped in a blanket coat, his hair straight and long, said something in Bannock.

"He says," MacTavish translated, "that these are his buffalo. He and his men are going to hunt here today."

"You tell him to go to hell," Potts snapped. "Ain't no goddamned Bannock gonna tell me what buffler I can take. "

"Shut up, Zeke," Cooper said, not looking at his friend. "We're outnumbered here. 'Sides these Bannocks have been friendly enough all along. No reason to antagonize 'em now. Duncan, tell him we saw these buffler first and have been huntin' here for several days as they should know. They're ours, and we aim to hunt 'em."

MacTavish did as he was told and then sat as the Indian rasped out a string of angry words in his own language.

"He says they're his buffalo, and he and his lads'll fight ye for them."

"Ain't no call fer fightin'," Cooper said, looking straight at the Indians. He paused while MacTavish translated, then said, "We been friends, and there's plenty of buffalo here."

"You're givin' in to 'em?" Potts asked in surprise as MacTavish translated.

"Ye ever seen me back down from an Injin?" he responded harshly.

"No."

"Then keep your trap shut. Maybe you'll learn something."

The Indians brightened, thinking they had won. Then Cooper said, "And since we saw these here buffler first, they're ours. You fellers can mosey on off and hunt somewhere else."

The Indians grew angrier as MacTavish spoke in their language.

Finally, the leader said sharply, "They're ours. Leave here or all will die."

Cooper's face never changed as MacTavish translated it. Then he calmly said, "Tell this son of a bitch—what's his name anyway?—that he'll be the first to go under." He patted the rifle lying across his saddle in front of him.

"His name's Lame Dog," MacTavish said, then translated what Cooper had said.

The Bannock leader sat, unblinking as he considered the situation. He knew of these men; knew how well they could shoot. All three would die, but at what cost? And that, he realized, would be too great. Then there would be the others to contend with. But he had to find some way out of this while still saving face.

Cooper smiled inwardly. He had the Bannocks where he wanted them, so he could be magnanimous, "I tell you what, Lame Dog," he said. "You let us boys do the huntin' today. Then you get your women to help with the butcherin'. We'll share the meat and hides with you. Tomorrow you can do the huntin' and our women will help with the butcherin' fer a share of the meat."

Lame Dog smiled. This white man was no fool. The trapper's idea was reasonable. "It is good," he said in English. He whirled his horse and, with his warriors on his heels, raced off toward his camp.

"Damn that was close," Potts said, uncocking his rifle.

"Not really, Zeke. Them Injins didn't want to fight us no more'n we did them. They were just seein' how far they could push us. If we had given in, they would've won. If we had commenced to fightin', they would've took our hair, but they would've lost a lot, likely all their warriors after our boys lit into 'em. This way, we both come out winners. We get some help and all we give up is some meat."

"Good work, lad," MacTavish said as they moved on toward the herd. "I could nae have done better."

"Reckon we only need to down a critter or two to keep our promise. We can let 'em have most of the meat," Cooper said.

They found their spot. Cooper and Potts hauled out their rifles. Brooks and the others come up behind them, and they saw the Bannocks gathering on the grassy hillocks to their left.

"What was that all about?" Brooks asked.

MacTavish explained.

"One each, then. And best be doin' your best shootin', boys," Brooks said. "Ye got yourselves an audience."

"You don't shut your trap," Potts said, "there ain't gonna be nothin' to shoot at—'cept you."

Cooper grinned and rested his cheek on the polished stock of his rifle.

TWENTY-ONE

COOPER WAS bone weary that night at the meat-making camp. So were most of the others as they slouched around small fires. Potts showed no ill effects from the hard dirty work; and neither did Sits Down, surprising Cooper. Despite them having worked as hard, if not harder, than the men, the women seemed none the worse for it and performed their daily tasks as usual.

Goes Far fed Cooper and then went back to work making a fancy shirt for him. Potts, Cooper, and Brooks sat around the fire, still nibbling on meat, or smoking their small clay pipes.

"How much longer you plannin' on stayin' here, El?" Cooper asked.

"Couple more days ought to be enough."

"Reckon so. We got us a heap of meat."

Brooks nodded. "I figure we do, but I ain't aimin' to take chances. Not after we damn near run out last year. Facin' starvin' times midway through winter don't shine with this chil' one bit."

"Nor with this one," Cooper said. "But we get so much meat now that it'll be hard for the animals to carry it all."

"We'll cache some, then."

"Where? Here? That ain't gonna do us much good. 'Less'n you're plannin' to winter somewhere nearby."

"Hadn't thought to."

"Got someplace in mind?"

"Well, I hear tell that southeast of here, toward where the Bighorn or Rosebud meet the Yellowstone, are some pleasurable spots."

"That's where we wintered a couple years ago, when," Cooper growled, "me and Zeke met. It wasn't a bad place, except for the damn Crows," Cooper spit, "some folks I don't much fancy either. And it's mighty close to..."

"I forgot that, Hawl. Well, maybe back the way we come. Seems we come across some reasonable lookin' places when we come through there. In the Elkhorns, maybe, or even down to the Bitterroots."

"Where we rid ourselves of those horse- and plew-stealin' sumbitches," Potts threw in.

Brooks nodded thoughtfully. "That was a fine place, as I recall," he finally said. "At least in the spring."

"Yep."

Brooks thought a little longer, then nodded. "We'll head southwest, see if we can find a place in the Elkhorns. If not, we'll mosey on down to the Tobacco Roots."

"Sounds reasonable," Cooper said. He rose, knocked the ashes from his pipe and slipped it into the heart-shaped buckskin holder around his neck. "It's robe time for this ol' chil'," he said, rising.

It was still warm this night, so he shucked his heavily fringed buckskin pants, plain calico shirt that had been white not too long ago, and moccasins. Naked, he slid into the comfortable bed of buffalo robes. Unashamedly, Goes Far slid out of her plain buckskin dress and knelt at his side. With fingers made strong working with thick, heavy buffalo hides, she kneaded his back and neck muscles, working down to his legs. It was as if she had done no heavy work during the day.

"Damn, you sure are good fer a man," he muttered in pleasure. In the dark, she smiled.

When she was done, he flipped over and pulled her to him, her breasts brushing his muscular chest. Later they laughed as they heard Potts shout, "Goddammit, can't you people ever keep from doin' that?" His woman still would have nothing to do with him at certain times, and it frustrated him.

Two days later, most of the work was done. Brooks called them all together in the sort of center of their camp, with a big fire. Cooper had brought down a buffalo cow that day and the best parts of the meat had been butchered out. Fresh tongues were roasting in the coals, and racks of ribs were skewered on ramrods and jabbed into the ground so the meat would sear on the outside while letting the insides stay red and juicy. Several yards of boudins lay on a hide nearby, ready to be put on the coals. Gourds served as bowls for marrow that would be spread like butter over the meat or biscuits baking in a few Dutch ovens.

"We'll be spendin' a day or two more here," Brooks announced, "to finish tannin' the hides we got. Then we'll be on our way. You boys done good this year, so I figured it was time we had is a feast. And some Lightnin'. He pulled a jug from behind him and plunked it down in front of him.

"This is all you boys are gonna get for a spell, so enjoy it." He pulled the cork with a pop, hauled the jug up on his left arm, resting on the crook of his elbow and took a healthy swallow. He smacked his lips. "Damn that shines." He handed it to Cooper, who sat to his right.

The jug made a circuit as the men talked and waited for the meat to get done, which did not take long. Soon the men were gorging on tongue, hump meat and ribs slathered with marrow, popping chunks of fleece into their mouths. The jug continued to make its way around the circle.

The women and children had their own fire and a good supply of prime meat.

Soon most of the men were sated on food, and the jug was getting considerably lighter. Sits Down soon fell over, overcome by tiredness from all the work, the little whiskey he had had, and his full stomach. He snored loudly until Cooper and Potts rolled him over, out of the way.

"That's a goddamned disgrace," Webster said loudly.

"Sure is," Cooper said with a grin.

"I wasn't talkin' to you, Cooper," Webster said nastily.

"I agree with him," Potts said, hardness in his voice.

"I wasn't talkin' to you, neither, boy. You just keep your mouth shut 'round your betters. 'Leastways 'til you and your friend there pull your weight like the rest of us."

"What's that supposed to mean?" Potts asked,

putting down the jug that had just arrived in his hands.

"Well now," Webster said slowly, relishing the fact that he had an audience. "Seems you two been spendin' a heap of time with your squaws, whilst the rest of us was breakin' our balls workin'."

"Hell," Potts snorted, "we work a damn sight harder than ye. Just 'cause ye ain't got a woman ain't no reason to disparage those of us who do." Anger began to burn in Potts's eyes.

"Most of us don't see it that way,"

Dave Wheeler agreed loudly. The other men were silent.

"You'd best watch what you're sayin', boy," Cooper said easily, though a warning was evident in his voice. He grinned tightly. "Ol' Zeke's woman is smack in the middle of her unclean time, and so she ain't been really sharin' his bed. That means ol' Zeke is gettin' right pent up about now, and you know how he is times like that."

"Reckon I do," Webster said almost agreeably. "Kinda makes him queery in the head, don't it."

"He gets a lot worse'n that..."

"Stay out of this, Hawley," Potts said. "Last time this goddamn fool started arguin' with me you stepped in. I ain't gonna let you do it again."

"Suit yourself," Cooper said, not bothered by Potts's statement.

"If you think Hawley messed you up, boy," Potts said in a voice hard with anger, never having taken his eyes off Webster, "just wait till I get through with you." He got up slowly, eyes burning into Webster's.

"Sit down, Zeke," Brooks commanded.

"Keep your distance, Cap'n. This ain't your affair."

Webster started to rise, hand reaching for the pistol

in his belt at the same time.

"You pull that piece. I'll blow a hole in your belly big enough for a buffler bull to run through," Cooper said.

Webster stopped in midrise, staring at the muzzle of Cooper's .54-caliber pistol. It was on full cock. Webster's hand fell to his side, and he finished rising.

"I told you to keep out of this, Hawley," Potts said.

"I ain't interferin'. Just makin' sure it's a fair tussle."

"That's enough," Brooks interjected, standing before this truly got out of hand.

"Like he said, Brooks," Webster snarled, "keep out of this."

"Goddammit, ye boys elected me your captain. Yee don't like it, unelect me. Till then, I'm in charge here. Now sit down!"

Potts looked at him, as if deciding whether to fight Brooks before taking on Webster.

"This here is supposed to be a fandango," Brooks said, more quietly.

"You're right, Cap'n," Potts said. He felt the anger ease up just the littlest bit. "This ain't gonna be the end of this, Webster," he said harshly. "But this ain't the time nor place fer it. There'll be another time."

"I'll be waitin'."

Potts sat first, then Webster. Brooks stood, then he smiled. "We need to get us a real shivaree goin' here," he said. "It's time we make this night shine."

Brooks headed off to his bedroll to get his dulcimer, and Jacques Dubois did the same to fetch his fiddle, while Paddy Murphy pulled his jaw harp from his possible sack.

Soon the music was playing, and the men were

dancing around the fire, a few with their Indian wives—who thought all this perfectly silly—others with other men, since there was no other choice. The children laughed and screeched in joy watching their elders. The celebrating lasted long into the night.

The men were groggy the next day from lack of sleep, but the workload was light compared with what it had been. Most of the men saw to their equipment—cleaning rifles or pistols, sharpening knives or tomahawks, casting lead balls, repairing clothes; making sure their traps were in good shape.

The only one who seemed not to feel the effects of the night before was Potts, who awoke crowing, whooping, and hollering. Cooper grinned over coffee, looking at Brooks. "I reckon his woman's clean again," he said.

"Would seem. Else she's found a new trick to use on him."

Both men chuckled, while Potts scowled—but only for a moment, before he laughed, too.

THAT AFTERNOON, the Bannocks who had camped nearby returned. They had moved off for a couple of days after sharing the hunt and meat with the mountain men, but now were back. And they invited the white men for another feast in their camp.

Brooks agreed. But when the Bannocks had ridden away, he said to Cooper, "We've got to leave a few men in camp. I don't trust them damned Bannocks."

"Me neither. I'll stay."

"Ye certain?"

"Sure. I got my woman here, and plenty of fresh

meat. I got no call to visit them boys."

"All right. Anybody else?"

"I reckon Zeke'll want to stay, too. I doubt he'd risk bringin' his woman over there with him, and he sure as hell ain't gonna leave her here alone."

"I stay, too," Beaubien said.

Brooks nodded. "That enough fer ye, Hawl?"

"Ought to be."

Cooper, Beaubien, and Potts caught two young Bannocks—boys, maybe fourteen—in the camp, looking to steal horses to impress their elders. But they'd take anything that wasn't tied down given half an opportunity. The two mountain men did not give them one.

The men returned well after dark, and Brooks made sure at least two of them stood guard through the night.

In the morning, Brooks said, "I was plannin' to cache some of these buffalo hides, some meat, and some supplies here fer spring. But I ain't so certain of it now."

"Yep. I figure they're lingerin' here for somethin' other'n they like our company," Cooper said. "They know how much meat we got. We leave here with a lot less'n that, they'll be prowlin' here soon's we leave lookin' for our cache. And no matter how good we hide it, those bastards'll find it sure as hell."

"I got the same feelin'." Brooks paused. "Well, hell, we'll haul all of it along. We'll cache whatever we want soon's we shed ourselves of them Bannocks. Might take a few days, but we can do it. Or we can make it damned uncomfortable fer 'em."

"That's where my stick floats too," Potts said.

"I was thinkin' of leavin' day after tomorrow, but with them Bannocks still loiterin' 'round here, we'll do so tomorrow," Brooks said firmly.

TWENTY-TWO

IT TOOK a week of riding almost, taking switchbacks, using rocky trails, crossing creeks and more to lose the tenacious band of Bannocks. But they finally did it. With a sense of relief, they dug a large cache in a copse of cottonwood and ash just off a creek in the norther part of the Elkhorn Mountains. Only Brooks, Cooper and Two-Faces knew the exact location.

That done, they worked their way farther south, working slowly through the Elkhorn Mountains. Along the entire route, they had found streams full of beaver.

It had pushed well into November and they had faced snow more than once, though not much of it. Rain, sleet, thunder, and lightning pounded at them several times, but they moved on slowly, trapping as they went.

The plews were prime, and with thirteen men—counting Sits Down, who was beginning to slack off in his work again and as he had all along, skipped trapping —they pulled in plenty of fur. At each camp they made, beaver pelts stretched on willow hoops hung from trees or lay scattered about drying. The women—Goes Far; Little Fox and Dancing Water, Beaubien's two wives; Slow Calf, Dubois's wife; and Bloody Hair, White's woman, both Nez Perce—had their hands full. The men could cure their own beaver pelts, and did so, but the women were quicker and better at it, making the hides shine with lush softness.

They tried to get Sits Down into trapping, but he would have none of it. "Not go in cold water, trap beaver," he said adamantly.

"You said you'd done so many times, back in the village," Cooper said when they took a few days to rest and let the horses recover their strength some.

"I not remember that."

Cooper shook his head in disgust.

After a few days, Cooper told him, "Sits Down, I warned you when you asked to come along that you had to pull do your part or I'd set you loose."

"I know."

"Well, you ain't been doin' it. You don't mind workin', it seems, when there's food to be had, like skinnin' buffler. But you don't want to be doin' other work. From now on, you'll either work or you'll go hungry. 'Less'n, of course, ye want to hunt for yourself."

Sits Down just grunted. But he disappeared the next morning and was gone all day.

"See, the sumbitch lit out on us," Potts said. "Soon's he learned there wasn't no free food fer him, he took off."

"He'll be back," Cooper said. "He don't know where the hell he is, and we're workin' into Blackfoot country. He ain't gonna want to be alone to face down a war party of Blackfeet half froze fer hair."

Sits Down was back before dark, looking rather content.

"I wonder what'n hell he's up to," Potts asked, exasperated.

Cooper shrugged, but he was curious, too. The next day it was the same and the day after. "I reckon, I'll follow him tomorrow," he told Potts. "He's got to be gettin' food somewhere, but I can't figure where."

Cooper had already run his trap lines and left the resetting to Potts and Brooks. He buried himself behind a bush where he could watch Sits Down's robes. Soon enough the Nez Perce got up, stretched, greeted the new day, though the sun had been up for some time already. He banked the fire and let the old black pot of coffee heat up, then drank some using a cup he found setting by the fire.

With a furtive look around after he finished the coffee, Sits Down slipped off through the nearly leafless aspens and cottonwoods, moving swiftly and surely. He zigzagged a bit, doubled back a few times, scrambled over boulders, but always headed toward the creek a mile or so from the camp. Finally, he made it. He sat behind a tree and watched, waiting, to make sure no one came along.

Cooper sat not far behind him and also waited. After about half an hour, Sits Down rose and walked to the bank. He quickly pulled up two traps and brought out two beaver. He followed the creek, always alert, before finding a spot hidden in the trees.

Cooper couldn't help but wonder where he got the traps. None of the men had reported any stolen, though from this distance he couldn't tell if they were metal traps or a more primitive, handmade variety.

Sits Down made himself a small fire, using flint and steel. He added very dry wood in small amounts, so there would be little smoke. He relaxed against a tree trunk and sliced the tails off the beaver carcasses. He roasted them one at a time, eating one while another cooked. He looked perfectly at ease.

Cooper watched for some time before stealthily heading back to camp, where he told Potts about it.

"I'll be damned," Potts said in wonder. "He can do somethin' when he wants to."

"I don't know about wants to," Cooper said. "It's more like he'll do damn near anything to keep himself from starvin'."

They moved on the next day, traveling through a horrendous rainstorm and cold temperatures. By afternoon the driving rain had changed to wind-whipped snow. They made a cold camp that night, with the wind making it impossible to keep a fire going.

The next day they pushed on through more snow. By noon, it was a full-blown blizzard. Drifts piled up taller than a horse along cliff walls. Horses and mules foundered in the deepening snow and the cold sliced right through the men's capotes and bearskin coats. The wind roared around the men, pounding them. Their breath frosted in the air; icicles formed on beards, mustaches, and eyebrows.

A mule went down under the weight of beaver plews, snapping its leg. Anderson, whose mule it was, dismounted and slogged through the swirling whiteness to get to the animal. He shook his head.

"Somebody help me move these plews," he shouted into the shrieking wind, the words ripped from his mouth individually.

Malachai Webster and Dave Wheeler struggled against the wind to get to him with another mule. They transferred the heavy packs and pushed ahead while Anderson quickly slit the downed mule's throat. It took an effort for him to get back into the saddle with the wind blowing so hard, but he managed it and forced the other animals to move along.

They forced their way along a slim path with a cliff wall to their left and a sheer drop-off of more than a hundred feet to their right. The horses moved slowly in a long string, not being able to bunch up on the slim trail. One of the extra horses panicked, jerking and jumping, until its feet went out from under it and the animal plunged, screaming, off the mountainside.

The men did not care. Most were on the verge of frostbite on fingers, toes, or noses. Their behinds hurt from sitting on frozen, rock-hard saddles that their behinds could not heat up any; their eyes crusted over with ice; and the wicked, freezing wind made breathing difficult. The women huddled in their buffalo robes, wrapping the thick, haired hides around themselves and their children.

The trail finally headed downward, and with another two hours of hard-fought traveling, they reached a valley that was pleasant compared with the rock wall to which they had been clinging.

A thick stand of pines and aspens ran alongside the left side of the valley and would provide some shelter and plentiful firewood. A creek ran through the center of the meadow, into the trees. Several buffalo were grazing by scuffing away the snow with their beards to reach what was left of the short, brown grass beneath.

The men entered the valley in hushed silence.

Though the wind still blew, its ferocity here in the valley was so diminished that it was quiet after the ear-shattering hammering they had received above.

While most of the men made camp, Cooper and Potts rode out and shot one of the buffalo. They dragged the carcass along the snow to the camp, where the men butchered out enough to feed everyone for a few days, then dragged the dead animal back to where they shot it, leaving it for the wolves and other scavengers.

Fires were going by the time Cooper and Potts hauled the carcass to the camp, and the men stood around them warming the hands, feet, and faces, getting as close as they dared to the flames. They hurried in the butchering, put meat on to cook, and went back to huddling near the fires. With fresh buffalo in their bellies, pipes full of tobacco, cups full of sweetened coffee and tea, they were mostly content. It was still a few hours before dark, but they continued to huddle around the fires for warmth. They stared out through the trees at the buffalo that still gazed placidly.

"It's somethin' how they get at the grass despite the snow," Potts said. "Regular cows're too damned stupid to do it. They'll starve to death when a buffler will live almost comfortable."

"Well, there's a limit to what buffler kin do," Brooks said slowly. His tone signaled to Potts and Cooper and Two-Faces and MacTavish that a tale was in the offing.

"I mind the time I was alone down to the Valley of the Great Salt Lake. You've all heard of that Salt Lake now, ain't ye?" He didn't wait for an answer. "It was spring when I got there, and a hell of a spring it was, too. Warm and sunny, and everythin' just a bloomin' all over. I come into this here pleasant valley. Leastways I thought it were goin' to be pleasant—I'd been there afore and always enjoyed it.

"Well, what do I see this time? My eyes have before them countless buffalo, all dead. The winter we just finished was the worst anyone ever heard of, I'd be sayin'. Fer certain. Snowed one time fer seventy straight days and nights. Never stopped. Slowed some occasional, of course, but never stopped. We had been there just after the snow stopped and we measured it. Now, ye may think I'm embellishin' things just a bit, but God's truth, we measured that snow at sixty feet deep. Sixty, I'm sayin'. Covered over every buff in the valley. I'm tellin' true now, boys, it was the damnedest thing this chil' ever set eyes to.

"Well, now here I am come back in the spring, and all that snow's done melted away and gone. So, what do I see? I'll just tell ye. I see millions of buffler lyin' dead all over the place from where that snow buried 'em. So's me'n my partner, we worked and struggled and grunted and groaned to push them buffler into the salty water of that big ol' lake.

"Took some work, too. Most of the summer we worked, shovin' them damned buffler carcasses into that lake. But when we was done, we stood there a wipin' our hands off after a good summer's work done, and I thought to myself, 'Now what're we gonna do for makin' meat for the comin' season?' And then I commenced to think on the problem. Well, it weren't long afore I realized what we had here was enough pickled buffler fer my boys and most of this whole damned country of ours, too.

"So we hired us up some wagons from Taos and

shipped a heap of them pickled buffs back to the towns."

"There no buffalo there," Sits Down said seriously.

"You been in the Great Salt Lake Valley?" Cooper asked.

"Yes."

"Well now, think about it for a spell, Sits Down, maybe it'll come to ye why there ain't no buffler there," Brooks said.

Sits Down's chubby face crinkled in thought while the other men talked softly and laughed at the story. Finally, Brooks said, "Still cain't think it out?"

The Nez Perce shook his head.

"Well, now, it was 'cause that damned storm for seventy suns killed off every last buffler in that valley. All them bufflers we pickled was all there was. And now there ain't no more and probably never will be again."

TWENTY-THREE

THEY STAYED THERE TWO DAYS, letting the storm blow itself out. They had to kill another horse—one belonging to Murphy—that had gone lame, and they had had to amputate the left pinky and ring finger of Little Fox, Two-Faces Beaubien's Flathead wife. She took it well, having been dosed well with whiskey. Two-Faces had done the operation himself. But she was ready to leave with everyone else, though she favored that hand for some weeks. They were lucky frostbite hadn't gotten more of them.

The sun finally came out and the temperature rose into the fifties. The snowmelt ran in rivers, down washes and gullies, making their journey all the more hazardous. They camped that night on the bank of a nameless—to them—river, watching the waters roar and tumble down. They worked their way along the bank and found several creeks running slow enough to be trapped. They spent three days in the vicinity, pulling out some of the best plews they had come across.

But Bill White lost a pack of beaver when crossing the river a week later.

"Dammit all," White swore as he fought to control the panic-stricken mule that had gotten caught in an undertow and was frightened all the more when the rigging holding the plews on his back came loose.

"We should've stayed in that valley, Cap'n," Webster said loudly, sarcastically emphasizing the captain.

"It was no good, and you full well know it."

"Hell, it had everything we needed."

"That's true. But not enough of any of it. Come midwinter and we run outta feed fer the animals we'd have faced starvin' times fer certain. And by that time there'd be so much snow we'd nary get out."

"But..."

"'Sides, ye should be smart enough to know there ain't enough beaver there to last another week, let alone the rest of the fall hunt."

Webster looked as if he was going to argue, but Brooks cut him off. "Go on and help Dan with the extra animals, Malachi, afore we lose more of 'em."

An angry Webster slapped his horse hard with the reins and hurried ahead.

"Malalchi almost had a point today, El," Cooper said that night at the fire. "Not that we should've stayed there in particular, but we best find a winterin' place soon. It looks to be a bad winter from what we've seen so far."

"I know," Brooks said with a sigh.

"I know you know, El. But you got to make a decision soon or we'll be facin' poor times fer certain. We got to build livin' quarters of some kind, put up feed for the animals, pile up firewood, and still trap. We wait much longer and whatever places that we've used before might be taken up before we can get there."

"We'll give it another week or two," Brooks said wearily.

The weather held fairly good as they rode slowly southeast, trapping as they went. But they never spent more than a day or two in one place. The nights were cold, but the days were mostly warm. The sun shone most of the time, but they did get some snow flurries and two days of light sleet.

They cached more supplies and three packs of beaver pelts, one each belonging to Brooks, Cooper, and Potts, each weighing ninety to a hundred pounds. They hastily threw up a makeshift beaver press whenever they stopped for a few days to compress the plews into manageable size. Once pressed tight, they were wrapped in wet buckskin, which bound them tightly once it dried.

About midafternoon two days later, they spotted smoke downriver.

"Most likely Blackfoot," Cooper said. "Which don't shine with this chil'. But they might be Crow, though, which could be just as bad, or Shoshoni, though this is some out of their usual territory."

"We'd best find out, I reckon," Brooks said, looking a little harried. "Might need to find a way around 'em. Zeke, you and Al take a *paseo* over that way and see what them Injuns are."

Potts and Alistair Wentworth rode out, horses kicking up clots of mud and hunks of stone. They were back about two hours later, animals breathing heavily.

"Shoshonis," Wentworth said. "About ten lodges."

"Then I reckon they're friendly."

"All of 'em I know are," Cooper said. "And since I'm one of them, we should be all right." He did not see it necessary to mention the band of Shoshonis that had refused to help him after Black Moon Woman had been taken.

"Think we should go around 'em anyway?" Brooks asked.

"Nope," Potts said. "Ain't likely anyway. The river heads down into a hole. That's where those Injuns are. A cliff rises this side. Onliest other thing we could do would be to cross the river, head mostly due south, then around."

Brooks looked over the wide, fast-moving, deep river and knew it would be foolish to even attempt it.

"Then let's drop by and see 'em. Maybe if you mention you're one of them, they'll be especially friendly."

"Rather keep it quiet at first, just to see how they feel about things. Up here they ain't likely to know Cheyenne Killer's band, so it could get a little touchy, though I don't see why it should. Still, it might pay to be cautious. If it seems all right, I'll bring it up."

"If that's where your stick floats. Not long though. Like ye said, we still need to find a place to winter up. And soon."

"Hell, I ain't sayin' we're gonna spend a week with 'em. A day, maybe two, and we'll be on our way. Won't lose no time at all spendin' a night or two with the Shoshonis. 'Specially if we can trade for some horses and maybe a few plews. 'Sides," Cooper added with a wide grin, "some of the boys is gettin' a might pent up.

While they ain't too loose, might be a few girls there maybe willin' to favor some of the boys here for a night."

A smile crept across Brooks' face. "I reckon one of them Shoshoni girls could take a shine to this ol' feller at that. Let's do 'er."

Potts whooped. "I knew ye couldn't go a whole winter without a woman, even as old and wretched as ye are."

"Ye just best stick with that little Nez Perce of yours. She's the only one that'll put up with ye. And if she was to catch you foolin' with one of them Shosho-nis, she'd have your balls hanging' from her lodgepole like a scalp."

Potts blanched for a minute, then recovered. "She keeps me busy enough. I reckon I don't need no other. But she'll be gettin' one hell of a run tonight." He whooped again and trotted off.

"That'll be the death of him yet," Brooks said with a laugh, joined by Cooper. "He's gonna have it out of his pants once too damned often and..."

"You're just jealous." Cooper laughed. "You ain't no young buck anymore."

"I'm young enough to tame any Shoshoni squaw they can drag out, ye fractious son of a bitch," Brooks said. "I'll match ye and that pup Zeke any day—or night —ye care to mention."

They both laughed and rode on. Before long, they were at the small village. They had ridden in under the watchful eyes of several warriors, and the camp was a little tense. But then Duncan MacTavish yelled out, "Hey, Slow Bull."

An imposing warrior standing in front of a large,

elaborately painted tipi, looked up sharply, and then smiled. "MacTavish," he said, butchering the word.

"Traded with him and his band a few years back," MacTavish said softly to Brooks. "I was nae sure he'd remember me."

They made their greetings, but then moved out from the village a mile or so where they planned to make their own camp. Not being sure of what to expect from this band, they did not unpack, just loosened saddles and quickly threw up a few picket lines so the animals could feed some but not move off. Bill White and Two-Faces Beaubien were left to guard the camp and their women and animals, while the rest of the men rode into the village. Several of them drifted off to find women willing for a night's dalliance. But Brooks, Cooper and Potts met Slow Bull and some of the other warriors in the Shoshoni's lodge.

They smoked a pipe of greeting and then talked comfortably, swapping yarns and crowing about war deeds.

"Ain't you awful far north?" Brooks asked Slow Bull as the tale telling dwindled a bit.

The Shoshoni shrugged.

"This here's Blackfoot country."

"And Crow country," Cooper added.

Slow Bull and the other warriors smiled. "We're not afraid of Blackfoot," he said in English. "Or Crow." Falling back into his own language, he said, "This is a good place. There is water here along Sage Creek, much game, plenty of wood, ample feed for our ponies. The weather is not too bad, the snow's not too deep, the wind not too strong. A good place."

"Sounds too good to be true," Potts muttered.

"Maybe we ought to consider winterin' up here, El," Cooper said. "It sure seems like a good place. And beaver shine here."

"I was thinkin' the same," Brooks said. "Slow Bull, would ye and your people mind if we were to winter up close to you? Trap beaver till the river and streams froze over and such?"

Slow Bull talked in a low voice with his warriors. Cooper caught some of it even as softly as they were speaking but did not interrupt or translate.

"It is good," Slow Bull finally said.

The talk drifted back to tales and heroics, and the men grew comfortable, eating, drinking coffee that the mountain men provided. The Indians wanted whiskey, but the whites were in no shape to deal with half-drunk Shoshoni warriors if the Indians took a mind to raise hair.

Suddenly the night air was punctuated by an angry bellow, "Come back here, you red-skinned bitch!"

There was a scream, a few moments of silence, then a gunshot and another scream.

Cooper was the first out of Slow Bull's lodge, followed closely by Brooks, Potts, Slow Bull, and the others. They stopped, searching through the darkness broken only by a three-quarter moon. Others were pouring from other lodges, looking around in confusion.

An Indian girl, perhaps fifteen, stumbled from inside the lodge into the cold night air. She clutched her midsection, and a wide, dark stain that was spread over much of her dress.

Webster bulled his way out of the lodge and tried to grab the girl but missed. She lurched a few steps and collapsed in a pile on the cold ground.

Cooper slung his rifle across his back, pulled a pistol and fired in the air as three warriors—one with a stone war club, the other two drew horn handled knives—sprang forward, heading for Webster. They stopped and looked around.

Cooper jammed that pistol away and grabbed his other one. He turned and threw his left arm around Slow Bull's throat from behind and squeezed. He jammed his pistol into the Shoshoni's side. "Tell 'em to back off, Slow Bull," he hissed. "Now!"

Slow Bull really had no right to order the warriors to stop, other than the respect he had earned through battle. But Cooper knew it was the only chance they all had of getting out of the village alive.

"Now, goddammit!"

Slow Bull yelled at the warriors in Shoshoni. The three, and now the rest of the village's warriors, stood rooted and turned to look at Slow Bull.

"That's not what you said," Cooper said in Shoshoni. "Tell them to back off!"

TWENTY-FOUR

SLOW BULL STIFFENED, then yelled again. The three warriors were still looking confusedly at Slow Bull. Another half-dozen who had started toward Webster from other directions, stopped and also turned toward Slow Bull. They saw their war chief's predicament and hesitated to do anything that might further endanger his life.

The other mountain men, some only half-dressed but all armed, were hefting their rifles or pistols, cocked and ready to fire.

"Now listen, Slow Bull," Cooper said in Shoshoni. "I don't want any fighting here. I don't think you do either. It'd mean a lot of dying on both sides."

"You may go," Slow Bull said in a choked voice. "But he will stay."

"I can't do that, Slow Bull, much as I'd like to. What he did was pure deviltry. But I can't just give over one of the boys to you. Now we aim to ride out of here—all of us. Any of your people try to stop us, there'll be a lot of dying, like I said. Understand?"

Out of the corner of his eye, Cooper saw a warrior creeping up behind Wentworth, ready to bash his brains in with a war club when Sits Down slipped up behind him and clubbed him with a meaty fist and dragged him behind a lodge. At least that's what Cooper thought he saw. He couldn't be sure.

"He must pay," Slow Bull insisted.

"Now look, it was only a woman he killed. It wasn't like he killed a warrior." He felt bile rising at the words, but he had to do it. To this Indian, it might sense in a way, and it might help them get out with their hair. "Now let's move, Slow Bull. Toward the horses, nice and slow."

Cooper moved back a step, pulling Slow Bull with him. The other mountain men fanned out a little, eyes alert, weapons ready.

"You speak my language well," the chief said quietly.

"I am *Too-Shah-Itsup-Mah-Washay*—He-Who-Is-the-White-Wolf-Killer, son of Cheyenne Killer."

"I have heard of him. And you. You are big medicine among the People."

"Then you know I mean what I say."

"Yes. But..." he hesitated.

"But what?"

"But it would not be right for one Shoshoni to kill another."

"No it wouldn't. But it goes for both of us, I suppose." He did not see fit to tell the war chief that Cooper, with the willing assistance of Cuts Throat, had killed the two sons of Black Moon Woman's father, who had objected to Cooper marrying his daughter.

Two of the mountain men slipped away and returned bringing their horses with them.

"Get on your horse, Malachi," Brooks ordered, voice dripping with anger.

Webster started to pull his other pistol.

"You cock that thing and I'll turn these warriors loose on you."

Webster looked around, hate and fear in his eyes. He shuffled to his horse and climbed on.

"You won't kill me, White Wolf, another Shoshoni," Slow Bull said.

"I will if I have to. Wouldn't like it though."

"I'll come with you. The others will not follow."

"My fellows aren't Shoshoni."

"They're under your protection."

"I'm not sure I can trust you."

"I would not lie to a Shoshoni brother."

"You'll ride out with us and not give me trouble?"

"*Oosh*—yes."

"And you'll tell the others not to follow?"

"*Oosh*."

Cooper hesitated, then said, "Have one of your warriors bring you a pony."

While they waited, the white men mounted one by one, so that only one at a time was occupied.

Before they were finished, a warrior approached warily with Slow Bull's pony. Stiffly the chief turned and easily leaped onto the animal's back and sat patiently, no sign of fear in him.

"Tell your warriors not to follow or you'll die," Cooper said.

Slow Bull did so. Cooper nodded, then climbed

onto his own horse. "Let's ride," he said, "you in front, Slow Bull."

BROOKS SENT Paddy Murphy racing back to their own camp to let the guards and the women know what was happening and to have them get ready to move. The men and women had little to do except tighten cinches and undo the picket lines, all of which they did swiftly though not frantically. When the others arrived, everything was ready.

They pulled out, and half an hour later, Cooper stopped the Shoshoni. "I didn't want it to be this way, Slow Bull," he said sadly in English. "None of these doin's shine with me. No, they don't. But what's done is over."

"I understand," Slow Bull replied in the same language.

Cooper turned in the saddle and watched as his friends pulled away from him. He turned back to the Shoshoni. "It'd be wise if you and your boys was not to follow us, Slow Bull." The Indian said nothing. "I understand what you're feelin'. Just remember, I could've easily killed you. Still could. But one of my boys took a life from your people. I'm givin' a life back."

Slow Bull nodded once.

"Word of this gets back to my clan, I might be unwelcome by them. I can say that the idea sickens me, especially when it comes at the cost of embarrassing you and saving that devil who killed that girl. Unlike that devil, you're an honorable man, Slow Bull. I wish you well."

The Shoshoni nodded again, this time curtly.

Cooper returned it in like fashion before whirling his horse and heeling it into a lope.

Before catching up with the others, Potts found him. "El wants us to watch our back trail, make sure we're not followed."

The other men pushed themselves and the pack animals, not slowing until they were some miles away to the north, back the way they had come. They kept on the trail through the night and the next day, pressing hard. They stopped only occasionally and then for just minutes at a time.

Brooks and Beaubien led them across the rocky, sometimes snow-covered ground, through a wide, boulder-strewn pass, and weaving sometimes through heavy stands of pine, cottonwood, ash, or aspen.

No one had followed, Cooper and Potts reported when they caught up with the others, and after almost twenty-four hours of running, Brooks called a halt. It had rained off and on throughout the day, and the night was cold and clammy, with a thick covering of clouds. But the rain had stopped, and they managed to get their tents up, fires going and food cooking.

Cooper and Potts rode in about an hour after camp was made. They noted with grim satisfaction the guards posted. They dismounted and gave their horses to their women to care for, then headed for the fires.

Cooper strode past the fire he would share with his usual cronies and went straight to the fire at which Webster, Anderson and Wheeler sat. All three looked up, Webster with a smirk on his face, and Cooper planted a moccasin sole full across Webster's face, snapping his head back on his neck. Webster toppled over backward.

"You are the dumbest fucking excuse fer a man I ever saw, you scabrous idiot," Cooper roared, using the rarely spoken epithet in his rage.

To his right, his two friends started to rise. Cooper backhanded Wheeler with his knuckles tight in a fist. Wheeler fell back and over. Anderson froze. The other men began to gather, and Wheeler thought better of trying to get up and face Cooper.

"You stupid son of a bitch, you almost got all of us killed. And, goddammit, you lost us one shinin' place to winter up," Cooper roared. "We had made a deal with Slow Bull to winter there with his people. There was plenty of wood, water, and feed fer all of us. But no, you, you goddamned scar-faced, stupid bastard, ruined it fer us all. You..."

Webster had done a back somersault when Cooper kicked him, coming to rest on his haunches, facing Cooper. Now he launched himself at the lank mountain man. But he was only halfway up when Cooper kicked him again, catching him in the crotch. Webster coughed, doubled up, and fell back. Cooper leaped on him, kicking and punching, pummeling him.

Finally, he stood and slowly drew his Green River. "Your days here on this earth are about over, boy," he hissed, taking Webster's hair in his hand, lifting his face and exposing the throat. The knife started to move forward slowly...

••• And stopped.

Brooks and Potts had grabbed him—Brooks on his knife arm, Potts around his middle. Using brute strength, they dragged Cooper slowly away, inches at a time. "Leave off, now, hoss," Brooks grunted, beads of sweat decorating his forehead from the exertion of trying to move an enraged Cooper. "Leave off him, I say!"

Slowly Cooper relaxed and his knife hand dropped.

"Can I let you go?" Brooks asked.

Cooper nodded tightly.

Potts and Brooks freed him, and Cooper took a deep breath to steady himself. "You should've let me kill that no-good son of a bitch. He's nothin' but trouble."

"Hell, Hawley, if we were to let you do that, we just wasted ourselves one hell of a good run. Nearly the clock around, case you don't remember. We wanted him dead, we could've just given him over to Slow Bull. Them Shoshonis would've let the rest of us go if we'd done that."

"I know," Cooper said angrily. "But..."

"You sure made ol' Webster come now, you did," Bill White said, moving up. "He's stove up real good, Hawley. Knocked out a few more of his teeth, broke at least a half-dozen ribs, I reckon, and who knows what all else."

"Goddammit, Hawley," Brooks said angrily. "Now see what you done. Dammit, he ain't no good to us this way. Don't matter to me that he can't trap for himself, but it does matter that he can't be guardin' horses, helpin' with other camp chores. Nothin'. And we'll have to cart him along on a travois. That'll slow us considerable. I'm of a mind to whup you my own self."

"Come on, then, El," Cooper said heatedly, his face red with rage. "You seen what I did to Webster. You don't think I could do the same to you?"

"By God, I'll teach you a thing..."

"Stop it, the two of you," Potts snapped, stepping between the two. "Lord a'mighty, you're actin' like a couple of unruly schoolboys back in the Settlements causin' some mischief. That don't shine with this chil', nor none of the others, I reckon."

Two-Faces Beaubien joined him, Potts facing Cooper, the half-breed facing Brooks.

"We 'ave enough troubles," Beaubien said. "We don' need no more. You stop, eh."

There was silence for some seconds, except for the drip of water off tree branches, the soft gurgle of the brook nearby and the crackling of the fires. All the eyes in the camp—except Webster's were on the two men facing each other—and the two men between them.

"Well?" Potts finally said in exasperation.

"We could just leave him," Cooper said softly.

"I already thunk of that," Brooks said sullenly. "But it wouldn't be fittin'. Even fer the likes of him."

"You'll come to regret this, El," Cooper warned.

"Might."

"And you might reflect on this: These doin's might just cost me my Shoshoni family if Slow Bull gets word to Cheyenne Killer."

Brooks's eyes widened. "I didn't..."

"Best see to Webster."

Brooks looked like he was going to say something else. But he did not. Instead, he turned and walked toward Webster to survey the damage.

Cooper turned the other way, heading for his tent. When he entered it, Goes Far hurried to the fire outside and returned in a few minutes with food for him—a chunk of pemmican and a steaming tin mug of coffee, unsweetened this time. He nodded thanks and took the bowl and mug. He ate and drank in silence.

"You should not fight with your friend," Goes Far said in English. "Is not good."

"What'n hell do you know about such doin's?" he asked angrily and was immediately sorry when he saw the hurt look on her face. He put down his bowl next to the mug and wiped his hands on his stained, tattered calico shirt. Goes Far stood and headed for the door. But he was up and caught her arm before she could get out. He pulled her around to face him, but she would not look at him.

"Dammit, Sally," he said softly, "I don't know what's got into me. I didn't mean what I said. I purely didn't. You were right, you speak true. Just like last time. It wasn't right for me to say what I did. I must be touched by the spirits." He circled his right temple with his right index finger.

Goes Far relaxed a bit and even managed the hint of a smile.

"I'm angry," he said. "Angry at all that happened." He sighed. "Come, sit," he said, tugging her down to the dirt with him. "I can't believe what I done today. Maybe what I did to Mal was necessary, and even right, but it sure didn't help none of us any. And then arguin' and fightin' with El. Then mistreatin' you. Damn, it don't make sense, and it don't shine. But these doin's have been poor bull, I'm sayin' and have torn apart my sense."

He looked seriously at Goes Far, longing in his eyes. It was not simply lust, but, he realized, possibly for the first time, love. She was truly some woman. She was, he realized, much like Black Moon Woman, maybe not in looks, but in the same gentle but stout heart. The way she cared for him, her easy manner around him, even her sassiness. He could not believe he had been so lucky to have found such a woman twice.

"You're not angry at me?" he asked, a tinge of worry in his voice.

"I think not, Hairy Face," she said, using the translation of the Nez Perce name she had given him. She had trouble pronouncing his English name anyway. She smiled, but then grew serious. "What you did was wrong."

"You mean what I done to Webster?"

TWENTY-FIVE

"NO. That was right. Fighting with friend is wrong. I will make medicine for you, so you not fight him no more."

"It'd have to be right strong medicine fer it to do a hard-headed ol' coon like me any good," he said ruefully.

"It will be strong."

"What if we meet up with some Blackfeet?" he asked, a twinkle suddenly appearing in his eyes. "I need to be fightin' then."

"I will make medicine that will stop you from fightin' with friends."

"That would shine." He stared at her plump cheeks, at her cracked, work-hardened hands resting in her lap; he watched the slow rise and fall of her worn, greasy buckskin dress over her ample breasts. She looked worn and tired, he thought, punished by the long trip, harsh work and the run from the Shoshonis.

"It's been hard on you, ain't it?" he asked softly, his feelings strong for her.

She raised her eyes to stare at his handsome face, covered now with a beard. It was a strong, manly face. "No," she said, a smile brightening her face. "Not hard."

She stopped, thinking. How could she tell him how she really felt, what he really meant to her? She did not know enough English, and his Nez Perce was imperfect. They could communicate well enough, but these feelings were too strong to explain under the circumstances. Had she remained in her village, she would have had a truly hard life. She was a little too independent for an arrogant Nez Perce warrior, one filled with pride and self-importance, as they all were. She would have done something to anger her husband, then maybe would have been lodgepoled. That and the harsh life of the Nez Perce village would have aged her, made her older before her time.

But it was different with Cooper. He did not beat her, as many men—white and red—did. He was not averse to occasionally helping her at her chores, though she would scold him for it—she thought it made him less manly in the eyes of others. Sure, there had been some hard times—days when hunger gnawed at them, moments of danger in encounters with hostile tribes and more. But she always felt safe and protected with Cooper,

Cooper was proud of himself, and he was proud of her. And he showed it in many ways—the way he treated her, the way he decked her out in the finest foofaraw available at rendezvous. In turn, she took pride in her appearance, always trying to look her best for him on special occasions. And she took pride in her man, too, making every effort to ensure that his fancy buckskins were made of the finest cured elk or buffalo hide, that the decorative beadwork and quillwork were the best in the mountains, that his moccasins were the softest, most comfortable.

No, she could not explain these things to him. She smiled again, and he returned it, his teeth sparkling from within the dark, lush beard—the one thing she did not like about him because it scraped her soft face and irritated her skin—but she would not tell him. He liked it and it was easier for him not to shave. There were more important things for him to do—trapping beaver, hunting, caring for the animals, fighting the damned Blackfeet, as she had learned to call them. He said it helped keep him warm in the winter, too. She was happy that he cared enough to scalp his face in the spring and at rendezvous.

"You are some woman, Goes Far," he said softly. "I reckon I'm the luckiest chil' in all these here Stony Mountains to have you." He pulled her to him. She came willingly, eagerly, giggling just a bit as they tumbled onto the thick, plush buffalo robes.

THEY BEGAN STRIKING the camp in the dark, and by dawn, they were ready to leave. Anderson and Wheeler gingerly laid a groaning Malachi Webster in a travois attached to a calm horse and made sure he was well-covered by a buffalo robe.

Cooper moved up alongside Brooks. "Mornin', El," he said quietly. It was the first time he had spoken to Brooks since their altercation the previous night.

"Mornin', Hawl." He grinned wide. "I never seen ol' Mal lookin' ever better."

"Me neither. Right peaceful too." He smiled, relieved.

"It's still gonna slow us up some, though," Brooks said thoughtfully.

"I reckon. Ye settled on a place to winter up yet?"

"Nope," Brooks said uneasily. "I ain't been up this way much before. Maybe some of the other boys have. Jacques has been around a spell, of course, as have Duncan and Two-Faces. I'll check with them."

"There is place," Sits Down said from behind them. They had been aware of his presence, but as usual, they had paid him little mind. The broad Nez Perce had done little around camp but eat, and all the men were disgusted with him. Cooper was, however, looking at Sits Down in a different light. He had seen something in Sits Down's eyes after their confrontation with the Shoshonis. That and seeing the way he had handled himself the day Cooper had spied on him had him thinking there was more to this melancholy, obese warrior than he was showing to the world.

"Where?" Brooks asked.

Sits Down pointed toward the northwest, toward a series of snow-covered peaks cut with passes. "Along Blackfoot River, between what mountains white man call Sapphire Mountains and Mission Mountains."

"How far?"

"Seven suns. Maybe little more."

Brooks sat in thought, then quizzed Cooper with his raised eyebrows. Cooper shrugged. They were not sure they could trust the Nez Perce. Not that he would deliberately try to harm them. They just did not think he could know where he was or where he was going.

"What the hell," Brooks said, running a hand across

his jaw. It was as good a direction to go in as any, he figured. "All right, Sits Down," he said, "lead the way."

They moved out of the mountains down a steep, rocky trail covered with patches of snow. The sun had risen and was bright for about an hour. Then clouds moved in fast, and it began to rain, a steady downpour that made footing treacherous. The men were silent, or they occasionally grumbled, swearing as water seeped under the compotes to trickle icily down their backs or chests. The rain changed to sleet, then snow as they made their way down into a narrow, rocky valley late in the day.

They camped near a small grove of poor cottonwoods. The next day they moved a little faster since the snow had stopped. Though the sun shone brightly, the temperature never rose above freezing. They worked their way slowly northwestward, past gigantic boulders. They camped in a flat, open spot with little wood or cover. The temperature plunged, but Cooper and Goes Far were warm enough in their small, hastily erected tent and under their thick buffalo robes. They chuckled as the sounds of enthusiastic lovemaking drifted over them from Potts's and Morning Song's nearby tent.

Alistair Wentworth lost a horse and Jacques Dubois a mule in the frigid, swirling water of a creek flecked with chunks of ice that was deeper and more treacherous than they had thought. But they made it. On the west bank, they made great fires and stood as close to them as they dared, letting their clothes dry and gratefully allowing warmth to seep into them.

The valley widened, allowing them to move faster. The next day, they came to the headwaters of Clark Fork, and they camped along the river after two long days' travel. It was a cold and miserable night. Just before the light failed, they had seen the smoke of a number of fires to the northeast.

"Blackfeet?" Potts asked.

"Might be mountaineers," Brooks offered.

"Might be," Cooper said, "but I'd be more inclined to think it's Blackfeet. I ain't about to go out there and take a looksee, though."

"Me neither," Brooks said. "But we best set a guard tonight."

A short while later they thought they could hear faint drumming, confirming Cooper's judgment. They posted a heavy guard that night, and all slept uneasily.

Nothing untoward happened, but they were on the trail before daybreak, Sits Down in the lead again. Webster was feeling a bit better and tried sitting a horse for the first time. He was quiet, though the men could see he was in great pain, and Cooper was often aware of his hate-filled eyes boring into his back. It made him uneasy at first, but he soon got used to it.

They followed Clark Fork's snake-like path, having to cross and recross it every hour, it seemed to the weary travelers. They did without incident, though their legs ached from the frequent dousing in ice-cold water. Two days later, they turned east onto the Blackfoot River.

"How much more?" Brooks asked Sits Down that night at their fire. They had shot two buffalo cows that day and had fresh meat, improving their disposition a little. Brooks had also brought out a jug of whiskey and portioned out a cupful to each man. It was almost a celebration.

"Two suns."

"Good. We'll take us a few days here. We ain't done

any trappin' these last days, and it's time we was gettin' back to business. There looks to be a heap of beaver in these parts. So, we'll just oblige 'em by takin' 'em. 'Sides, it'll let us catch our breaths a bit."

The men agreed.

They spent three days there, hauling in a fine catch of lush, thick beaver pelts. As they often did, they made wagers among themselves as to who would bring in the most furs. Cooper and Brooks won it two days for working together. The other day, Cooper, working with Potts this time, won again. He crowed around the camp about his victories, much to the amusement of most of the others.

"By God, I made them beaver come now, I did. I told you boys I could make beaver shine, didn't I? Well, I showed you—all of you—for certain. I'm the best damned beaver trapper in all these here Shinin' Mountains."

"Sit down and shut up, you goddamn idjit," Wheeler said. "I'm plumb tired of you and your claptrap."

Cooper stopped in midsentence, glaring at Wheeler. His eyes sparkled with excitement, glory and anger. "I'll crow all I damn well please, boy," he said sharply. "I'm a better man than you, and I can prove it any way you like. Come agin me, boy, and I'll show you how to shine, I will. You saw what I did to your amigo there, and I'll dish out the same to you if you set your sights agin me."

Wheeler started to stand but thought better of it. "Just quiet down, dammit," he said lamely. "There's sick folks here and they don't need your loudmouth, jabberin' nonsense."

Cooper let out a war whoop and did a war dance around Wheeler, Anderson, and Webster at their fire a few yards from the one shared by Cooper and his usual companions. Webster's face was stamped with loathing. The other men laughed—even, much to the surprise of all—Sits Down. Cooper plopped down cross-legged at the fire. His booty—an otter fur possibles bag, otter-fur hair ties that one of Two-Faces' women had made, two Green River knives, a shot pouch, a bone pipe choker—was piled before him. With a smile, he handed the hair ties to Goes Far, who thanked him and Dancing Water. She thanked Cooper much more personally that night in their robes, until he swelled his chest with pride in his manliness.

The next day the group moved deeper into the mountain, and the day after that they turned north on a wide, crystal-clear creek. They worked their way through a narrow cut in rocks rubbed smooth by the passage of millions of buffalo on the narrow trail over millions of years. In late afternoon, Sits Down, riding ahead of the others, stopped, and pointed.

Cooper, Brooks, and Potts rode up and looked. An even narrower trail led through a tall, sheer cliff on their left and a short, jagged one on their right. Over the latter, they could see a pleasant-looking valley several miles long by a few wide. A good-size stream snaked through it, fed by a half-dozen small creeks. A wall of the mountain rose sharply at the far side, with a band of aspen, cottonwood, and white oak running along the foot of the cliff. Another stretch of trees ran along most of the northern side of the grassy meadow up to a rocky slope on the northwest. A small herd of buffalo was feeding on the brown grass where it poked through the light coating of snow.

"Damn, that's a purty sight," Potts said in delight.

The others agreed.

"How'd you know this place was here?" Brooks asked suspiciously.

"I come before."

"When?"

Sits down shrugged.

"What were ye doin' here?" And where is it exactly? This place seems a far piece from your land, boy."

Sits Down pointed to the northwest. "Flatheads, three suns ride. Friends."

The three mountain men glanced at each other, shrugged, and then Cooper said,

"Lead the way, Sits Down."

TWENTY-SIX

THE SNOW LAY deep and thick on the land, but the mountain men, their women and their animals were comfortable enough. It had edged into January as best they could figure it, but they had had no time to celebrate the most solemn and festive occasion of Christmas.

As soon as the men had ridden down into the valley, they had started working on their winter camp, alternating between chores and trapping. Trees were felled and mules hauled the trunks to where the cabins would be built hard against the mountainous cliff.

Cooper and Potts rode out, searching for lodgepole pines. It took a while, but they found some and chopped down nearly fifty of the tall, straight, slender trees. They tied them into two bunches and had a pair of mules haul them back to camp.

Cooper and Potts chose a nice spot, protected, but not too closed in. They would be a little distance from the others—enough to keep away the smells that would soon be wafting from the cabins, but not so far that they would be inhospitable.

Two-Faces had picked the spots and stayed behind to clear brush, leaves and snow while Cooper and Potts had gone to get the lodgepoles. He, too, would be living in a tipi. The three men worked over the lodgepoles, hacking away branches, smoothing them, shortening them to the proper length. While they were doing that, their women were speedily finishing stitching tough buffalo bull hides together. They had been working on these tipi covers when they could while traveling. As usual, they all pitched in, laughing and chattering as they worked. They were almost done with the second. With all six women working on them, all would be done quickly.

Bill White and Jacques Dubois, along with their women, set up their tents the first night because it looked like a snowstorm was brewing. It turned out not to be as bad as expected, but they did waken to a coating of snow maybe two inches deep. Grumbling, the men went back to work. Except for two of the men: Webster, who was progressing quickly and probably could lend a hand but preferred to sit and watch balefully as the others worked, and Sits Down, who disappeared.

Since he had become the de facto second in command of the group, Cooper got the first tipi made. The women raised it quickly and with no fuss the next morning. The men hastily pegged it down, and Cooper moved his possibles in. Later he would furnish it. But there was much to be done yet.

Two days later, Beaubien had his lodge, and three days after that, Potts went up. He had griped about the long time it seemed to take, and he had but little privacy, but the others ignored him.

The same day Potts got his lodge, the rest of the men raised their first cabin. Despite the extra work, they had put a slightly canted roof on it, having learned that a flat roof allowed snow to accumulate to unsustainable—and dangerous—depths. It didn't stop the leaks, but at least some of the snow and water in those infrequent times when it rose above freezing ran off instead of all of it landing inside. Once done, half of them set to filling in the gaps—and there were many—with mud mixed with what straw they could find. The other half went about building the second.

While they were doing so, Brooks joined Potts, Cooper, and Beaubien in running trap lines. It was hard, long work, since they set everyone's traps, not just their own, while the other men were occupied. Only Webster complained, almost accusing the others of stealing his pelts despite having been given five or six a day, same as everyone else.

Each evening for almost a week, Cooper entered his lodge with his legs aching from the cold. He would strip off the buckskin pants that had blanketing for legs from the knees down and Goes Far would rub his legs near the fire, using a piece of blanket to help warm him. Sometimes he would sit up afterward and put on his heavily fringed buckskin pants and eat the warmed pemmican or hard-as-stone jerky or, rarely, fresh buffalo. Occasionally he would bring home a beaver tail or two for them to roast and enjoy. Other times, he did not bother with his buckskins, just either rolled into the warm robe and fell asleep or would joyfully pull Goes far into the robes with him.

The sight, smell, and feel of her naked body next to him never failed to excite him. He could detect subtle changes in her body—and her attitude—as the child she had only two weeks ago announced was within her grew, though she was still showed little.

"We will have a good son," she told him. "He will be big and strong like his father. And brave. None will be braver than our son."

Cooper smiled. He liked hearing her talk that way.

Within another week, the second cabin was up and chinked with mud. The men happily moved in—just in time for a blizzard that swept over the mountains to the west and rolled over them. By the time it stopped three days later, they had several feet of snow on the ground, with drifts piled up on the sides of the cabins and over the roofs.

Cooper laughed when he saw it. It was a laugh of humor mixed with relief that the storm was over and they would not be cooped up any longer. They had been unable to run their trap lines during the storm, and now, though the air was still bitter, they could get back to work.

Soon they would have to leave off trapping for the winter. The creeks would freeze over, which they were showing signs of doing, and the beaver would be nestled in their snug lodges, unwilling to come into the freezing water unless necessary. Trapping would be futile until spring.

They had lost two horses, one belonging to MacTavish and one to Wheeler, and a mule of Webster's in the storm, so Brooks said, "We got to make us a shelter of some kind fer the animals. We can't afford to lose no more of 'em."

So the men went back to work. The four best trappers—Cooper, Brooks, Beaubien , and Potts—ran everyone's trap lines. The pelts they brought in were as fine as they had ever seen—thick, lush, heavy with fur.

"I ain't ever seen plews so prime as these," Potts said happily. "By God, we ought to come here every year."

"Blackfoot might take a dislikin' to that," Brooks said.

"Hell with the Blackfoot. We ain't seen any. All we seen is sign, and not much of that."

"Them Blackfoot ain't gonna leave off this valley forever," Cooper said.

"Bug's Boys might not be disposed to us settin' on their land if they find us after we whupped 'em good last year," Brooks added.

"Bunch of yellowbellies, I'd say," Potts said with a grin.

Brooks did not smile as the other two did, even when Cooper playfully tossed a dirty piece of cloth that he had been using to clean his rifle at Potts.

THE OTHER MEN built up a brush and post enclosure for the animals. It ran in a semicircle under an overhang on the mountain wall. It would keep the animals protected as much as possible under the circumstances. They would be let out daily, unless the weather didn't allow it, to run along the snow-covered meadow. Two or three of them men would watch over them at such times lest the animals wander too far off.

That done, they built two log storage sheds—one for their food supplies, extra traps, trade goods, robes, cured pelts, and such. The other would store feed for the animals for when the weather got really bad. The men peeled willow and cottonwood bark from hundreds of trees, working with those farthest away. That way, if they needed more in the heart of winter, they would have a supply close to hand. They kicked away snow and pulled up grass and tender shoots, and anything else the horses and mules would eat.

They worked against time now. Christmas had long since passed, and the weather was bitter cold. Two of the smaller creeks were frozen over, and it looked like several others would be soon. They had suffered through another blizzard—one not as bad—as well as a day of hail mixed with sleet. The days were short and often gray. And the work kept them too busy to celebrate Christmas.

Past the halfway point of January, they were done with what they could do. The horses and mules would have to stick it out as the winter worsened, just like the men, the women, and the children. The traps were coming up empty more often now.

"Dammit," Potts grumbled, "This don't shine at all. Freezin' my ass off every single day and fer what? Two goddamn plews this week. It don't shine, I tell you."

As every night, the usual group—Cooper, Potts, Brooks, Beaubien, MacTavish and Sits Down—were gathered in Cooper's lodge.

"Ye ought to be used to it by now," Brooks said. "It's the same every year this time."

"'Sides," Cooper said with a snigger, "it makes your woman have a heap of sympathy fer you. You come in all a-soppin' wet, wore out from all your hard work..." He did a pretty good job of mimicking Potts. "...And she feels all sorry fer you, rubs you down some with her toasty warm hands and then she..."

"Stop!" Potts said with a strangled look in his eyes. "Don't go on like that!"

"What's wrong?" Cooper asked innocently.

"Dammit, you made me lose my thoughts, and you put other ones there. I don't..." He jammed to a stop. "Aw, hell, Betsy, come on over here."

When the woman came up, he grabbed her hand and pulled her from the lodge. The others doubled over with laughter. They did so again a few minutes later when they heard Potts's rutting passion from the tipi nearby.

—————

LESS THAN A WEEK LATER, they all came up empty on their traps two days running and called it a season. But that did not mean their work was done. Brooks and Cooper made a sturdy press to bundle their pelts, traps had to be repaired, rifle balls made, saddles fixed, and more.

The women, now with some of the men helping, tanned the last of the plews taken. Some of the men cut more firewood. Anderson, Wheeler, and Murphy had care of the horses and mules.

Webster had mostly recovered, and though he was still a little weak, his strength was coming back rapidly. He most often spent time with Wheeler and Anderson, tending to the animals.

Sits Down disappeared mostly every day, trying to skip out of work, and reappeared every evening in time for something to eat.

"We need more jerky and pemmican," Beaubien said frequently to Potts, approaching him wherever he was with an empty parfleche.

The others thought it hilarious, especially Cooper, who laughed every time Beaubien arrived.

"You should have listened to me, boy, when I said I'd take care of that no-good brother-in-law of yours," Cooper said with a laugh. "But no, you had to insist that since he was family, he was your responsibility. And now you got to suffer fer it. We got us another two, three months of winter facin' us, and you're gonna have starvin' times fer certain you keep feedin' that lazy bastard. I'm tellin' you..."

"Goddammit, shut up," Potts said.

However, since he was responsible for bringing Sits Down along, Cooper decided to speak to the Nez Perce a few days later. Mountain men ate enormous amounts of food when they could but Sits Down could easily outeat any two of the men here. Come February, it would really start to tell on their supplies if he didn't ease up.

Cooper didn't know how much good it would do talking to the big Nez Perce, and he was somewhat surprised when Beaubien did not show up at Potts's lodge for several days looking for more food.

"I don' know what's got into zat chil," Beaubien said. "'E just stop eatin' one day. Jus' little bits now."

Cooper smiled. "When did he start this?"

"Four, five day ago, I t'ink, eh." He frowned. "Why you smile like zat, eh? You know somet'ing?"

"I had a chat with him just about that time, told him he was gonna bring starvin' times to us all he didn't ease up some."

Beaubien scratched his hair under the wolf-head hat. "Must've done 'im good."

Cooper thought so, too. But he also wondered where the warrior was getting food. He could not be doing without. The next morning, he carefully checked the supplies in the storage cabin, but he found nothing amiss. So the next day he did as he had done once before some months ago and silently followed Sits Down as the Indian left camp before dawn.

More than a mile to the west there was an indentation in the mountain wall. Not a cave really, just a section of the mountain wall a few feet deep. From a little distance away, Cooper sat and watched as Sits Down pulled a deer carcass from up in a tree where the wolves could not get it. With a tomahawk Cooper had given him, he hacked off a large haunch. Then he built a fire and roasted the meat. While he was waiting for it, Sits Down reached under a bush and brought out a sinew-backed bow wrapped in mountain lion fur with the feet dangling. A matching quiver was next. From it, The Nez Perce pulled several arrows, some finished, some not.

"I'll be damned," Cooper muttered as Sits Down began working on one of the unfinished arrows, straightening the stick with a round stone with a hole in the center. He ate and worked all day. Finally, about two hours before dark, he finished the last of the deer meat he had cooked, carefully hid the bow and arrows, hauled the deer back up into the tree with the help of a handmade grass rope, and headed back toward camp.

Cooper waited until he was well gone before finding the bush where Sits Down had cached the bow and arrows. The bow was superbly made, tough, strong, backed with many wrappings of tough elk sinew. The bow itself was made of stout wood augmented by horn, and Cooper thought he would have trouble drawing it. He wanted to slide the bowstring on and try, but he decided not to.

The arrows were of the same quality as the bow, their shafts straight and true, smooth. The arrowheads had been carefully knapped from fine flint. The feathers were straight and attached to last with a thick coating of glue made from boiling down buffalo hooves and horns.

Cooper stood for some while, staring at the items and looking back toward the camp. There was definitely more to the obese Nez Perce than he was letting on. And it made sense now that Sits Down had kept a mighty keen eye on his buffalo robe, which hung lengthwise on one of his ponies instead of crossways behind the saddle. He must have kept the bow hidden there all along. It was disturbing to Cooper. He shrugged. It would work itself out eventually, he supposed.

He put the bow and arrows back exactly as he had found them. Sits Down would never know he had been there as he headed back to camp, brushing his trail behind him.

It was past dark when he returned and Goes Far scolded him, something she rarely did. He accepted her sharp rebukes for a while, but finally had enough. He looked at her, ready to retort, to tell her that she had no right, as a woman, to tell him, as a man, what he could do, or when he should return to the lodge. She should know these things, and he thought she did. But she was forgetting her place and...

He realized something was wrong with her. Something was bothering her, and she was using this excuse to lash out at him.

"That's enough," he said. "Maybe I done wrong, but you've let me know it now, and it's over."

She wound down, and he asked, "Now what's wrong with you? This ain't like you to be doin' such things."

"Nothing wrong," she said, dropping her face.

"Like hell there ain't, woman. I know you better'n that. You got somethin' in your craw, you'd best let it free. I can't help you less'n you tell me what it is."

But she would say nothing. He was angry, and it became a sore spot between them over the next several days.

TWENTY-SEVEN

BROOKS CALLED the group together one afternoon, and the men crammed into one of the cabins. "We've had us a good fall hunt, boys," he said. "We've all brought in a heap of plews. We got a fair amount of meat made and a comfortable camp. And since we didn't have much of a celebration to pay homage to the Good Lord for Christmas, nor to welcome in the new year, I reckon we deserve a real celebration."

He waited while the men whooped and hollered before he continued. "So I reckon we're gonna have one."

Again the room erupted with war whoops and shouts. "Day after tomorrow, we'll meet right here and..."

"Cabin's kind of small, ain't it?" Wheeler said.

"Ye got a better place in mind?" There was silence. "Didn't think so. We'll make do. I'll bring the whiskey."

There was more cheering as the men drifted out.

Early the next morning, Cooper and Potts saddled up and rode out. After a month or more of the men being here, game was rather scarce, but the two were hoping they might spot some buffalo or at least an elk along the southern edge of great meadow several miles from the camp. Going was slow in the deep snow, but they were in no hurry. A couple hours later, they could hear the unmistakable snuffling grunts of the buffalo, and they shifted course a little to come up on the animals from upwind.

Cooper took the first shot and Potts the second. Two cows went down. They hurriedly began butchering the beasts. They did not have the time—the wind was picking up and snow flurries had begun—nor enough mules to carry much, so they took only the best cuts, and some lesser ones to make boudins, the meat stuffed intestines that served the mountain men as sausages. They left the rest of the carcasses to the wolves, which were already circling at a little distance.

The two men and their laden mules beat the storm back to camp, but not by much. The arrival of the fresh meat was greeted with cheers. Leaving the bounty with a few others to be unloaded and stored for the night, Cooper tended to his horse and then headed for his lodge. He was cold, tired, and hungry. As he pushed through the flap, anger burst inside him. The fire was burned down to mere embers, and there was no food warming on them. The lodge had not been cleaned, nor items put away.

"Dammit," he muttered. He and Goes Far had been at odds for more than a week but he figured they would work things out. And she had tended to her chores throughout it all. Until now.

Over the howling of the wind outside, he heard sobbing. "Sally?" he called softly. "Goes Far?" He moved deeper into the lodge, and the sobbing grew louder. Then, in the dimness, he could see her in a heap on the buffalo robes. "Sally?" he said, urgency and dread springing into his voice.

He hurried to her. Kneeling at her side, he pulled her resisting body around to face him. Her face was a mask of tears and grief.

"What is it, Goes Far? Tell me, dammit."

She fought weakly against him, trying to turn her face away again. But he would not let her.

"Tell me, goddammit, what's wrong?" He was filled with fear, more fear than he had ever known.

He saw blood on her buckskin dress near the midsection. But the dress was pulled up and twisted some so he was not sure where it was from.

"Are you hurt, dammit? Tell me," he ordered, voice quivering. "Did somebody hurt you? Tell me!" he roared, shaking her.

"Baby," she wailed. "No more baby. Baby gone." She was reduced to blubbering, her face a mask of pain.

"What do you mean baby gone?" he asked, confusion mixed with worry.

She tried to explain, but he could not understand. He knew nothing of these matters.

"Someone hurt you?" he asked. "Somebody hurt the baby?"

But all she would do now is howl and cry. Cooper held her, feeling the shaking of her young body. He became aware of someone calling his name from outside.

"Go away," he snapped. "Ain't no time for visitors now."

"What's wrong?" he heard a voice and realized it was Potts.

"None of your damned business. Now leave us alone."

"Like hell I will," Potts said, breaking etiquette and entering. "What in hell's wrong?" he asked in surprise.

"I don't know," Cooper said helplessly. "I found her hollerin' and cryin' here when I come in. I been tryin' to find out what's wrong. Somethin' about the baby bein' gone. But I can't understand her."

"Baby gone? She was with child? I didn't know."

"Nobody did 'cept us. She was sure only a couple weeks ago. Only been two months, maybe a bit more, she figures."

He put a hand on his friend's shoulder. "I'm sorry, Hawl." He pulled the hand away. "I'll be right back." He stepped outside and bellowed for Morning Song, who came running from inside her lodge, fear in her large, soft eyes.

The two entered Cooper's lodge, and Potts said, "Find out what's wrong with Goes Far, Betsy."

The woman kneeled next to Cooper and fired questions at Goes Far, who answered between howls. "She lose baby," Morning Song said, grief covering her face.

"What do you mean, lost the baby?" Cooper demanded.

"Baby no more inside."

Cooper looked at her blankly. Then he began asking her questions. The young woman struggled to answer in English or simple Nez Perce. Finally Cooper's eyes widened. "Something happened to make the baby come out when it wasn't supposed to?"

"Yes."

"But what happened to it?"

"Not can see when it happened. Too small. Too early to grow."

Cooper tried to digest that. It was alien to him. Men didn't deal with such things. "How did it happen?"

"She not say, but something happened. Someone hurt her, I think."

Cooper nodded dumbly. It was going too fast for him. It did not seem real to him, but he knew Goes Far's pain was real.

He was not aware of Potts taking Morning Song's arm and pulling her quietly from the lodge.

Cooper did not know how long he sat there, but he finally realized it was quite dark, and had grown cold in the lodge. The wind still roared and whistled outside.

"You got to stop this bawlin'," he said quietly to Goes Far. "It's over and done, and that can't be changed. We got to go on."

She quieted a little. "You not mad?"

"Mad at you? Why'n hell would I be mad at you?"

"For losing baby."

"Ain't your fault far as I know. Now you rest a few minutes." He laid her head down on the robes and went outside. It was bitter, and the wind ripped at him as he picked up a good load of firewood. Back inside, he stamped his feet to restore feeling in his legs and got the fire built up. Before long, its brightness and warmth flooded the lodge.

TO THE SYMPATHY of the other women and most of the men—a few were annoyed—Brooks canceled the party for that night, telling the men they would still have their celebration, but it would be in a few days considering Goes Far's condition.

Cooper roasted some of the meat that night and made her eat. She made a face when she tasted the half raw, half charred flesh, saying, "This bad."

"Well, dammit," he said, his feelings hurt some, "I ain't no cook. It tastes all right to me."

She smiled wanly and ate a little. Before long, she fell asleep and Cooper sat, staring into the fire, trying not to think. In the morning, Goes Far was feeling a little better, but he still was the one to make the food. As he did the next day and the one after that.

"Your friends will laugh at you," she said in Nez Perce.

"Ain't nobody here 'cept you'n me. They don't need to know," he said testily.

After she had eaten, he said, "Tonight's the party. It'll give you a chance to put on your fancy dress, the one with all the foofaraw I bought you to rendezvous."

"I not go."

"The hell you won't, woman. I ain't goin' by myself, and I sure as hell ain't gonna sit here with you all weepy and suchlike."

A stubborn expression spread across her face.

"Don't you go givin' me that kind of look, Sally. 'Sides, I know you're just itchin' to put on that nice dress, all fancied up like it is and show it off to the other women. Two-Faces's fat ol' squaws'll choke on their buffalo stew when they see ye in that getup.

A faint—very faint—smile tugged at Goes Far's lips. *It would be all right,* she thought, *if only...*she shrugged mentally. She could not refuse to go, so she would put on her best face and her best dress and make her man proud of her. She nodded.

They spent the day getting ready, cleaning themselves as best they could under the circumstances. Cooper trimmed his beard and slicked his hair back with bear grease. Goes Far sent him away after a while so she could tend to her needs in private.

"But, Sally, I seen ye naked afore," he argued. "Why're ye actin' like this?"

But she was adamant and pointed to the tipi's entry flap. "Go," she ordered. So off he went and spent the day leaning against a tree with a good fire in front of him making another willow backrest for inside the tipi.

Finally he figured it was time, and he went back to his lodge. "Can I come in?" he called after looking around to make certain no one was watching.

"Yes."

He entered and stopped, smile building. "Damn, you shine, Sally, you purely do."

She stood looking demure in a buckskin dress that reached a little below her knees. It was tanned so it was almost white. Small silver-colored tin cones that clacked when she moved ringed the bottom hem. An intricate, colorful pattern of beads, dyed porcupine quills and shells decorated the bodice. An inverted triangle tapered to a point several inches above her navel. An ermine tail dangled from each of the three points.

She turned slowly, showing an identical design on the back. Both sleeves were heavily fringed on the underside. A choker of interspersed black and white bone hair pipes set off with large white beads and golden metal ones circled her neck. A shank of horse-hair dangled from the beaded rosette in the center. She had wrapped her braids in otter fur as usual and painted the center part with vermillion.

She wore moccasins tanned to the same color as her dress. The puckered toes were decorated with beadwork that matched any made by Crow women, who were renowned in the mountains for their bead and quillwork, and there was an arc of tiny bells across the instep of each. Above them were leggings that matched.

"You like?"

"Yes, I like," he said, mouth gone dry. He moved toward her, but she placed a hand on his chest, holding him back, and said, "Not good now." Her eyes implored him.

He nodded after a few moments.

She had laid out an outfit for him on the robes, and he donned it quickly: Cream-colored buckskin pants with three elk-horn buttons, black suspenders to hold them up, and a buckskin war shirt of the same color. Strips of beadwork and quillwork from the bottom up the back and over the shoulder and down the front, about halfway on each side. Like her dress, the sleeves were fringed and had a beaded strip on the upper side of the sleeve. Scalps dangled from rosettes at the upper part of the chest, just below the shoulders and on each upper arm. His moccasins were similar to Goes Far's, with beadwork and bells.

A wide, thick leather belt went around his waist. It was studded with brass tacks in diamond designs and had a sheath in a slit through the back into which he slipped one of his Green Rivers, and his tomahawk went alongside it. A small possible sack was hooked on it at this right hip. He slid the metal hook of his pistols onto the belt, one to each side.

A gun fired loudly, rising even above the storm that still blew. "Ready?" he asked.

She nodded, hoping he didn't see the pain and fear in her eyes. Cooper reached for his capote but Goes Far stopped him with a touch on his arm.

"What?" he asked. "I can't go out, even just that little bit without my capote."

"Wait."

She went to the back of the lodge and reached into a large parfleche. She turned with something in her hands. Coming to him, she held it out. He took it and let it unfold to its full length. His eyes sparkled, and he smiled as he put on the coat. It was of the finest elk skin. It reached below his knees and had an irregular cut at the bottom. Fringe ran around each shoulder and more down the sides of each sleeve. The lapels were wide as was the belt. Buttons ran the length of it. The fur had been left on the inside for warmth. It was the most comfortable thing he had ever worn.

"Do you like?"

"Yes, ma'am. It purely shines." He grinned.

"Then you say no more."

As he put on his broad-brimmed felt hat with the beaded headband and the feather dangling off the back, she grabbed her blanket and wrapped it deftly around her. Out of the corner of her eye, she watched him and tried to calm the sickness she felt inside.

Cooper looked at her and marveled. To him there was no sign of the turmoil at the miscarriage that had burned within her just three days ago. He nodded and smiled.

Goes Far smiled wanly back, letting him think that she was fine. He could not know that pain she still carried in her heart. But she was determined to make sure he did not see it.

They stepped out into the swirling snow and blustery wind, which carried the aroma of cooking meat and the faint sound of music. The inside of the cabin was stifling, and Cooper left his fancy coat on just long enough for everyone to admire it before he took it off and hung it on a peg on the wall.

Jacques Dubois was scratching at his fiddle, Two-Faces Beaubien was puffing into an ocarina, Duncan MacTavish was squeezing a concertina, and Paddy Murphy hummed on his jaw harp. The music they produced was rough but harmonious enough for this crude gathering.

Buffalo meat was roasting in the fireplace, and in the embers to the sides, biscuits and cobbler were baking in Dutch ovens.

It was crowded and water dripped from the roof in places, but to the revelers, it was festive.

"Care to dance?" Webster asked Goes Far, bowing, then turning his smirking face to hers.

TWENTY-EIGHT

GOES FAR SHRANK BACK from him as Cooper
said in a low voice that only the three of them could
hear, "Back away, Webster, or I'll carve your heart out
and eat it with a few of them biscuits cookin' over
there."

Webster looked at Cooper with cold, hateful eyes.
But fear was there, too, as Cooper's gaze bore into him,
making all the old wounds hurt anew.

"Maybe later," Webster mumbled, trying for a smile
but failing miserably.

"You ever come near her and there won't be enough
left of you fer the crows to pick over." He shoved past,
bumping Webster on the shoulder, Goes Far in tow, her
eyes downcast.

Cooper boiled, but within a few minutes, Two-
Faces Beaubien shoved his ocarina into his possibles bag
and was twirling around the cramped, steamy cabin
with Dancing Water, his Nez Perce woman, who was
not in the least graceful. Nor was Beaubien. But the

two did not care. They spun and stomped and danced their own steps, banging into other men and women in the crowded cabin. Soon Cooper and all the others were smiling.

"Come on, Sally," Cooper finally said. "Let's dance."

"I can't..." The words were ripped from her mouth as Cooper yanked her forward and began swinging her around recklessly, not letting her finish telling him she was in no way ready in body or spirit for such frivolity.

"Wait," she said softly. "I don't know..."

"Neither do any of these others," he said jovially, ignorant of the pain he was causing, which he had not let her express.

The night passed in fun and jollity for most. Music never sounded better; buffalo never tasted better, and Taos Lightning was never quite as smooth as on this night.

Only two fights broke out—once when Luis Gamez tried to dance with Bill White's Nez Perce woman and once when Wheeler, with too much whiskey in him, insulted Beaubien's two women—Dancing Water who was with him, and Little Fox, his Flathead woman who was in the other cabin watching over all the children.

Both fights were broken up quickly, and the night roared on. Bolstered by warmth, music, whiskey and food, the people easily forgot the raging elements outside, and the heat and leaky roof inside. Goes Far managed to make it through with great difficulty, which she was able to keep Cooper from seeing. Nor would she let him see her pain when they were in the robes together.

The men dragged around camp the next day, hungover and bloated from the previous night's festivities. All but Sits Down, who had not been seen at all during the revelry. But the day after, they found themselves back at work—they tended their own animals, and all took part in the camp chores—collecting fodder for the horses and mules, cutting firewood. Then there were the personal tasks—repairing traps, saddles and other tack, mending clothes and more.

So as winter dragged on, they passed hours as men had done through the ages in such times. They talked and argued, fought sometimes, yarned, recalled their exploits both glorious and not, slept, ate, fornicated, and gambled. While the men would bet on anything, euchre was popular, as was the hand game learned from the Indians. Potts was particularly good at the former and often won. Some said he cheated, but not to his face, as most of them knew that even if he was known to cheat on occasion, he would not do so playing with friends.

Cooper, Potts, Beaubien, MacTavish, White, and Brooks were engaged in a game of euchre in Cooper's lodge almost a week after the party. It was early morning, so the men were wide-eyed, full of energy, making it a lively game. As usual, Sits Down had not been seen, though after all this time of him disappearing, the men paid no attention to the fact.

With a gourd in hand, Goes Far left the lodge to get water. Cooper nodded and smiled at her as she left. She had seemed all right to him since the night of the party.

Potts made his bid, grousing at the poor cards he held.

"Hell," MacTavish said good-naturedly. "We've

been here less than an hour, lad, and ye've won three times."

"It ain't the cards he's complainin' about, Duncan," Cooper laughed. "It's his woman again."

"That time, eh, laddie?"

"Yep. Damn women," Potts grumbled. "Have the damn thing every other week, or so it seems to me. It wouldn't bother me none to have at it whilst she's that way. But she won't have no part of me durin' it, I'm likely to go plumb loco afore long she keeps this up."

The others chuckled. They knew what he was going through, as their women had the same condition every month that the men had to endure, which they generally did without too much complaint.

"Knock her up." White laughed. "Then she won't have that problem fer a spell."

"Hell, that'd only bring on another passel of troubles."

"You need another woman, *mon ami*," Beaubien said. "Like me. When one has zat time, you can have at ze other."

They all laughed, and the card game continued, the men talking easily. They knew each other well, and had faced danger and hardship together, making their chatter friendly, even when joshing each other.

A scream suddenly rent the air, stopping the friendly jibes,

"That's Goes Far!" Cooper snapped. He jumped up and bolted out of the lodge, heedless of the freezing air. The others boiled out of the tipi just behind him into the overcast day. Another scream split the air, and Cooper headed toward where he thought it had come from. But with the wind making it hard to tell exactly where the sound came from, the other men spread out to search. After running a few more yards, Cooper stopped and frantically called, "Sally? Goes Far! Where are you?"

He heard something in the thickets among the cottonwoods along the river. He ran, heart thumping. Several panthers had been spotted in the area recently, and he worried that perhaps one of those beasts had gotten her.

He spotted a flash of color and crashed through the thicket, thorns tearing at him. He suddenly dug in his heels and stopped, then spun and retraced his steps.

He found her lying in a heap, coat open, dress thrown up almost over her head, exposing her leggings and womanhood. He yanked the dress down moments before the other men started charging up. He thought he heard someone running the other way, but he was not sure.

Cooper pulled Goes Far around. Her cheekbone and the eye socket were discoloring where someone had hit her.

"What happened?" Cooper asked, trying to keep the urgency, fear and anger out of his voice. He could read sign, and there was no real indication that another man had just had his woman. But he could not be sure. But he knew that if that had happened, she had not been a willing participant.

"Nothing," she said weakly, eyes on the ring of concerned men gathering around her.

"Like hell," Cooper exploded.

"I fall. Hurt face."

He was about to protest, say something sarcastic about her dress being up over her head, a possible sign of another man having taken her. But he caught himself. He would say nothing here in front of the others. They had not seen her the way he found her. They need not know.

"All right," he said, forcing calmness and gentleness into his voice. He scooped her up and carried the shivering woman toward their lodge. Though his thoughts were awhirl, he suddenly realized that whoever had attacked Goes Far had not had enough time to do what he had first suspected, what he had feared. Inside the tipi, he placed her gently down. "Now, tell me what happened," he said, his voice no longer gentle.

"I fall," she said again, trying to rise.

He pushed her back down. "I ain't a damn fool, woman," he snapped angrily, eyes burning.

"Please," she pleaded, "let me clean face and..." she sputtered. "I all right."

"I don't give a damn that you're all right. I..." He paused, drawing in a deep breath and let it out slowly. "That ain't true, and you know it," he said more calmly. "I do care. But you got to tell what's gone on."

"I can't," she said, hiding her face.

"Yes, you can. You got to." He waited but she still said nothing. Then he said softly, "If what happened was what I fear it was, I don't love you any less for it." He realized with a small jolt that this was the first time he had told her that he loved her. "If it's true, I know you didn't bed whoever it was willingly. But I don't think it is. He didn't have enough time to debase you."

"He not do..." She fought to control her shivering.

"He try, but I scream, he hit me. Then we heard you and others coming. He jump up and ran."

Cooper felt a sense of deep relief, but it did not lessen his anger any. Whoever did this likely would try again, and Cooper would not let that happen. Whoever it was—and he was certain he knew—would try again if Cooper didn't end it now. "You got to tell me who done it. I'll take care of it."

"I can't. Before he run, he say if I tell, he kill me and you."

"Ain't nobody in this goddamn camp I can't take," he said vehemently. "Ain't nobody here gonna kill me. Or you."

"But he say."

"Don't mean a goddamn thing what he said," Cooper roared. "You doubt me as a man? As a warrior? That it?"

"No," she almost wailed. "You brave. Strong."

"Then tell me who did this to you." His voice was low, but there was fury there, and strength.

"The one..." she started, faltered.

"Was it Webster?"

"Yes." Her voice was barely a whisper.

Cooper started to rise, nostrils flaring and eyes burning with rage. The thought of revenge seared through his soul. He could feel his hard, calloused hands around Webster's neck, see the fear in the man's eyes above the puckered scar, feel...

Her hand stopped him.

"Let me go, dammit," he hissed.

"Wait," she pleaded.

He forced his muscles to relax.

"There's more," she said.

He nodded, realization flashing on his face. "This here's about the baby, ain't it? Last time?"

She nodded weakly and pushed herself up so she was sitting across from him, cross-legged. Her eyes worriedly searched his face. She nodded again. "He catch me last time. He try to do...to..."

"I know what he tried to do," Cooper said tightly.

"I not let. He try to hit my face, but I hide it. So he hit me two times. Here..." She pointed to her belly. "He throw me down. Hard. I try to get up. He kick me in same place. We hear someone come. He kick me again, stepped on me hard, then run away. I stand, feel blood, much pain. Liquid come from belly. Come back to lodge, lay for a long time. Hurt much. Baby gone. Baby no more. Baby..." She started to cry.

He took her tenderly in his arms and let her sob. He stroked her hair softly, saying, "It's all right, Goes Far," over and over.

Finally she began to quiet down. He pushed her to arm's length. "Now, I want ye to go to Morning Song's lodge. You don't need to tell her anything if you don't want. Have her tend to you, if you need it."

"Where you go?"

He did not answer her. He stood and made sure his Green River was in its sheath, the tomahawk was in his belt and his pistols were ready. He grabbed his Dickert rifle, then said to her, "Go on to Morning Song's now. I'll come fetch you later." His face was as hard as the granite wall of the mountain outside.

He stepped out of the lodge. Brooks, Potts, and Beaubien watched intently. "What're ye you gonna do, Hawley?" Brooks asked, stepping in front of him.

"Get the fuck out of my way, El," Cooper said

through compressed lips, using the rare expletive in his rage.

The two stared at each other for a moment. Then Brooks asked, "What is it, Hawley?"

"None of your concern."

"Like hell it ain't. I'm booshway of this outfit, and don't you forget it. Somebody attacked her, didn't they? Who was it, Hawl? I'll take care of it."

Cooper looked at him in disbelief and shoved past. Behind him he could hear Potts and the others following him, and Potts mumbling, "How goddamned stupid can you get, El?"

Cooper marched to where the two cabins stood a few feet apart. He did not know which one Webster was staying in; he had not paid attention. He stopped more or less between them and bellowed, "Webster!"

The word hung in the air like a fog, heavy and unmoving. The door of each cabin opened. From one, several men peered out. From the other came a disembodied voice, "What you want, boy?"

"Get out here, you scabrous festerin' pile of buffler shit, or I'll burn down the whole goddamn cabin with you roastin' inside."

Webster appeared in the doorway, cocked rifle held in both hands. He stepped out, followed by Wheeler and Anderson.

"Throw down your rifle, shit pile."

"So ye can just shoot me down?" Webster asked with a sneer. "I ain't that goddamn foolish."

"You got to be a goddamn fool to think you could get away with what you done."

Webster shrugged and moved a few steps closer. "Hell, I figured on killin' you afore long anyway."

"If ye somehow got lucky and managed to kill Hawley, ye'd nary get away with it," Potts said. "I'd put ye under fer certain."

"You would've never known it were me who done it."

"Wouldn't take much figurin' to know."

Sits Down silently came around the corner of the cabin. Suddenly the big warrior was between Webster and his two friends.

"Drop your rifle," Cooper ordered again.

"Like hell I will," he snarled. But the scowl turned to surprise when Sits Down reached around him and snatched away Webster's rifle, which he had been bringing to bear on Cooper. Sits Down gave the mountain man a hard shove in the back, sending him stumbling forward. He stepped down and shoved Webster forward a few more times. The Nez Perce's move surprised everyone—except Cooper.

Webster fell to his hands and knees in front of Cooper.

Cooper grinned, half-turned, and tossed his Dickert to Potts, who deftly snatched it out of the air.

"I should've done this a long time ago, Mal," Cooper said, drawing his Green River. He pushed off Webster's hat and grabbed the man's greasy long hair and yanked his head back until Webster could look at him. There was fear in Webster's eyes now. Stark terror. He had planned to shoot Copper in the back and be the cock of the walk. Now here he was in the snow, his hands and knees freezing, about to die.

"I..." he started.

"Don't say a word, boy," Cooper snapped. "Nothin' you say can save your sorry ass now." He raised the knife and brought it forward, until it touched Webster's forehead, just below the hairline. "Your scalp first," Cooper said in a voice that chilled even his friends. "Then I'll remove some other parts."

"Shit, look!" Wheeler suddenly shouted, pointing well behind Cooper.

TWENTY-NINE

WAR CRIES TORE through the air as the men turned to see almost a dozen Blackfeet come barreling at them across the valley's blanket of snow.

"Goddamn," Potts muttered, tossing Cooper's rifle to him.

Cooper dropped Webster's head and caught the rifle. "I'll tend to you later," he snapped. Then he ran for the skin lodges and tents where the women and children were. Potts, Beaubien, Bill White, and the aging Jacques Dubois hurried after him. Brooks and most of the others dashed into the safety of the nearest wood cabin, which was only fifteen yards or so away. Sits Down disappeared around the back of the cabin, tossing Webster's rifle away as he did.

Cooper glanced over his shoulder and cursed when he saw Dubois falling behind on aging legs.

"Zeke!" he bellowed as he turned and dropped to one knee.

He fired and Potts did the same. Two Blackfeet fell dead off their ponies. Then the two were off again,

Dubois having managed to pass them by a couple yards, Cooper skidded to a stop behind a large cottonwood. Potts was a little farther into the woods, and Beaubien was close by, too, near his lodge. White and Dubois knelt behind trees near their tents, calling for their women to stay put and to tend to the children.

"No need tell that," Dubois's wife, who was far younger than he was, said, her face appearing outside the tent for just a moment. "I hear."

Goes Far and Morning Song stuck their heads out of Potts's tipi flap, then right back in. Dancing Water darted out of her lodge and handed Beaubien a bow and quiver, then dashed back inside. The half-breed slung both over his shoulder and was back behind a tree, firing his rifle in seconds.

A warrior stopped in front of the two cabins. Showing his bravery, he hopped off his pony, planning to scalp Luis Gamez, who had gone down with three arrows in his back in the first few seconds.

Cooper drew a bead on him, but a rifle spoke from inside the cabin, and the Blackfoot was knocked back, clutching at the throat that was no longer there.

Cooper nodded and took aim at a blanketed Blackfoot with a buffalo horn headdress as the Indians headed back for the strip of woods a couple hundred yards across the meadow. The warrior tumbled over his horse's nose as a ball from Cooper's rifle ball plowed deep into his back.

Several other Blackfoot went down as gunfire popped from the mountain man's camp, the men firing through rifle ports.

Cooper reloaded swiftly, eyes on the Blackfoot, who

pranced their ponies just in front of the woods across from them.

"*Mon dieu*," Dubois said, "there are more of zem zan there were a few minutes ago."

"And there's more comin' down the trail into the valley," White said. "Damn good thing that trail's so narrow. It weren't, we'd be ass deep in Blackfeet already."

"Hey, Hawley," Potts called. "Ain't that sumbitch with the wolf skin on his head the same feller who was leadin' that passel of Bug's Boys we had a tussle with last year? The one we never could manage to get a bead on to take him out?"

"Seems like."

"Think ye can take him down now?"

"No trouble."

"Figured so. Put him down. I'll put that one with the yellow face paint under."

Cooper settled his furry cheek against the maple stock of his Dickert rifle and sighted down the octagonal barrel. He set the rear trigger so the front one would need only a light touch. He waited as the Indian moved back and forth, shouting what Cooper supposed were taunts. The warrior finally stopped, facing the mountain men's camp, shaking his coup stick at them.

Cooper fired. An instant later, the Indian toppled backward off his horse and lay in a crumpled heap in the beaten-down snow. Seconds later, Potts's gun roared, and another Blackfoot slumped off his horse. A cheer went up from inside the cabin.

As Potts and Cooper reloaded, the former yelled over, "How many you figure there are?"

Cooper shrugged. "A heap more of 'em than I like," he said dryly. "And more are still comin'."

At least a dozen Blackfeet were racing across the open land again, lying on their horses' necks, not presenting much of a target. They zigzagged when they were halfway across, six rifles fired from inside the cabin, and five more from in the woods. Six Indians went down, while two horses fell, tossing their riders.

The others did not slow, though they swung toward the trees where the three tipis and two tents were nestled.

"Damn, they're coming straight fer us," Potts yelled.

"I can see that, ya damn fool," Cooper snapped. "Reckon they figure they can ride right over us, take our hair, and get to the horses. And the women."

"Well, I ain't gonna make it easy for zem," Dubois shouted. "I 'aven't stayed alive in zese mountains all zese years to go under like zis. Not without takin' a bunch of zose *maudits diables*—damned devils —with me."

He fired, wounding a warrior, and hurriedly began to reload.

Cooper took more care with his shot, making certain of his target. He knew he would only get one shot with the rifle. There would be no time to reload this time.

His shot was accurate, and he dropped the rifle next to him. He grabbed his pistol and fired at a warrior less than twenty yards away. The ball knocked the Blackfoot off his horse, but Cooper was not sure the man was dead. And he had no time to find out. As he leaped up and out of the way of a charging Blackfoot, Cooper was vaguely aware of Beaubien firing his rifle and Potts yelling.

Cooper grabbed the rope rein on the Blackfoot's horse and yanked hard, making the horse tumble.

The Indian scrambled up, snatching out his war club, but a bullet from White's rifle blew out the Blackfoot's brain.

Cooper was about to yell his thanks when an Indian slammed into his side, and they both crashed to the ground, grunting under the impact. Cooper worked an elbow free and rammed the Indian in the nose. The warrior fell off, and Cooper spun, kicking out, catching the Indian in the stomach. There was not much force in the blow, but it slowed the Blackfoot enough for Cooper to grab his knife and stab him as the Blackfoot struggled to get up.

"Bastard," Cooper muttered, ripping his knife free and spinning, waiting for another attack. He saw Beaubien club a Blackfoot with his rifle, and then swing around to catch another on the side of the head.

White and Dubois each fired a pistol. One missed, the other merely wounded the Blackfoot, who stumbled out of the trees and was helped onto a pony by a fellow warrior.

The five faded deeper into the woods, making it more difficult for the Blackfeet, who had to come in by foot.

Potts had two Blackfeet closing in on him, one on each side. He stood, a tree branch almost as tall as he was in his hands, swinging it back and forth. "Come on, ye shit-eatin' demons," he shouted, showing the warriors that he had no fear. "Ye just come on ahead! I ain't afraid of ye boys. No, I ain't. This chil' ain't one to take lightly. No, siree."

Beaubien had dropped his rifle and fired two arrows within the blink of an eye. Both sank deep into the chest of one of the two warriors, staggering him. The Blackfoot clawed at the fire in his chest for a few moments before shuddering to a stop.

Potts whooped and charged at the other Blackfoot, who was armed only with a knife. Potts swung the long tree limb in a wide arc, backing the warrior up. So intent was the Indian on keeping out of the way of the wild-swinging branch that he backed right into Cooper, who grabbed him and slit his throat.

The other Blackfeet, their number considerably reduced, were racing back toward the other woods. More shots rang out from the cabins, and two more fell dead off their horses.

"Waugh!" one of the men yelled from inside the cabin.

The cabin doors opened, and the men tumbled out, whooping and shouting insults at the fleeing red men.

"We sure made 'em come now, boys, we sure did," Brooks said.

Cooper smiled, but there was little joy in it; only relief that he was still alive. He deftly scalped the Blackfoot at his feet, then retrieved his rifle and loaded it and his pistols.

The other men had continued yelling, but suddenly they fell silent. Cooper looked up, alarmed. "Shit," he said softly.

"*Mon dieu*," Beaubien muttered, following it with a string of French mixed with Sioux.

In front of the other woods sat what seemed to be

more mounted Blackfoot warriors than there had been and still more were slowly coming down the trail into the valley. They were painted for war, and their horses decorated. Most wore capotes or blankets wrapped around them, though a few wore bear or buffalo skins.

"This here's poor goddamn bull," Cooper said as he watched his friends across the sward scramble back into the cabin.

"That's a fact," Potts said tightly. "Now you keep an eye on them boys for me."

"What for?"

"I'll be scalpin' those bastards layin' out there."

"No, Zeke, your business is to get the women and young'uns into one of the cabins where they'll be a lot safer than in skin lodges. You and the others should know that."

"And what'll ye be doin'?" Potts asked.

"Tryin' to protect you while you get the women and children to safety."

"You're a pain in the ass when ye make sense, Hawl."

Sits Down strolled up, his face blank.

"Where'n hell ye been, you chicken-hearted bastard?" Potts snarled. "It ain't bad enough we got to feed ye and put ye up in one of our lodges, now we got to fight fer ye, too. You lazy, no-good sumbitch."

Sits Down said nothing.

Neither did Cooper, who noticed that the Nez Perce warrior was carrying the elk-horn bow and wore the quiver filled with the finely crafted arrows. He nodded almost imperceptibly, and the look in Sits Downs' flat eyes made Cooper almost smile. *He knows,* Cooper thought. *He knows I followed him, and he knows I know about the bow and arrows*. But he decided not to say anything.

"Hey," White suddenly said, "why ain't they goin' for the horses? Most Injins do that right off and then leave. Maybe if they get the horses they'll take off."

"If I was to guess, I'd say these boys're on a hair-raisin' quest, not a horse stealin' one. I reckon they're not goin' for the horses now because they don't need to," Cooper said. "Or think they don't. I figure they plan to overrun us, capture us and take us back to whatever devil's den they call a village. Or raise out hair. And they'll take the horses—and the women—with 'em." He shook his head, looking thoughtful, then added, "But it might be that if these are the same hellions we battled last year and are out for revenge, we'd be the target, not the horses or women. Those would come later, after we men were defeated."

"Any more good news, Hawl?" Potts asked sarcastically, not expecting an answer.

"Zeke, you, Jacques, and Two-Faces herd the women and young'uns to the cabins. Me and Bill will give you what protection we can from here. El and the others'll do so from inside if they figure out what's goin' on."

The three men nodded, then Dubois stopped. "I'm not sure I like zis idea, 'Awley. I don' run so good as you see before. I say maybe we should leave ze women and *les enfants* 'ere while we go to ze cabins. I t'ink maybe I don't want to go under tryin' to protect zem, even if my wife and children are with zem."

"And we just leave 'em to the tender mercies of the Blackfeet?" Potts demanded.

"*Oui*. I t'ink zey will be safe. If not..." He shrugged.

"You jeopardize this duty, I'll shoot you in the leg so you can't run at all, ye old fart, and leave *you* to the lovely ministrations of these savages," Potts growled.

While he had talked, Potts made sure his rifle and pistols were loaded, and the half-breed, with rifle in one hand and bow still slung over his shoulder, headed to the lodges. With hesitation, Dubois walked slowly toward his tent.

"We're ready," Potts called a few minutes later.

"Slit holes in the back of the lodges," Cooper shouted back. "Slip out that way and into the trees here. Work your way around to where you can keep the cabins between you and those Blackfeet as much as you can."

"*Oui, m'sieur*," Beaubien responded.

Five minutes later, Beaubien called, "*Nous allons* —We go."

A moment later, the women, carrying all the children but one, who was old enough to run on her own, burst out of the trees. Beaubien was on one side, Potts and Dubois on the other. Three tense minutes later they were inside a cabin.

"All right, Bill, time for us. Let's go." Cooper darted out of the woods, racing across the open expanse of snowy field, followed by White. Suddenly Sits Down lumbered up beside Cooper, surprising the mountain man with his speed. Then those three were also in the cabin, everyone crammed into one.

THIRTY

"WHAT THE HELL are those devils waitin' for?" Alistair Wentworth asked, voice quivering the littlest bit.

"They're scared," Malachi Webster responded. He had regained some of his arrogance, and his voice was filled with disdain. "Them red-skin bastards ain't got the stomach fer goin' against white men who know how to use our rifles."

"Were you born this stupid, or did the whore who spawned you teach you?" Cooper snapped.

"Why, you son of a bitch." Webster started to rise, but the curved butt of Cooper's rifle on his throat stopped him.

"Drop your weapons, Mal," Cooper said in cold, hard tones. "Paddy, tie him up."

"Hey, you can't..."

"Shut up."

"You said we need every gun, Hawl," Brooks said. "And we do with all those Blackfeet out there. If..."

Cooper ignored him. "All right, Paddy, go ahead."

"I ain't lettin' you tie me up." Webster pulled a knife. So Potts whacked him with his rifle barrel. It didn't quite knock him out, but he could offer no resistance.

"Dave, you're his pal, but if you try to help him, I will put a lead pill in your brainpan, even if it does mean we're down two guns. Now, are there any fusils in here, or are they all out in the storage shed?"

"Box of 'em in the corner there," Wentworth said.

Cooper nodded. "Load 'em up. You women, keep ball and powder handy and reload as quick as you can when the time comes. This way, we'll have extra firepower."

"WHY ZEY NOT ATTACK, 'AWLEY?" Dubois asked.

"If I was to guess, they're countin' their losses and contemplatin' the situation. And I expect they figure we're in here sweatin', wonderin' when they're gonna attack."

"Well, we are," White said with a rueful grin.

"That's a fact. I suppose they're waitin' for more warriors to come down that trail—and for dark," Cooper said deliberately. "They can overrun us with their numbers now, but they lost a dozen men, maybe a few more, already. They ain't hankerin' to lose more. They know that if they come ridin' across a wide-open meadow against this many rifles with men who know how to use 'em a heap of 'ems gonna be with the Great Spirit soon. So I expect they'll wait for dark, lettin' us sweat throughout the day. They'll figure we're tired and worried so maybe we won't be able to shoot well, especially at dusk or in the dark. They'll attack then and maybe try to set fire to the cabin here and shoot or capture us when we run out."

"I don't like ze sound of zat," Dubois said.

Cooper didn't think that needed a response. He sighed. "I also think they're waitin' for more warriors to join the fun."

"Which they are," Beaubien said from the rifle port through which he was keeping watch, "though they've slowed considerable with the snow comin' down."

"Ye boys got any good news on any of this?" Brooks asked with little humor in the sarcasm.

Cooper shrugged. "Maybe if we get lucky, they'll realize tryin' to get us will be too costly and they might just settle for stealin' the horses. Ain't likely though. I reckon Bug's Boys are out to raise our hair and nothin's gonna stop 'em 'til they get it."

"Can't we do anything?" Anderson whined.

"We attack them while they're sittin' there waitin' for dark, if that's what they're doin'," Potts said urgently. "They won't expect us to take the fight to them."

"Ye goddamn fool," MacTavish said sharply. "We're outnumbered four to one, maybe more. They'd cut us doon like wheat under a scythe."

"Any other ideas?" Brooks asked.

"We could skedaddle," Wheeler said, eyes wide and bright with fear. He had faced Indians before, but it had never looked so helpless. "Run out, grab the horses and ride like hell."

"If you thought for even just a moment," Cooper said harshly, "you'd remember that the only way out of this goddamn valley is up there." He chucked a thumb in the rough direction of the narrow trail that wove up the mountainside. And as you could see if you used El's lookin' glass like Two-Faces there's warriors still comin' down. Ye aim to fight Blackfeet on a narrow trail like that if we even get that far?"

Brooks suddenly turned angry eyes on Cooper. "You certain that bastard," he started, pointing to Sits Down, "wasn't in collusion with them Blackfeet? Maybe that's why he brung us here. So's they could come and raise our hair and take all our plunder?"

Cooper felt all the men's eyes on him. They were angry eyes, scared eyes, suspicious eyes. Cooper pulled a twist of tobacco from his possibles sack and bit off a small chunk. He chewed it slowly, working it into his cheek, making the others wait. Finally, he spit and said, "That's the dumbest goddamn thing I ever heard you say, El. You've known Sits Down longer'n I have. Where'n hell would he have gotten friendly with the Blackfeet?"

He paused, letting that sink in, then said, "'Sides, if he were in collusion with those Injins yonder, do you think he'd be sittin' here now with the rest of us? He'd have took my scalp and Zeke's before hightailin' it over to his friends.

"Like I said, maybe that fight with us last year got their dander up. They either found us, maybe knowin' we're the ones who sent 'em packin' and want revenge, or maybe they just saw a group of mountaineers and figured to raise hair on any they come across, just like usual. Hell, I got no idea. Don't matter anyway."

"Then you're sayin' we just set here and wait 'til them devils come and make wolf bait of us all??" Paddy

Murphy asked. He did not seem frightened, only interested.

"That's one choice. If the Blackfoot—or any other Injins fer that matter—take a shine to settin' out against an enemy, they ain't likely to set there fer long. But if I'm right in my thinkin', they'll only be waitin' till dark or just before, which with the snow comin' might not be too damned long."

"Then what do you suggest?" White asked.

Cooper spat, the tobacco juice making a brown path across the dirt floor. "Well, ol' Zeke here might've hit on somethin'."

"See, I told you boys I wasn't crazy fer sayin' we ought to attack them bastards," Potts said smugly.

"Doin' it your way would be certain to get us all sent to the Happy Huntin' Grounds," Cooper said. "But if we do to them what I think they're plannin' fer us, we might be able to get somewhere."

"You mean sneak up on 'em just as dark's comin' on, and steal their horses?" Brooks asked, warming to the idea.

"If we can. Likely wouldn't work though. Be nice to get close enough to take the fight to them somewhat."

"Why don't we just send a few boys up the trail out of here, and come down behind 'em and maybe start pickin' 'em off one by one?" Alistair Wentworth said.

Cooper shook his head. "Like I said, them Blackfeet have been comin' down that trail all mornin'. Maybe they've slowed some, but even if they stop usin' it altogether because of the dark or the weather, there still might be a mighty big passel of 'em loiterin' up there just waitin' to use it again." He sighed. "I wish there was another way up there."

"There ain't such a thing," Murphy said.

"I know."

"Be nice if we could fly," Murphy said with a rueful grin.

"I know way," Sits Down said quietly.

Everyone turned to look at the warrior. "Where?" Cooper asked.

"I show."

Cooper nodded. "Big enough for horses?"

"No. Small trail. Go on foot. Horses can't go."

Cooper nodded, accepting it. "Can we ~~ye~~ get ~~us~~ there in the daylight?"

"Yes."

"That should do," Potts said almost eagerly.

A quiet mumble through the others supported that.

Then Cooper shook his head again. "Won't do us no good to get to the top of that cliff unless we got a way down," he said.

"There is way."

"There are three trails in and out of this valley?" Cooper asked, startled.

"Just two. Main one we use. Blackfeet use now. Small one, where no horses can go. We use now. Other not really trail, just a small cut in mountain. Very steep. Many rocks. Not even coyote can use."

"But we can?" Brooks asked. He sounded skeptical.

"Hard. Very hard, but we can do."

"How do ye know this?" Brooks suddenly asked suspiciously.

"I look around one day, find it."

Cooper leaned back against the wall, gazing out through a rifle port across the expanse of white, to where the Blackfeet were making their medicine. The other mountain men talked and argued amongst themselves, as if he was not even there. He did not mind. It gave him time to think. He was certain he was right about the Blackfoot plans, and he was certain he was right in this being the only thing they could reasonably do. What he wasn't sure about was the actual getting there.

Finally, the men quieted, and Brooks asked, "Well, Hawley?"

Cooper nodded, making up his mind. "Seems like the only thing we can do other than sit here and wait for those bastards to come get us."

"How many was you thinkin' of sendin' against those sons of Satan?"

"Just me'n one other. The rest of you are needed here to protect the women and children, makin' sure they don't fall prey to the Blackfeet if we go under."

"Who's goin' with ye?" Brooks asked.

"I canna let ye go alone, lad," MacTavish said firmly. "I'll go wi' ye."

"Thank you, Duncan," Cooper said before anyone else could speak. "But I'd rather have Zeke along. It's nothin' against you, you understand. I just know Zeke better, worked with him more."

MacTavish nodded, a little relieved but a little disappointed too. It would be better, he figured, to go under, if that was indeed his fate, fighting the Blackfeet rather than sitting here in the cabin waiting for death to come to him.

Cooper looked over at Potts. "Well, Zeke, ol' hoss, you reckon on comin' with this chil' to raise hair on Bug's Boys?"

Potts scanned the faces around him, making them

wait. Then he grinned, breaking the tension that had built up. "Well, hell, somebody's got to go with ye to make certain ye don't lose your hair, and if you're damn fool enough to ask me, then, by God, I'm damn fool enough to agree."

"Then it's settled," Brooks said. He was feeling some easier now. He, too, would have gone, and done so without hesitation, if need be. But he thought he might be getting too old for such things. Maybe it was time to ride down out of the mountains, to a town back in the States, take up with a woman and settle down. But first, this had to be taken care of.

"I go too," Sits Down said, his bass voice a rumble under the hissing of the growing snow. "Need to show way."

"Figured so," Cooper said.

"No goddamn way," Potts snapped. "He can just tell us the way to go, Hawley, I ain't takin' that walkin' bucket of lard against a large Blackfoot war party. No, sir. My mam didn't raise a chil' so foolish as that. If ye..."

"He comes," Cooper said easily.

"Now wait a goddamn minute," Potts shouted. "I done said that I wasn't goin' with..."

"You can sit here with the women if you like," Cooper said. "Me'n Sits Down can take care of them Blackfeet by ourselves if you're too scared of 'em."

"Now just hold on there, goddammit. Ye know I ain't scared of no Blackfeet, nor Crows, nor Cheyennes nor anyone else..."

"'Cept his Nez Perce woman," White said, and the men chuckled nervously.

"...But it'd be pure foolishment to take that fat, stupid sumbitch out there. He'll get himself kilt."

"That's his concern," Cooper said with a smile.

"Hell, ye think Mornin' Song's folks'll ever let me back into her lodge if her brother gets his dumb ass kilt and I don't bring 'im back fer a proper buryin'? You want to be the one who carries that fat carcass out on your back?"

The other men were laughing now, their tension lifting for a few more moments, at Potts's vehemence.

"He goes," Cooper said. "We don't let him, he might not tell us how to get where we need to go, and we can't make him, I don't reckon. Even if he tells us, there's no guarantee we'd find it right off. He comes, he can show us, and we can be certain. You want to come along, you'll be welcome. You want to back out after makin' your commitment, you can do that, too. Duncan's already volunteered."

"Oh, goddammit, Hawley," Potts said in exasperation, "ye know goddamn full well I ain't lettin' ye go out on that venture with only one fat, useless Nay Percy to keep ye safe from those hordes of Blackfoot."

"Good. Now that you've made up your mind, shut your gums. You see anything, Two-Faces?"

"*Non.* Zey just sit zere. A few more have joined zem, but not many."

"What do ye need, Hawl?" Brooks asked.

THIRTY-ONE

"SMALL SACK of jerky for each of us. Plenty of powder. A trade gun for each of us, so a couple of ye boys need to start makin' some balls straight off for 'em. This snow keeps up, we'll need snowshoes."

"I'd like to carry an extra pistol or two if someone will lend me his, or who's got an extra," Potts threw in.

"Ye can have mine, lad," MacTavish said.

"And mine," White said.

"Thanks, boys," Potts said.

"I'll need some too," Cooper said. "I feel like a fool now for havin' lost my extra ones gamblin' at rendezvous last year."

"We got enough extra, Hawl," Murphy said.

"Thanks, Paddy. Time to get to work, boys."

Late in the morning, using a swirling snowstorm as cover, Cooper Sits Down, and Potts darted behind the cabin, then hurried across the small open space into the trees where the lodges were. They slipped along the cliff wall behind the trees, the Nez Perce leading the way.

Not far from where Cooper had seen Sits Down working on his bow and arrows, the Nez Perce led them on foot up a very narrow, rocky animal trail that twisted and wound up the side of the mountain. They had their extra rifles and their snowshoes—hurriedly made in the cabin from what materials lay around—strapped to their back.

After more than two hours of slipping and struggling past rocky outcroppings on the snow-covered trail, they reached the top. From there, Sits Down led them east. It was about three miles around the rim of the valley to where they needed to go. The Nez Perce moved fast, Cooper following, Potts last.

The wind was worse up here, with little to block it. The gusts screamed at them, whipping at the fringes, long tassels, and bottoms of their capotes, which they had retrieved on their dash into the woods, slipping in through the slits in the rear of the lodges. It blew the snow in crazy patterns in front of their eyes.

They struggled along, each immersed in his own thoughts, cursing or bemoaning the troubles that had brought them here. They stopped after a short while and donned their willow snowshoes, and they made good time, schussing along. Cooper wondered which was worse, the scrabbling up the narrow trail, fighting for footholds on slick snow—and ice—covered rocks or battling the howling bastard of a snowstorm.

Thoughts of Goes Far helped warm him a little.

Shortly before he had left, Goes Far rose and tentatively walked to Cooper. "You still want me?" she had asked urgently in a whisper, searching his eyes with fear in her own.

"Always."

"You won't send me away?"

"What for?" he responded in kind.

"Because...of..."

"Hell no, I won't send you away," he said bluntly, letting her know that even though they were whispering, there would be no argument about it, no recriminations. "Soon's I get back, I'll see to Webster."

"But the others..."

"It ain't their concern. Nothin' happened to be concerned about. Let the others think what they want, it won't make any difference, but I don't think anyone here will say anything about any of this. They do, they'll regret it. Don't you go frettin' over it no more."

She had smiled and hugged her man, though a tinge of fear licked at the corners of her mind at what he would soon be doing. But she had faith in him and in his abilities. He would come back to her.

It was a pleasant memory to Cooper, who smiled at it behind the cover of the beaver fur that protected his face from the cold and stinging snow. His hat was tied on with rawhide thongs, and like the others, he wore thick mittens of soft martin fur. To protect his rifles from the elements, he carried them in cases—his Dickert in the buckskin case with beaded designs Goes Far had made for him. He was proud of it, and it saddened him when he had to cut down the two-foot-long fringes that ran from the tip of the narrow end halfway down its length so they would not hinder him.

It took less time to cover the three miles east and then south to the other side of the valley than it had to make their way up the steep path out of their camp. There were still a few hours before nightfall, though the daylight was considerably dimmed by the thick clouds that still spewed forth snow.

Removing their snowshoes, they started down a thin, barely discernible trace of a trail that made the one that had climbed up look like the road through South Pass on which supplies were brought to rendezvous. They gingerly wove around or climbed over bounders, stumbled on rocks, slid on patches of snow, scraped their shoulders where the rough, rocky sides of the mountain closed in enough to make it hard to squeeze through. There were times they had to turn sideways and unlimber their rifles and snowshoes from where they laid across their backs to slither past a bounder or two, barely making it. Even though Cooper could see Sits Down, he could not understand how the bulky Nez Perce was making his way through such obstacles. But he was and seemed none the worse for wear for it.

After an eternity or perhaps two, Cooper felt, they reached the bottom. They swiftly slipped into the dense stands of pines and aspens behind where the Blackfeet had amassed. As they had planned before leaving, Cooper swung northwest until he reached the tree line, where he had a clear view of the main trail leading into the valley. He left his snowshoes and musket slung across his back and pulled the Dickert from its protective covering and stuffed the case inside his capote.

With a grim smile, he picked off three Blackfeet as they rode into the valley at the bottom of the trail. The flow of Indians stopped but Cooper waited. He heard several shots from deeper in the woods and knew Potts was at work.

Ten minutes or so later, a Blackfoot eased his way warily off the trail onto the valley floor. Cooper let him go unmolested, as he did the next one. The third was not so fortunate. Nor were the first two. After Cooper shot the third, he turned his rifle on the other two, whose luck suddenly ran out.

He reloaded again and shoved the rifle back into its case. He hurried southeast and then east, deeper into the woods. Much of the underbrush had died off, easing his way a little as he flitted between the trees. It wasn't too unpleasant here in the trees. Though the aspens were barren of leaves, the thick pines and their needles cut the wind considerably and blunted the snowfall a little.

Within minutes, Cooper could hear Blackfeet talking and he stopped. He checked his surroundings, then eased his way forward, knowing the hissing of the snow would mask what little sounds he made. The voices were louder, and suddenly Cooper saw four Blackfoot warriors sitting around a small fire, talking and applying paint. He slipped the case off each rifle. The two arms would not freeze up in the short time before he would use them. He patted himself, making sure the three pistols he had were tucked under his capote, within relatively easy reach.

All four warriors were wrapped in Hudson's Bay blankets and wore various skin and fur hats.

Cooper's lips and mouth were dry, so he scooped up a little snow and popped it in his mouth. The cold was sharp and gave him a jolt. He rested the trade gun against the tree trunk behind which he stood and raised the Dickert. The four were only thirty yards away; there was no possibility he could miss. He drew a bead on the Blackfoot farthest away, the one who was sitting almost opposite him, the one who would see him first if he killed one of the others. He fired, and the Blackfoot's head burst from the impact of the .54-caliber ball. The other three sat stunned for a moment, enough time for him to drop the Dickert and grab the trade rifle. He fired quickly, killing another warrior.

The other two Blackfeet were moving, grabbing their weapons, and running, shouting warnings or for help or likely both, Cooper figured. He did not care.

The mountain man grabbed the Dickert and ran to another tree, hoping he might have a shot at the fleeing warriors. But they were not to be seen.

Cooper reloaded both long arms before making his way slowly through the trees again.

He heard a shot, then two more from his right, the first in a little while. Each was accompanied by a scream. *Zeke's busy again*, he thought, then flattened against a tree trunk as he heard someone running toward him. A Blackfoot burst from the covering trees, coming from Potts's direction, running hard. He had lost his blanket and was wearing only a war shirt, buckskin leggings, and moccasins.

Preferring not to use one of his firearms lest he give away his position, Cooper set his two long arms down and leaped at the Indian as he ran past, slamming into the Blackfoot, with his shoulder down. The Blackfoot tumbled, falling sideways into the snow. Cooper tried to keep his feet but slipped on the slick snow and fell. He pushed himself up with his left hand, yanking out a pistol with his right. The time for being silent was gone. The Indian was still trying to get up, his eyes glittering with hostility. Cooper fired, and the Blackfoot was slammed onto his back by the impact of the shot.

"Damn," Cooper muttered. He glanced around, making sure there were no other Blackfeet nearby.

The action and adrenaline had warmed him, so he slid off his capote and the snowshoes. He hung both from a tree and put his shooting bags over his shirt. With the heavy buckskin shirt and the activity, he figured he should be warm enough. He dropped the two rifle cases before setting off again.

Several screams came from his left, and he smiled grimly. Maybe Sits Down was a warrior after all, he thought, for he was certain that they were not Sits Down's screams.

He had heard horses to the right ahead of him and headed that way, hoping to find the Blackfoot herd. If he could get to the animals, set them running...

———

POTTS HAD MOVED to within ten yards of three Blackfeet sitting around a small fire, eating jerky and making what Potts took to be small talk.

The sounds of battle could be heard from the mountain men's camp. Then Potts heard Cooper's heavy Dickert.

The three Blackfoot looked up, surprised. Potts opened his capote and pulled two pistols. Calmly, he stepped out from behind the tree and fired both, then dropped one pistol. Two Blackfeet crashed backward. The third, eyes suddenly wide, reached for his lance, craning his neck to look behind him. He saw the strange white man calmly reloading a big pistol. He jumped up and with a war cry, charged at Potts, lance held in both hands, point outward, before him.

Potts rammed the ball home, then fumbled with the cap. "Dammit," he muttered, dropping the pistol in the snow. He danced a step to the side and grabbed the lance as the Blackfoot bore down on him. With all his strength, feet planted as solidly as possible on the slippery ground, he yanked and turned his body, throwing the Blackfoot off balance.

Potts wound up with the lance in his hands. He smiled evilly. He raised the lance and threw it as hard as he could. It sliced a deep furrow through the Blackfoot's leg.

"Damn," Potts said in annoyance. He had expected that in using the lance it would be easy to kill the Indian. The Blackfoot tried to get up, blood welling from the wound in his leg. But Potts took two steps and kicked him in the face, then drew his Green River and emotionlessly slit the Indian's throat.

He considered taking all the scalps, thinking Cooper might be keeping score, but he decided this was not the time or place for it. He cleaned his knife off on the warrior's coat. He heard someone coming and snatched up his pistols and ducked behind a tree, where he grabbed his main rifle. Two Blackfeet came into the small clearing, and he shot one of them through the forehead. Before he could grab his trade gun, the other took off into the trees, heading toward where Cooper would be. Potts ran after him, but lost the warrior in the brush and thick knots of trees.

SITS DOWN flitted through the trees like a shadow. He had discarded his buffalo robe, the beaver fur covering his face and his snowshoes. Stripped down to war shirt, leggings, blanket breechclout, and moccasins, all of them having been kept well wrapped and hidden during his travels, he moved on. The trade rifle hung across his back from a buckskin strap. In his hand was the elk-horn bow. The quiver of a dozen arrows was also across his broad back. He held one arrow loosely nocked and three more in his left hand, held against the sinew backing of the bow ready for instant use.

He could smell the Blackfoot horses and began making his way there. He could also hear some shots from the mountain men's camp. He figured some of the more adventurous warriors were making forays against the cabin though it was still daylight. He thought they would be testing the white men's resolve, and withdrawing under heavy fire,

He heard, over the sighing of the snow, someone urinating. With a grin, Sits Down moved up behind the Blackfoot. When the Blackfoot had readjusted his breechclout and turned, he stepped into eight inches of cold steel attached to an elk-horn handle. His eyes widened in shock, and he slumped against the heavy Nez Perce.

Moments later, with a bloody scalp dangling from his thong belt, Sits Down moved forward. Two warriors were chatting, each rubbing down a blowing horse. Within seconds, they were dead, managing only a short burst of scream when the arrows pierced them.

Sits Down yanked his arrows free and moved on, heading for where the horses would be. He spotted Cooper moving in the same direction and nodded. This hairy-faced white man was nearly as good as a Nez Perce in the wilderness. It had taken a lot to be certain

Cooper had followed him into the forest because the mountain man had made it so difficult to know. But he had and Sits Down knew that if any of these white men could get to the Blackfoot horses, it would be Cooper.

He moved on, making his way toward where Potts was. He knew the Blackfeet had heard the gunfire from Cooper and Potts and he figured the Blackfeet would be thinking that another force, perhaps larger, was attacking them from the rear. And if Cooper had been successful in his initial attack, there would be no help coming from the trail anytime soon.

Blackfeet were starting to filter through the trees, bent on counterattacking the whites. Two strayed into range of Sits Down's bow and paid for it with their lives, though they never knew where death had come from.

Sits Down heard a struggle, then silence. He moved swiftly toward it.

THIRTY-TWO

COOPER WAS VERY close to the horses now. He had dodged several enemies while making his way toward the remuda but one surprised him. He was lucky. The Blackfoot slipped on a patch of ice at a crucial moment, and Cooper was able to grab his tomahawk and plant it deep in the Indian's head.

The Blackfeet presence was growing, though it seemed the attacks on the cabin were lessening. Cooper figured more warriors were spreading through the woods searching for him and his partners.

Cooper almost bumped into a Blackfoot who, himself unaware that he was not alone, was leaning against a tree. So silent and still had the Indian been that Cooper had not seen him until the last second. He clamped a hand on the warrior's mouth and plunged his Green River into the Indian's back, twisting it to ensure a quick, sure death.

He moved off a little way, where he could watch the horses and guards. There was another shot off to his right but then little sound other than that of Blackfeet moving through their camp and into the forest. He had the horse guards spotted now. It was time to move in.

POTTS WANTED MORE Blackfoot to kill. Let Cooper and Sits Down worry about the horse herd, if that's what they wanted to do. He wanted...

A Blackfoot clubbed him in the side of the head. In was a glancing blow because he had been moving, but he staggered to the side, eyes unfocused for a few moments. As he struggled to clear his vision, he fired his rifle blindly, hoping he would hit whoever had hit him. But there was no sound.

His vision cleared in time to see a warrior two feet from him, war cry on his lips, bone war club raised, hovering in the split second before descending.

There was a hiss, and the point of an arrow suddenly appeared in the Blackfoot's chest. The Indian stumbled and fell. Potts skipped out of the way, noticing the feathered end of the shaft protruding from the warrior's back. He looked around, a little queasy. He had been too close to death this time.

Then he saw Sits Down, bow in hand, coming toward him. In surprise, he watched the heavy Nez Perce roughly tear the arrow from the Blackfoot's body, cleaned it on the Indian's blanket coat, and shoved it back into the quiver.

"I good warrior," Sits Down said, a twinkle in his eye, though his face was solemn. He took the Blackfoot scalp and disappeared into the trees.

"Goddamn," Potts breathed. Shaking his head in wonder, he moved ahead.

COOPER SLIPPED the Dickert over his shoulder from the buckskin strap. This would be close in work, and the rifle would be nearly useless. It was dark now, and he slipped up behind one of the horse guards and, with the Green River in his left hand, stabbed the Indian. The Blackfoot half-turned and started to scream. Cooper slammed him in the face with the butt of the pistol he held in his right hand. The Indian crumbled.

Cooper screamed as loud as he could and fired the pistol into the air. Several horses startled, bucked , and snorted, shoving away from the sound. Others, frightened by the sound and the pressure from horses behind them, snickered and started to run, galloping away from the camp through the trees.

Blackfeet shouted in alarm, chasing their horses, which fled across the snow-covered meadow. They were like a swarm of bees, Cooper thought as he ran the other way, through the trees, swearing each time he was scratched by a branch he could not see in the darkness.

Cooper crashed into someone, saw a hairless face and began kicking, biting and punching without thinking. It had to be a Blackfoot, he knew, since Potts had a small beard, and the warrior was much too small to be Sits Down. He smashed a fist into the Blackfoot's mouth, shutting him up. But others were on their way, and he had little time. He quickly stabbed the Indian, leaped up and ran again.

THE NIGHT WAS a kaleidoscope of sounds: horses whinnying, Blackfeet shouting after them, muffled hoof beats, the crack of trees exploding in the cold, the soughing of the snow through the trees, angry Blackfoot voices, gunshots.

Cooper ran and hid, ran and hid. He was reluctant to stop for too long in any one spot. He worried that he would be too easy to find, even in the dark, and he might freeze to death. He managed to find his capote and put it on, grateful for its thick warmth. He moved on again for a little while, then stopped, deciding to risk being seen for a bit. He and pulled out some jerky, wishing it was pemmican. The fat-heavy food was much better for a body at a time like this. It would provide energy, which he could use. But jerky was all he had, and it would have to do.

He dozed but woke suddenly when a body crashed to the ground near his feet. His eyes popped open to see a dead Blackfoot and Sits Down calmly walking toward him, grinning.

Cooper gave him some jerky. Sits Down nodded and sat nearby. The former's worries being found resurfaced, but he figured that if they were mostly quiet and stayed only a short while there would be little danger. Within a few minutes, Potts suddenly appeared, his face looking almost blue in the dark. He was breathing heavily.

"This don't shine at all," he said plopping down. "Gimme some of that jerky."

"You got a sackful."

"Lost it."

Cooper shook his head and handed him some of the dried meat.

Potts tore off a piece and chewed. "We'd best get out of here, Hawley. Them goddamn Blackfoot are like buffalo shit. They're all over."

"We'd never make it across the flats, either way we went," Cooper said.

"Like hell. It's so goddamn dark they'd never see us if we was to head for the trail outta here."

"Trail watched," Sits Down said. "And more Blackfeet still at top."

"How in hell would ye know, ye fat..." He stopped, remembering what Sits Down had done. "You sure?" he added rather contritely.

Sits Down nodded.

"Damn." Potts tore off another piece of jerky. "Well then, what'n hell're we gonna do?"

"Keep movin'. Harass 'em as much as we can just like we've been doin'. Enough to keep 'em from a full out assault on the cabin. If we get lucky, sooner or later, they'll decide they're medicine's gone bad and they'll leave."

"I sure as hell hope so."

"Me, too." Cooper grinned, though there was little cheer in it.

"I told El my will from last time still stands," Potts said quietly.

"I know. I did the same and he told me."

"What're our chances, you figure?"

Cooper shrugged.

"You do know," Potts said flatly, "that if we don't scare 'em off tonight, we'll be in a heap of trouble come light? You do know that, don't you?"

Cooper nodded. It did not deserve an answer. Suddenly he stood. "This ain't good. We can't get caught all of us together. We'd best split up again, do what we can against these devils. We done all right so far."

"Where'll we meet?" Potts asked.

"It don't make a hell of a lot of difference, does it?" Cooper said. "We chase 'em off. We can meet anywhere. We don't..." He let the sentence hang there and moved off into the trees, swallowed up instantly by the darkness.

"Thank ye for what ye done, Sits Down," Potts said. "I..." He had been watching Cooper leave, and he turned to where Sits Down had been. But the Nez Perce was gone.

Potts stood, the cold of the bitter night settling on him. He shrugged and moved off.

———————

THE NIGHT WAS long and cold, though the snow had stopped, and the clouds had broken up, allowing some light from the moon to shine through. It wasn't much here in the trees, but Cooper thought it would be welcome across the meadow, giving his friends enough light to fend off a charge.

The game of hide and seek they played in the dim forest was deadly. Cooper moved almost constantly, afraid to sit still for more than a few minutes at a time. But he hovered around the fringes of the Blackfoot camp. Sporadic firing still came from the cabin. Since it was intermittent, Cooper figured it meant that the Blackfeet had not made a full-scale assault on the men there. More steady firing would have meant the mountain men were desperately trying to hold off an onrushing horde. He also thought, maybe a little arrogantly, that the efforts of himself, Potts and Sits Down had been enough of a distraction that it kept the Blackfeet from fully attacking the cabin, especially with the three of them drawing more attention. They were also busy chasing horses. And without many—if any—reinforcements coming down the trail, the odds were looking slightly better. He began to think that the Blackfeet would not charge the cabin, that they would want to destroy the enemy behind them, then they could turn their efforts toward the cabin. The men there were not going anywhere.

He often roamed near the fringes of the forest at times, where he could see Blackfeet around their fires, which were growing fewer and fewer as the night rolled on. Whenever he did, he fired, as often as not hitting the target. Occasionally he could hear Potts doing the same, and twice he saw Blackfoot warriors fall, pierced by arrows. Between the three of them, Cooper hoped to keep the enemy on edge, thinking there were more of the mountain men behind their lines than just three.

As the number of fires dwindled, Cooper figured many of the Blackfoot were as cold as the mountain men and the Nez Perce, which likely would make them angrier. And he hoped that might make them careless.

Cooper saw some of the warriors returning with perhaps a dozen horses of the forty or so that had gotten away. Combined with the dozen or so brought back by their riders, they were not doing too bad. He was also surprised that the warriors had not brought in some of the white men's horses. Surely they would try to raid the herd with their own horses being scattered. But with the herd visible from the cabin, maybe the mountain men had fended off a raid or two.

Cooper moved a little closer, hoping he could send the regathered herd running again, keeping the Blackfoot more occupied in chasing horses than in chasing him and his two companions.

He watched the guards carefully. There were more of them than before and they were more alert. The chances were not good. He decided to bide his time just a little.

He was slammed from behind with a war club. Only his thick fur hat saved him. He went to his hands and knees in the snow, losing his rifle. He groaned once as the ground spun.

Cooper heard the Blackfoot shout something, and in his suddenly dim brain he figured the Indian was telling his friends he had caught one of the enemies. He froze in terror for a moment. There was one thing that had been drilled into him since he had been in the mountains: If you think you'll be taken alive by the Blackfeet, kill yourself.

Almost unconsciously, he reached inside his capote for a pistol. If he could keep his hand steady, he could manage it. He heard others yelling, whooping, shouting, coming toward him. He must be quick.

His thoughts became jumbled, and he tried to sort them out. Goes Far flashed into his mind, and Webster. Brooks made a brief visit, as did Potts, his family back east.

He felt a rough hand reach out and grab him under the chin and yank his face up. He saw two Blackfoot in front of him. They were laughing.

THIRTY-THREE

THEN HIS BRAIN began to function again. Without thinking, he surged up on weak legs, yanking out two pistols as he did. He fired both, almost as the same instant, killing the two in front of him. He spun and kicked as hard as he could. The Blackfoot who had originally hit him was caught by surprise. He doubled over, hissing in pain as the kick caught him full in the testicles.

Cooper felt his mind starting to go on him again. He reeled as the world lurched before his eyes. "Damn," he groaned. He shook his head, clearing it a little, though it sent a new burst of pain through it. He pulled his tomahawk and brained the warrior with it.

He heard more voices heading his way. "Time to move," he mumbled. He scooped up his rifle and two pistols and stumbled off into the darkness.

He wandered, aimless, weapons clutched to his chest, stumbling into trees, unaware of the thorns and branches that tore at his flesh and clothing.

COOPER WAS cognizant of great cold. He sat up quickly and sucked in his breath as pain seared through his head. He slammed his eyes closed and grabbed his head. He let out a muffled grunt, then opened his eyes slowly again. Either he was dead or he was still in the woods. And he didn't think being dead would be this painful.

With great care, he turned his head an inch at a time. Then he saw Sits Down. "What?" was all he could say.

"I find you walking. Blackfoot chase you. You fall down many times. You not right here." He touched his head.

Cooper realized he still wore his capote, but he was also under a buffalo robe. The last time he had seen Sits Down, the Nez Perce had not had the robe. With his mind still fuzzy, he didn't care where the warrior had come up with it, only that it was helping to keep him warm.

"You safe now," the Nez Perce said.

Copper nodded after bracing himself for the wave of pain that was to come. It did, and he rode it out. He rubbed his temples with his fingertips and took several deep breaths. "I been out long?"

"Not long."

There was a gunshot from far off to the right, and Cooper grinned. He huddled under the robe, knowing he should give it back to Sits Down, who was exposed to the cold, but reluctant to do so. Finally he forced himself to stand. "Good lord, almighty," he muttered as pain rampaged through his skull. He sucked in air, trying to steady himself. "Here," he said, holding out the buffalo robe.

"You keep."

Cooper gingerly nodded and ~~He~~ walked around a little, mostly to see if he was able to do it. He looked up to clearly see the almost full moon and plenty of stars. He was surprised that there was no canopy of trees. It was a blessing and a curse.

Something turned in his mind. Finally it jelled. Blackfeet. There were Blackfeet about. And here they sat. "We'd best be movin'," he said urgently.

"No."

"We got to. The Blackfeet'll be on us any time now."

Sits Down shrugged.

They were in a tight thicket, maybe ten-foot-tall not easily seen by prying eyes. And it would look, he decided, almost impregnable, so it would not likely be checked too closely, especially since he figured they were some distance from the Blackfoot camp. Sits Down had chosen well again, though Cooper did wonder how the Nez Perce had managed to get them inside it. It was another mystery about the large Nez Perce warrior.

But while he was sitting here and, even if not entirely sound, Potts was out there alone. "We got to go, Sits Down. Zeke'll be needin' us.

"More time."

"We ain't got much more time."

"You wait."

Cooper argued but Sits Down was adamant.

While they sat there, Cooper said, "You're a hell of

a warrior, Sits Down. You've done real fightin' here today. And that bow of yours is top-notch."

The Indian nodded.

"Why do you let people think the worst of you?"

The Nez Perce hesitated, then said slowly, "I fat when boy. Others make fun of me. I can't use weapons. I decide to do nothin', let the others make fun. But uncle sees, then teaches me to be warrior when no one looks and teach me to make bow, arrows. He was patient, made it easy to learn."

"But why...?" Cooper waved a hand at the big man, indicating his still poor clothes.

"Uncle want me to join warriors, but I say no." He shrugged the great humped shoulders. "I don't know. I just let people still treat me bad, make fun. I accept." He smiled a little. "But I follow warriors sometimes against enemy. Stay behind them, attack by self. Kill some. Sometimes I go alone. People think I run away, but I just make war by self."

"And you do a hell of a great job at it, too. What you've done here today is the best fightin' I've ever seen." Cooper paused. "But why did you want to come with us?"

"Watch over sister."

"Zeke does a good job at that."

Sits Down nodded. "But if something happens to husband, she needs someone to protect her against other warriors, maybe, and white men."

"Why now? They've been together five, six years now."

"I have vision. See bad things happenin'.

"The mountain man's eyes widened, then he nodded. "You're not only a hell of a warrior, you're also a hell of a man, too, Sits Down." He smiled. "But maybe after this, if we're still alive, we should give you a new name."

"Old name good."

Cooper stared at him a few moments, then nodded.

An hour later, Cooper was thankful the Nez Perce had made him stay. He was feeling considerably better, his vision had cleared, and he could think more rationally. He knew that if they had left when he had wanted to, he would have collapsed before getting fifty yards. He was still wobbly, but now it was time to move, and he told Sits down so. The warrior nodded and shoved their way out of the thicket.

POTTS FELT BETTER NOW that the snow had stopped, and he could see a little by star- and moonlight. He had spent much of the time earlier just trying to keep from the clutches of the Blackfeet. He had never been so scared, and he did not like the feeling.

Then he had found Sits Down, who was carrying a limp Hawley Cooper. "Damn, what happened to him?"

"I not know. I find him. He act strange."

Potts looked Cooper over. "Hell, we gotta get him back to camp."

Sits Down shook his head.

"Now, you listen to me, goddammit." His voice rose, then suddenly stopped. "Damn, what a fool I am. Every damn Blackfoot in the mountains must've heard me."

"I know place to take him."

"You'll be safe there?"

"Yes."

"Where is it?"

Sits Down jerked his head off northward. "Mile."

"You certain you'll be safe?"

"Yes."

Potts nodded. "All right. You take him there. And fer chrissakes, stay with him. I'll keep them goddamn Blackfeet from findin' you."

Sits Down trotted off, carrying Cooper lightly. Potts watched them for a moment. Then he grinned. *Hell, there's nothin' to be afraid of*, he thought. *Just a couple dozen goddamn Blackfeet is all.*

More relaxed, he took the fight to the Blackfoot, rather than wait for them to bring it to him. A shot here, another there. A scalp taken to show his contempt. A knife running smoothly across a struggling man's throat. *This is more like it*, he thought.

MORNING BROKE PALELY, throwing feeble light through the thick branches overhead. It was still bitter cold, and the weak sun posed little threat of warming the day much.

Cooper and Sits Down had separated shortly after leaving the thicket. Now the mountain man carefully worked his way from bush to tree, tree to bush. He picked up his pace. With the light up, he wanted to make his way to the horse herd. He hoped to scatter the ponies again and the Blackfeet with them. He wondered how many Blackfeet were left. He and his two companions had killed many, he figured the men in the cabin had also gotten at least a few. And the enemy had not had reinforcements. He began to think they all might get through this alive.

His head still throbbed, but it was not enough to slow him too much. He could ignore it. He had recovered his face with the swath of beaver fur, leaving only slits for his eyes, nose and mouth. Ice caked the flesh side of the skin facing out, and it was hard to breathe in the cold.

He had heard a flurry of shots about an hour earlier, and he knew Potts was taking care of business. But he had heard none since, and he worried for his friend.

Cooper was close to the horses now and could hear their hooves stomping and their snorting and whinnying. He saw half a dozen warriors mount up and others drifting toward the animals. Through the trees, he could hear a war chief exhorting his men. Though he did not understand the words, he knew what he was shouting about.

"They will come for us," Sits Down said in Cooper's ear, startling him. He had been alone a moment before and never heard the Indian approach. "All spread out, look for us. Not one, two at a time, here, there, like night. They find us in day."

"That's what that ol' bastard is sayin', ain't it?" Cooper whispered. When Sits down nodded, Cooper said, "Any ideas?"

Sits Down pointed at the horses.

"I count six guards. It ain't gonna be easy."

"Seven."

"Where's the other?"

Sits Down pointed to their left. Cooper pulled down the protective mask so his eyes were clear and looked. He could see nothing. Then he spotted the slightest movement of a feather. He nodded.

Sits Down stabbed his finger at three Blackfeet. "You take them," he said. He held out his trade rifle. "You use. I don't want."

"You certain?" Cooper asked though he knew the answer. Sits Down had not used the musket all night. But he had done more admirably with bow, arrow, knife, and war club.

"I will kill rest," the warrior said matter-of-factly. Cooper did not doubt him.

"Then what?" Cooper asked, warming to the idea of the task.

Sits Down shrugged and grinned widely, showing a mouth of bright teeth beneath his large, fleshy nose. "All hell break loose," he whispered. He set the trade rifle against the tree, turned and once again disappeared into the forest.

Cooper grinned. He raised the Dickert, settled his cheek against the stock, pushed back the thumping in his head, and calmly blew away the back of one Blackfoot guard's skull.

The others dropped behind cover, so Cooper took his time to reload the rifle.

He waited, rifle ready, eyes sweeping the positions where the other two guards had been, as well as keeping alert to the rest of them since they were all probably on the move.

There was a movement, a slight rustle of a bush that was not caused by the light wind. Cooper smiled again and fired into the bush. There was a muffled grunt and the sound of a body falling against the bush, whose branches cracked loudly.

Cooper caught a fleeting glimpse of Sits Down between trees as a Blackfoot burst from behind cover twenty feet away charging at Cooper, war club raised, mouth wide in a war cry.

"Shit," Cooper muttered, dropping the Dickert. He snatched up one of the trade rifles—Sits Down's—and pulled the trigger. There was a loud snap but nothing else. "Hell and damnation," Cooper said. He tossed the rifle up, catching it by the muzzle end, and used it as a club, smashing the Blackfoot's face, feeling a quick sliver a fear as the Indians' war club missed his temple by less than an inch. The Blackfoot's momentum carried him into Cooper, knocking him down.

Cooper struggled under the weight of the Indian, but he finally managed to get free. He was sweating under the heavy capote. He threw it off. Without emotion, he slit the Blackfoot's throat and then lifted his hair. He had not done so all night, but now he figured it was time for a trophy.

He left the trade gun where it lay; it would be too much trouble now to try pulling the ball out, drying the barrel and then reloading. Instead, he wiped the inside of the Dickert's barrel with a dry patch in case any snow had gotten in it when he dropped it. Then he shot off three caps to dry the inside of the nipple before reloading. Finally he grabbed the dead Blackfoot's blanket. He jumped out from behind a tree, screaming wildly and flapping the blanket for all he was worth.

The horses neighed in fright and surged away from him, toward the open prairie. Snorting and whinnying, the animals fled, reaching a gallop in seconds.

Cooper stood, smiling as he watched the horses run. The Blackfoot would never catch them now, even though some of the warriors were already mounted and sitting on the prairie. Those warriors shouted and gave chase, as did some of the others on foot. The one Cooper had seen exhorting his warriors, spotted Cooper standing in the clearing where the horses had been. He let loose a blood-curdling war cry and headed for Cooper, lance in hand. He was followed by half a dozen more. With his peripheral vision, Copper could see others heading in his direction.

Cooper gave a moment's thought to fleeing back into the trees. But he instantly decided against it. They would catch him easily this time. He would have to make a stand. He lifted the Dickert, but before he could fire, he heard a shot and saw one of the Blackfeet fall with limbs akimbo, dead.

He smiled. "Ol' Zeke," he muttered before shooting one of the warriors in the chest. He dropped the rifle and snatched his own trade rifle from his back. Another warrior went down, two arrows in his side. Cooper fired, killing the war leader, an imposing man with his face painted all in black with speckles of white scattered across it.

Through the widely spaced trees, he saw Potts at the edge of the clearing seventy yards to his right. Potts fired again, and another Blackfoot dropped. Two went down under Sits Down arrows, before the huge-bellied Nez Perce broke into the clearing from the other side, behind the Blackfoot. In less time than it would have taken Cooper to reload once, Sits Down had shot his remaining arrows, killing four more Blackfoot and wounding three. He screamed a war cry as fierce as any uttered by the Blackfoot and pulled out his stone war club.

He ran forward, heading for a small group of Black-feet who had stopped at the sound of the war cry and turned. They, too, yelled, and charged forward. Sits Down shifted the war club to his left hand and scooped up a lance with his right. He stopped short and threw it with all his weight behind it. It caught one of the Black-foot in the chest, tearing through him so that the steel point stuck two feet out his back and driving him back-ward a few yards before falling.

Some of the Blackfeet also swerved off, aiming for Potts, who laughed, "Come on, ye dog-eatin' sumbitches."

He caught an arrow high on the chest, on the right side. The force knocked him down, but he bounced back up. "You'll have to do better'n that, damn ye," he roared, a pistol in each hand. "Don't stop now, boys," he yelled. "This chil's just startin' to have fun."

Cooper was too busy to notice. The main group of Blackfeet was still heading for him. He hissed in pain as an arrow thudded into his left thigh. He fired his pistol, dropped it, pulled another and fired. Then a third time. Each time, a warrior fell. But there was no time for him to reload.

As he snapped off the shaft of the arrow in his leg, he caught sight of Sits Down surrounded by Blackfeet, swinging his war club with reckless abandon. His deep voice could be heard above the battle as he sang his death song.

To Cooper's right, Potts, with the arrow still sticking out of his chest, drew a bead on another of the dozen enemies heading for him. Cooper's heart sank in despair as an arrow landed in Potts's throat, knocking him down. His friend struggled to rise but failed.

THIRTY-FOUR

"GODDAMMIT, NO!" Cooper roared. He snatched up his pistols, jammed them in his belt and darted into the thicker trees hoping to draw the Blackfeet away from Potts. His lanky legs carried him well despite the wound. He raced, heart thumping, arms pumping, the pain in his head forgotten. He sucked in bitter cold air, feeling it slice into his lungs. He did not care. His only thought was to get to Potts, to save him.

He left behind most of the Blackfeet and kept on running. He burst out of the trees near Potts's position. The young mountain man was not moving. But Sits Down stood a few yards away, a lance and a war club still clutched firmly in his meaty hands. The Nez Perce was surrounded and co do nothing to help Potts. Three other Blackfoot were just bending over Potts, knives out. One had Potts's hair in hand, ready to lift the scalp. Another was stretching out Potts's left hand to chop it off, and the third was slicing through Potts's buckskin pants to emasculate him, as was their way.

Cooper had never slowed, but he somehow managed an extra burst of speed, screaming at the top of his lungs, which felt like they would shatter with the effort. As they looked up at the sound, startled, Cooper dropped his weapons and dived, smashing into all three Blackfeet over Potts before they could do any damage. He could not get up before they swarmed over him, knives still ready. He had his Green River out and was deadly with it. He swung it and his fist, and kicked, kneed, bit, and scratched, spit and roared, bucked and squirmed,

The Blackfoot could not get a good hold on him, and he was too strong for them to subdue easily even with his aching head and wounded leg. He kicked one away from him, rammed his Green River to the hilt into another's stomach and ripped it upward. He shoved that Blackfoot away and struggled up. The third warrior was running now, as were the ones left living after attacking Sits Down.

Sits Down was bleeding from a gash over his left eye and from several small stab wound about his torso. Cooper was exhausted but Sits Down looked like he had just woken from a refreshing nap. Cooper stared at him a moment; neither needed to say anything. Then he bent over his friend.

Potts still clung to life but only by a thread. His chest was coated with blood from the frightful throat wound. Cooper went to break off the shaft of the arrow, but Potts shook his head weakly, croaking, "No."

"I got to get you back to the others, Cooper said, voice strained. "Mornin' Song and Goes Far can fix you."

"No," Potts croaked again. "I'm gone under fer certain." He coughed, spraying Cooper with blood. His eyes were bright, showing no fear of death. "We made 'em come now, didn't we?" he said, voice faint and gargling.

"We sure did, ol' hoss. I..."

"They come," Sits Down said.

Cooper looked up to see a number of Blackfeet rushing through the trees at them. He rose, wishing he had time to reload what guns he had left. He was surprised when the Blackfeet stopped and began spreading out to surround them. They moved slowly, thinking it would intimidate the enemy. They were in no rush now.

"What'n hell're they doin'?" Cooper wondered aloud.

"We are mighty enemies," Sits Down said with a sardonic smile. "Maybe want to take us alive. We be much sport for them in their village. We pay for killing so many of them. But maybe they just try to make us afraid before killin' us."

"Well, it's workin'," Cooper said as a chill splashed over him. But he quickly began loading his pistols, pouring powder recklessly and hurriedly ramming balls home. He grabbed the three Potts had been carrying and had dropped and loaded them too as the Blackfeet, a grinning malevolence written all over their faces, closed in. He wanted his rifle, or even the fusils, but they had long ago been abandoned. He shoved one pistol into his belt, which he would use on himself should that time come. He kept two pistols in hand and piled the others in front of him.

"Come on, boys," Cooper said. "I'll send at least five of you to the Happy Huntin' Ground afore I go under." Over his shoulder, he said, "Thank you for your help, Sits Down. You shine, boy, you sure do."

The Nez Perce grinned. He knew death was at hand, but he did not fear it. He was proud to have fought next to such a man as Hawley Cooper, who also had no fear of going to the land of the Great Spirit. "You good man, Hairy face," he said with a smile. "Like Nez Perce."

Cooper nodded, accepting the compliment.

The air was cold on them now that they had stopped fighting, though the adrenaline still burned hotly in them. They stood back-to-back, waiting for the rush. They likely would go under in minutes, but they had already made the Blackfeet pay dearly.

A war chief, face painted with yellow and red hail, a buffalo horn headdress perched jauntily on his head, howled and led the charge. Cooper waited, calmness settling over him. Sits Down began his death chant again, the voice somehow comforting his white ally.

Cooper fired once, aiming carefully, grinning madly in satisfaction as a warrior fell dead. He fired the second pistol in hand, and another warrior went down. He grabbed another and pulled the trigger, but the gun misfired.

"Damn," he muttered.

The Blackfeet were closing in rapidly. He tossed it away, grabbed one more pistol and fired without even trying to aim. But the Blackfeet were so close now that it mattered little. He picked up the final one from the pile and fired. A Blackfoot warrior's face burst into a bloody mask before he and Sits Down were swallowed up by the horde of enemy warriors.

Cooper fought like a demon in the snow swirled up by the battle. The air was icy in his lungs. He battled almost unconsciously, automatically, lashing out with a bloody knife and stained tomahawk. He could feel Sits Down's back leave his, and he was momentarily afraid when the reassuring bulk was gone. But still he fought on, only dimly hearing Sits Down's war cries interspersed with the monotony of his death song.

Cooper grunted under the blows he received from coup sticks, lances, and hands as the Blackfeet swarmed around, darting in and out individually to count coup on the fierce white man or his huge companion. The two men's fierceness—and the fact that the Blackfeet would want these two men alive for sport—kept the two from a swift death, at least for now.

The mountain man was unaware of the pain and the rising color over much of his body from the many coups counted on him. His mind was far away, and his body fought on. He hoped to die soon, so he was prepared for it.

The daring attempts by the Blackfeet to count the coup were costly. Several went down under the keen blades of Cooper's knife and tomahawk, or the dull power of Sits Down's war club. One finally tackled Cooper, landing atop the white man. He crowed in victory at having captured the mountain man. His joy was short-lived as Cooper's Green River sliced deeply into his abdomen. He howled in surprise before trying, with his last breath, to hit Cooper's head with his war club, but he collapsed, dead. Cooper struggled to get out from under his weight and stand as two more Black-feet bore down on him.

One hit him high while the other grabbed his legs and fought to get a grass rope around Cooper's ankles. The mountain man kicked, spit, and punched at both. His foot connected with the teeth of the one holding the rope, jarring him loose. With a mighty effort, Cooper fought to rise still in the grasp of the second warrior.

Suddenly the Blackfoot let him go, slumping to the ice- and snow-covered ground. Cooper shook his head in wonder, then saw Sits Down's gleaming face. The blocky Nez Perce had seen him in trouble, spun and shattered the enemy's head before grinning once and swinging back into battle.

Another Blackfoot raced up and slammed Cooper across the back of the shoulders with a lance, whooping in victory.

"Damn," Cooper mumbled, wondering, *Will this never end?* He lashed out blindly and felt some satisfaction as the blade of his tomahawk bit into the Indian's right arm. The Blackfoot stumbled away, clutching his blood-spurting limb.

Cooper was bone weary from the crushing blow to his head earlier, the constant pounding, the roar of warriors, the blood, the fighting. "Goddammit, leave us the fuck alone!" he roared into the brittle sunshine.

But they came again, three on his side and, from the sound of it, the same on Sits down's side. Cooper shook his head in weariness and hopelessness. It would end soon, he figured. He had little left inside him. He was drained, but, still, he raised his weapons and waited.

Two of the warriors charging at him suddenly went

down in heaps, amazing Cooper. They seemed to have fallen dead for no reason. The third did the same moments later, though this time Cooper was aware of the bright red blood on the Indian's chest. Then it filtered into his exhausted, battle-drugged mind that he had heard gunfire.

He craned his neck to see most of his fellow mountain men come charging up through the heavy stands of trees into the clearing on foot.

The few remaining Blackfeet fled, rushing for the scarce horses they had left or filtering through the forest, not bothering to try taking their dead and wounded with them as they went.

Cooper felt no joy at the sight, only the weight of his fatigue. But he did grin weakly as he saw Sits Down, on foot, charge after the fleeing Blackfeet in the company of the mountain men.

Absentmindedly, Cooper wiped his knife and tomahawk off on his pants and slid them away. The pistols could wait. Slowly he walked the few feet to where Zeke Potts lay.

The young man was dead, his body stiffening already from the freezing temperature. Cooper felt the bite of the frigid air and the sting of the increasing wind as he knelt next to his friend. "Dammit, Zeke," Cooper said sorrowfully as he touched Potts's pasty cheek above the sparse beard. "Why'd you have to go and get yourself killed like this. Dammit all, I told you to watch what you was doin'. I told you you'd come to a no-good end someday if you didn't watch your hair. Why'n't you ever listen to me when I talked to you. Dammit, I..."

He realized he was babbling and clamped his lips shut. He sat that way for some minutes before the coldness began to seep into his bones, and some of the mountain men began drifting up. "Damn fool," he mumbled and stood, not sure if he was addressing Potts or himself.

"Anything we can do?" Elson Brooks asked as he walked up.

"Not fer ol' Zeke here. He's gone under, and there ain't a thing can be done about it."

Brooks clapped him on the shoulder, making Cooper wince. "I'm plumb sorry, Hawley. I know what Zeke meant to ye, but them's the ways of the mountains. Ye should know that."

Cooper nodded. Potts had been an impetuous sort who often stood on the rim of trouble, willing to jump into that gully with both feet. It was a good way to live, but too often costly. "Yeah, El, I know that. Ol' Zeke did shine, he did. I can say that for certain. He made them fucking Blackfeet come sure as hell and he shined right to the end."

"I wouldn't have thought otherwise."

"Hey," Cooper said with a sudden twinge of fear. "Where's Goes Far and Mornin' Song? You leave 'em back to camp unprotected?"

"Ye think I'd do something that damned foolish? Do ye?" When Cooper shook his head, Brooks added, "'Course not. I left Two-Faces and Ol' Bill back there with the womenfolk and the children and with Webster." Before Cooper could say anything, Brooks added. "Fear not, Hawl. Webster's still trussed up."

"His friends? Wheeler and Anderson?"

"They're here with us, but Paddy and Al are keepin' an eye on 'em lest they try to sneak back and help Webster. Don't seem likely though. They've been actin' mighty contrite since this fandango started."

Cooper nodded, but the recent past came rushing back at him. Webster! He still had to deal with that son of a bitch. But that could wait. First there was Zeke Potts to take care of.

"Everybody else all right?" Cooper asked.

"Yep."

"Why didn't they attack you? Try to burn you out like we thought."

Despite the sorrow of the moment, Brooks laughed. "Damnedest thing. Seems most of 'em were back in the trees tryin' to drive off the horde of mountaineers attackin' from behind. That'd be ye three. Ye had them boys flummoxed, I'm sayin', as best I can tell. They must've thought there were dozens of ye. They come again us several times, but the storm had stopped, and the clouds drifted off, so we could see enough to blast a heap of those devils before they could do any mischief. They made a concerted run at us an hour or so ago. We got a few of those tryin' to fire the cabin—just the one; we nary did send anyone to the other, and Bug's Boys must've known that because there was no firin' comin' from that one. They finally managed to get two or three spots fired up. Then snow fell from the roof, put those fires right out. Heat from all us in the cabin along with the fire must've loosened it up, and it just slid off. Good Lord must've been watchin' out for us."

"Not for Zeke, though."

"God has mysterious ways, Hawl. Ye should know that."

Cooper nodded. "We lose any horses? Plews?"

"No plews. Don't think the Blackfeet knew they

were in that storage cabin. Doubt they were interested in 'em anyway." Brooks grinned. "We lost a fair number of horses. Seems when you three scattered the Blackfoot ponies the second time, those devils raided our picket lines and run off quite a few before we blasted enough of those savages that they left off tryin' again. Most of 'em came wanderin' back, havin' avoided the Blackfeet. I imagine the rest will do so, too. Those horses ain't about to try to get up that trail on their own, so they'll still be around the valley here. We can catch 'em all. We can replace any that're lost with Blackfoot ponies." He grinned. "And we should be able to collect us a heap of those ponies to use for trade.

Cooper nodded again, knowing Potts's death was not in vain.

MacTavish and Wentworth showed up with several horses, all without saddles, just basic rope reins, in tow.

"Mount up," Brooks said softly.

"I got to take Zeke."

"I know. Ye get mounted, and we'll hand him up to ye."

Cooper did as he was told, with much-needed help from MacTavish. Brooks and MacTavish lifted Potts's body. Cooper took it and almost dropped it, so weak was he from all his exertions.

"I take," Sits Down said, riding up alongside Cooper.

The mountain man nodded and handed the body to the giant Nez Perce, who cradled Potts carefully.

The men moved out, happy with their victory but silenced by the death that had come among them. Sits Down rode in the lead bearing Potts's inert form.

Cooper and Brooks came next, riding side by side. The other men followed.

"How'd ol' Sits Down do?" Brooks asked with a smirk tinged with bitterness. He had no real liking for the warrior, and he had been fond of Zeke Potts. He would rather have seen the Nez Perce go under and Potts live. And he blamed Cooper in his mind for Potts's death.

THIRTY-FIVE

"WEREN'T FOR HIM, ye'd have two dead mountaineers on your hands," Cooper said more than a little harshly. "Maybe more. He saved my life more'n once, and I know he done the same for Zeke. Hell, weren't for him, me and Zeke would've been dead an hour after we got behind the Blackfoot." He smiled wanly at Brooks's shocked reaction. "You should've seen him, El. I'll never doubt that man's ability again. He was the best fightin' warrior this chil's ever seen."

"Well, I'll be damned," Brooks said in wonder. They rode in silence a while before Brooks asked, "How're ye doin'?"

"I'll be all right, I reckon. Gotta get this arrowhead out of my leg. That might slow me down a bit for a spell." He shifted his weight on the horse's back. "I'll be mighty sore, considerin' the thumpin' I took, and my head hurts like the devil himself is dancin' on it with all his minions. But I reckon I'll be right as rain in a few days. 'Course, I'll feel a heap better after I've spent some time with Goes Far." He smiled a bit, lightening his mood a trifle. It was something Potts would've said.

"What're you gonna do about Mornin' Song?"

"She's your concern now, El," Cooper said, almost with delight.

"The hell she is."

"Damn right she is," Cooper said, voice hardening. "You remember Zeke's will, don't you? He done give her off to you whether you take a shine to it or not."

"What'n hell am I gonna do with a young squaw like her? I ain't used to havin' me a full, all the time woman to care fer and such. It goes against my grain. And my poor fortune."

"You'll care for her or you'll face me, Elson Brooks," Cooper said. "Come rendezvous, you can trade her off to someone or give her back to her family. But fer the rest of the winter and the spring hunt, she's your concern."

"Dammit all, Hawley, why'd ye and that damned Zeke Potts have to make me out the one in your wills? Maybe Duncan'll want her. Or one of the others..." He sounded almost desperate.

"It's your duty, El. You can't go back on it. Just treat her decent till summer."

Brooks grumbled, but Cooper knew he would do what was required of him.

A cold wind had sprung up again, and Cooper shivered under his capote, which one of the men had found and brought to him, along with his Dickert rifle and his own pistols.

"Why'd you come after us, El?" Cooper finally asked.

"Got tired of settin' and waitin'," Brooks responded with a shrug. "It wasn't easy just settin' there knowin' ye boys was out here facin' them Blackfeet devils alone. we'd hear some firin' and such, then nothin' for a long spell, then more shootin'. It tells on the nerves, I can assure you. Ain't comfortin' at all."

"I know. We felt the same about you fellers in the cabin when we heard shots, then didn't for a spell."

"Reckon ye did. Two-Faces kept an eye out with his lookin' glass and finally announced that a few Blackfeet had made it up the trail and joined those that were there in runnin' off. Broke their medicine, ye did, I reckon. So finally, Duncan said we ought to come and rescue ye boys if you was still alive, or avenge ye if you'd gone under."

"Well, I don't know about ol' Sits Down, but I was plumb glad to see you and the others. I was tired of fightin' and hurtin' all over. Just before ye boys showed up, I was ready to meet my Maker. It was some wearyin', I tell you."

"I reckon so. But from what me'n the boys seen, ye and your two *companeros* sure made those damn Black-feet come, I'd say." He almost chuckled with joy. "Damn, there were Blackfoot dead all over the place. That ought to keep them demons peaceable fer a long spell."

"That'd sure shine with me."

As they neared the camp, they could see the women come out of the cabin and nervously watch them approach. Cooper finally spotted Malachi Webster tied to a tree just outside the cabin.

The women watched the procession intently,

wondering whose body Sits Down was carrying. They couldn't tell Cooper or Potts was riding behind Sits Down. It wasn't until they were fairly close that the women realized whose body it was. Morning Song sank to her knees, wailing, her voice an ululating screech of pain and sorrow that carried far on the wind, chasing after the Blackfeet who had killed her man.

Sits Down handed Potts's body to Murphy and slid off the horse. Then he took the body back and stopped in front of her. He said a few quiet words in Nez Perce, then walked off toward Potts's lodge, a howling Morning Song in his wake.

"Best go see to her, El," Cooper said.

"Like hell I will, Hawley. Not now. Sits down can take care of her 'til she quiets down some. I can't deal with the god-awful screechifyin'. And I reckon she don't want no one but her own kind 'round her now."

But Cooper was no longer listening. He slid off the horse, almost falling, near Goes Far. She said nothing, but her eyes spoke of many things, mostly of her deep and abiding love for this tall, lanky man.

"I'll take your horse, Hawley," Paddy Murphy said, taking the simple rope rein from a grateful Cooper.

"I see to Mornin' Song?" Goes Far asked timidly. She wanted to be with him, but her friend was suffering in a way Cooper could not understand. "I come back tonight."

Cooper started to protest but saw the look in her eyes. He nodded and managed a small smile. He wanted her to minister to him, but he could see that she thought being with her friend was important.

Cooper greeted Beaubien and White. "He give you

boys any trouble?" Cooper asked, chucking a thumb in Webster's direction.

"Does it look like it?" White said with a sneer.

Cooper walked to Webster. "My business with you ain't finished, boy," he said tightly. "I'll be seein' to it directly. Soon's Ol' Zeke's been taken care of."

"Gone under, is he?" Webster scoffed. "Can't say I'm too displeased. If only it'd been you."

"Was it me," Cooper said tightly. "Ye'd have to face Zeke, and more'n likely Elson, too, stead of just me."

"And me," Beaubien said.

Cooper turned and took a few steps before turning his head to look back. "Was I you, Webster, I'd be reflectin' on my life, fer ye've got precious little of it left to you."

As he walked away, he heard Webster yell, "You gonna leave me tied up here whilst you stick your Green River in my guts? That's what it'll take for you to kill me, Cooper."

Cooper stopped and looked around at him. "You'll get more of a chance to fight than you gave Goes Far," he said in a tone that was colder than the frigid air around them.

He entered his lodge and sank down on some buffalo robes. Exhaustion swelled over him, and he groaned, grateful to be out of sight of the others. Pain flooded in on him now that he was free to stop denying it. He sat, unable to move any longer, for some minutes. Then he steeled himself and sat straighter, managing to slip off his capote. He reached up and tried to peel the shirt over his head. Then he decided it was not worth it. He dropped back onto the robes and fell asleep.

When he awoke, the fire was down to embers. He

struggled up and shivered in the cold. He was trying to gather up the small amount of firewood that remained in the lodge, moaning softly with the pain, when Goes Far came into the tipi.

"What're you doing?" she scolded in Nez Perce.

"What'n hell do you think?" he snapped.

She easily knocked the wood out of his hand and pointed to the buffalo robe bed. "Go," she said firmly.

"But..." Then he nodded weakly. She rarely used that tone of voice. "Yes'm," he mumbled and went back to sit on the robes. He started to peel the blood-caked shirt over his head. He was halfway through it, moaning softly with the pain, when Goes Far hurried over and pulled it off him. "Now you wait," she said firmly.

She hurried out and was back within minutes with a load of firewood. She dumped it atop the little pile in the lodge, then put some on the fire and stoked it.

Soon the warmth of the fire burned the chill off the lodge and Goes Far put some frozen meat in a pot of water to boil. Coming to him, she pushed him gently onto his back. She sliced through his buckskin pants to expose the arrow shaft in his thigh. Her fingers prodded and felt, touching softly despite their hardness, testing.

"Can you get it out?" he finally asked, realizing he had been holding his breath.

"Yes. But maybe hurt much."

"I can take it," he said with more confidence than he really felt. Then he grinned. "I hurt in so many places, another pain ain't gonna make a difference."

She smiled at him. "I'll be back." She covered the shaft with a piece of buckskin, stood, put on her capote and disappeared into the late afternoon. She was back quickly. With her was Brooks, who looked uncomfortable and carried a jug of whisky.

"Best take some of this," Brooks said after he and Goes Far had shucked their capotes and knelt at Cooper's side. He held out the jug, and Cooper gratefully took it and swigged deep.

"More," Brooks ordered.

"Nope. You'n Sally just get that arrowhead out. I'll do just fine."

"You certain?"

"Yep."

Brooks shrugged and nodded at Goes Far. She laid bare the wound again. Brooks gave Cooper a piece of wood to bite on. Goes Far pulled on the short piece of broken arrow shaft. It was tentative, but Cooper broke into a sweat. She tugged a little harder, and Cooper moaned. She stopped.

"Pull the damned thing," Brooks said.

She nodded and yanked a little harder, afraid to hurt Cooper.

"Goddammit, get outta the way," Brooks said, shoving her aside. He grabbed the shaft in a powerful hand and yanked once, hard. Cooper's eyes bugged and his scream was cut off by his lips tightening around the stick in his mouth. His chest heaved and his body bucked, then slumped. The stick slipped from his mouth, and he moaned, "It out?"

"'Course it's out," Brooks said in mock derision.

"Good," Cooper gasped, reaching for the jug. He drank deeply, smacked his lips, then said, with more vigor, "These doin's are poor bull for certain."

"I wouldn't think otherwise. Now you mind Goes Far here. I'll leave the jug, 'case you want it."

Cooper nodded thanks, and Brooks left. Goes Far applied a poultice she had made of yarrow root and other herbs to the big wound and then bound it up in cloth and buckskin. She used more of the poultice on other wounds. Then she asked, "Can you eat?"

"Yep." He realized how hungry he was.

Goes Far brought his willow backrest and he propped himself up. The woman made sure he was well-wrapped in robes before she brought a bowl of the boiled meat and the broth. As he ate with his horn spoon, she banked the fire, making a cheery glow inside the lodge.

"Was it bad?" she asked.

"I thought I'd go under fer certain," he answered. Between mouthfuls of food, he recounted the story, thankful for her understanding and the feelings she had for him. Her face showed that she fought every battle with him, endured each separate pain, and there were tears in her eyes, as there were in his, when he recounted Potts's death.

He asked for more food, and she gladly brought it for him, silently thanking the Great Spirit that her man was still alive. She felt sorry for her friend Morning Song and asked Cooper what would happen to her. While he ate, Cooper told her about their wills, first having to explain what such a thing was, and how Morning Song would be taken care of by Brooks, even if he didn't like the idea.

When Cooper had finished his meal, Goes Far took away his backrest so he could lie down again. With the arrow shaft gone, she could easily slip his buckskin pants off. She covered him with a heavy robe. Exposing only small areas of his body at a time, the woman gently worked to soothe the aches and pains. Cooper's body was a mass of black and blue and purplish-yellow bruises, and he realized his head still throbbed. He forced himself to relax as best he could, to let Goes Far's ministering fingers do their work.

THIRTY-SIX

Winter 1835-1836

COOPER AWOKE, sweating, filled with fear, not knowing where he was. Then he saw Goes Far enter the lodge with more firewood. She smiled at him, and everything was fine as his mind cleared, and he realized several days had passed, days that were a blur of pain and often confusion. He pushed himself into a sitting position, huddled in the robes against the cold. He ached and his muscles were stiff and unyielding.

Goes Far took off her capote and then brought him food—a bowl of boiled meat and a little pemmican whose greasy heaviness would stick to his ribs and fill him.

He ate with relish and a strong appetite, grateful once again that he had found this Nez Perce woman and that she was his. "Damn, you're a good woman," he suddenly said. *As good as Black Moon Woman*, he thought, realizing how lucky he was to have found two such women.

"You damn good man," she responded with a smile, making him laugh.

He finished his food and put the bowl down before wiping his hands on the robe. Goes Far reached for the bowls to clean then, but he said, "Leave 'em." When she looked up, uncertain, he said softly, "Come here."

She smiled coyly and stood. With one quick motion, she pulled her buckskin dress over her head and stood before him naked save for leggings and moccasins. As she slipped into the robe next to him, Cooper felt a momentary twinge of sadness. There were no sounds of lovemaking from the nearby tipi. He had become used to hearing Potts and Morning Song making love most nights and usually most mornings, too. It was odd and dismal without them.

But Goes Far's presence quickly overwhelmed him, and he pushed the morbid thought from his mind.

Two hours later, he stepped from his lodge into the frigid air and sparkling sunlight. He breathed the cold air deep into his lungs, reveling in the sharpness of it, giving thanks to the Great Spirit for being alive. He felt warm despite the day's coldness and happy despite knowing he would lay his friend to rest today.

Brooks wandered up and greeted him.

Cooper returned the greeting, then asked, "What happened with all the Blackfeet bodies? I don't see none around."

"The ones in the woods we left there. The others, well, we drug 'em to be with their brethren. Last few nights, we've been serenaded by the howlin' of wolves and coyotes, who had themselves a feast like they've never had before."

"Thought I heard such a chorus, though I was still some groggy. We found any live ones?"

"Had found two. Seems they were thinkin' of maybe gettin' revenge on us one at a time. We removed that notion—and their scalps. Three wounded ones, who were taken care of too. Other'n that, no. Bill even made his way up to the top there to make sure the rest were gone."

Cooper nodded. "Luis?"

"Buried him the mornin' after the big ruckus. Only Wheeler and Anderson were sad to see him go."

Cooper nodded again. Luis Gamez had never been popular with most of the men in the group. After a few moments, he said, "I best go and look for a place."

"Want company?"

Cooper shook his head. "No. I got to do this by myself."

"I understand."

Cooper put on snowshoes and shuffled off. He was in pain, his whole body one giant ache, but it had been only three days. Still, he was alive, and so he would accept the pain. Less than an hour later, he found what he wanted and headed back to camp. There, he saw that Morning Song and Sits Down had prepared Zeke's body. It had been difficult, but they had managed to get his fancy buckskins on him, with his favorite cap—skunk fur with head and tail attached—and the soft, beaded moccasins Morning Song had made for him. They had wrapped him in a fine buffalo robe and strapped him on a litter.

Cooper nodded his approval, then asked, "He got everything he needs for his journey to the Afterworld?"

"Yes. Except horse," Sits Down said in his great rumbling voice.

"His horse'll go with him. And a mule."

"I'll bring 'em," MacTavish said.

Morning Song and Goes Far piled things onto the mule that Potts would need for his trip to the Great Beyond—his rifle, which someone had found after the battle; some powder and ball; his shooting bag and possible sack; his pipe and a bit of tobacco; a small gourd of water and one of whiskey; a blanket, his capote; fur mittens.

Cooper, Sits Down, Brooks, and Beaubien carried the litter on their shoulders to the spot Cooper had selected. There, in the fork of a large, old cottonwood, they placed the litter.

As Cooper killed Potts's favorite horse and a pack mule, Sits Down, Goes Far and Morning Song chanted prayers over Potts. With the soft chanting still going on in the background, Brooks said some words for Potts's soul. Then Cooper talked a short while about his friend, saying his goodbyes.

The other men drifted away, each with his own thoughts.

It could have been any one of them, they knew. It came with these wild and savage mountains. And at times like this, each felt his vulnerability. But they were thankful, too, that it was someone else gone under, and not them.

Cooper shed but a few tears; indeed, he almost smiled at the thought of what Potts would have said had he seen tears in Cooper's eyes. Finally he put his arm around Goes Far's shoulders and they walked back to camp.

THIRTY-SEVEN

"GET YOUR ASS OUT HERE, WEBSTER," Cooper bellowed.

The door to the cabins opened. From one, a group of men came out, faces grim. From the other, Webster emerged, propelled by someone within. He was followed by the pushers—Beaubien and MacTavish—who continued shoving him closer to Cooper. The mountaineers had released him from the tree an hour after Cooper had returned, but kept him bound inside the cabin, under someone's watchful eye the whole time.

It had been a week since Potts's burial, and while Cooper's body was still colorful, the bruises were fading, and he felt mostly recovered.

"If you remember any prayers, Webster, best get 'em said," Cooper snapped as Webster stumbled to a stop near him.

"I ain't scared of you," Webster said with a snarl.

"That's good. I hate to have to skin me a coward. Now, I told you I'd give you a chance, and I will. I'll even let you have your choice of weapons. What'll it be?"

Webster looked around at the other men, seeking support.

There was none, not even from his usual allies—Dave Wheeler and Dan Anderson. The two shuffled their moccasined feet and looked down, or up or left or right, anywhere but at him. They had already apologized to Cooper after Potts was laid to rest for often siding with Webster.

"You ain't gonna get no help here," Cooper said harshly. You've rolled out your robe, now ye've got to sleep in it."

Webster shrugged. He had been alone before; this was nothing new to him, being deserted by friends when the going got rough. He didn't need them, any of them. "'Hawks," he said firmly with a smarmy grin.

Cooper was not surprised. Webster was one of the best with a tomahawk. He would have to be wary, but he was not concerned. "Done."

MacTavish tossed Webster's 'hawk toward him, and it landed in the dirt. Webster picked it up, eyes narrow slits of hate.

Cooper shrugged off his capote and pulled his tomahawk. It was not a fancy weapon, like some carried. His was a plain, razor-sharp, serviceable weapon, as was Webster's, though Malachi had wrapped fur around the hickory handle and bound it with rawhide. A feather dangled from the butt end.

The men formed a rough circle. They were quiet—this was deadly business, not just some drunken brawl at rendezvous. And they made no bets to argue over; Webster had no support among the men. All wanted

Cooper to win. Brooks, Beaubien, and MacTavish each rested a hand on his pistol, just in case.

Cooper and Webster faced each other, tomahawks held lightly. Cooper had his Green River knife in the belt sheath, and Webster had a large knife in his belt. Cooper had given his pistols, shooting bag, and possible sack to Brooks so they would not hinder him. The others had taken Webster's other weapons long ago, though the knife was returned this morning in case that was the weapon to be used.

No one had to say anything. By mutual, silent agreement the two combatants warily moved out and began to circle cautiously ten feet or so apart. Suddenly Webster reared back and let fly his tomahawk.

Cooper was half expecting it, since Webster's accuracy at throwing a 'hawk was well known in the mountains. He reacted swiftly, knocking the weapon out of the air with his own. He smiled as he picked up Webster's tomahawk with his left hand. "You forgot something," he said with a sneer. He tossed the tomahawk easily to Webster, who angrily snatched it out of the air. He rushed at Cooper, chopping the air with the stout weapon.

Cooper fell back, fending off the wild blows, as steel clanged on steel. Each hit of blade on blade or blade on hilt sent a shock through Cooper's arm. He had pushed away the stiffness and pain, but the assault's shock was beginning to bring it all back.

But Webster, who had not been treated kindly by the camp for all those days, who had been tied up the whole time, was weakening, too.

Cooper's left leg—the one with the arrow wound—buckled under him and he went to one knee. He just had the ability to whip his tomahawk up to catch the brunt of a wicked slash Webster aimed at his head. He shoved, pushing Webster back, and stood, panting.

"Gettin' old, Cooper?" Webster sneered.

Cooper stood, waiting, saying nothing.

"Come on, Cooper," Webster invited tauntingly. "You wanted to face me, so come on. Less'n you're not much of a man. Could be," he said, smiling wickedly, glancing around to see if he had an audience. "I reckon that's why that Nez Perce slut of yours asked me to give her this"—he grabbed his crotch with his free hand— "begged me for it."

There was a gasp from the men, and Webster smiled inwardly in satisfaction. "I figure it would be the first time she had herself a real man, one who knew what he were doin' with a woman. What do you think, eh?"

Anger roared through Cooper's head, almost blinding him with its impact. But he forced himself to remain still, to keep his features calm. Only the tightening of his lips indicated the depth of his hatred.

"Christ, boy, what do I got to do to get you to fight like a man?" Webster waited, thinking the men were on his side now. So blind was he, that he could not see the stark hatred on their faces, and the knowledge that his jibes had done nothing more than seal his fate, for Cooper would never forgive these insults to himself and his woman. And if he somehow was able to kill Cooper, there were eight mountain men and one giant Nez Perce warrior who would make sure he paid for it. Webster was a walking dead man.

Cooper moved then, eyes glinting. He moved easily,

with the fluid grace of a cat, the tomahawk jumping eagerly in his hand.

Webster smiled his oily smile, thinking he had Cooper where he wanted him. There were few men in the mountains who could match him with a tomahawk, and now he figured he had Cooper so riled up that he would not be able to think properly. He waited, hunched over, weight on the balls of his feet, as Cooper closed in. Suddenly his hand flashed and the 'hawk leaped into play.

He was shocked when Cooper easily blocked it and almost knocked it out of his hand. Cooper's weapon sliced a thin, not very deep gash across his abdomen. Twice more Webster feinted and swung, slashing at Cooper, and twice more the blow was blocked, and Cooper's tomahawk opened another bloody line across his torso.

Webster realized with a sudden chill that he was in serious trouble, had badly overestimated his abilities and his opponent's weaknesses. Fear clutched at his intestines and he almost stumbled. The fear grew when he saw the cruel slash of Cooper's mouth and the deadly, knowing look in Cooper's eyes.

He gulped and felt a huge knot in his throat, making it difficult to breathe. Suddenly he bent and scooped up a handful of snowy dirt and flung it at Cooper's face.

Cooper blinked once but was not thrown off.

Webster sucked in a lungful of air and let it out in an explosive yell as he leaped across the few feet separating him from Cooper, swinging his tomahawk wildly.

Metal rang on metal as Cooper calmly fended off Webster's powerful swings of the weapon. The two men were nearly nose to nose now, their 'hawks locked. Their breath frosted in the air.

"I'll kill you, you son of a bitch," Webster snarled, spitting in Cooper's face.

Except for a small reflexive flinch, Cooper ignored the spittle and the threat.

Webster tried to knee him in the groin, but Cooper deftly blocked it and shoved Webster away. Webster fell, and Cooper kicked him in the teeth as he tried to rise. Webster's head snapped back and cracked on the hard ground. He shook it off and jumped up.

Cooper punched Webster in the face with his left hand. Webster rocked, stumbled back a step, then another as Cooper punched him again. Cooper punched him a third time, and Webster fell, sitting hard, the jarring on his rump and on the hand that went down to help brace him, shook the tomahawk loose. Cooper kicked it away.

"Do it," Webster said, dejection overriding the fear in his voice.

Cooper hesitated just an instant. The desire to crush Webster's skull with the tomahawk and be done with it was great. But that was not his way. "Not yet," he said in a voice that chilled Webster more than the frigid air and ground. Cooper tossed his tomahawk away. "Get up."

Webster pushed himself slowly, awkwardly to his feet. But in the process, he pulled his belt knife. He grinned wickedly. "You're a damned fool, boy," he snarled.

The cocking of a pistol was loud in the new silence, and then Brooks said, "Throw down the knife, boy, or I'll put a lead pill right in the lights."

"Let him be, El," Cooper said quietly. He pulled out his own knife. Holding it so the sunlight glinted off the sharp blade, he said, "This here Green River's counted coup on one hell of a heap of Blackfeet and Crow. I reckon it won't have no trouble raisin' the hair of one stinkin' son of a bitch like you."

Webster realized he had made another serious mistake. He might've been able to outfight Cooper with a tomahawk had he not been so cocky, and maybe even with fists. But Cooper was more than his match with a knife, and he knew he was in trouble. He had only one chance, he thought...he raised the knife high, held in his right fist, and charged.

Cooper stood with his knife blade held upward in front of him. As Webster's knife arm swung downward, Cooper crouched and reached up, blocking that arm with his forearm. He pushed up with his legs, the right one bearing the brunt of the effort as he favored his wounded left leg. His knife darted out and punctured Webster's stomach.

Webster's eyes widened in shock and his breath burst out. "Damn," he muttered as his legs buckled. He sank to his knees, Cooper's blade tearing a path through Webster's innards as he did until it clunked off the bottom of the breastbone.

Cooper yanked the blade free and stepped back. Without his support, Webster crashed forward with his face landing in the snow. He still clung to life, though a widening circle of his blood stained the snow around him.

Cooper stepped over him, straddling Webster's back, facing his head. He grabbed Webster's greasy long hair with his left hand and brought the knife around to take his scalp.

Brooks grabbed his arm. "That's enough, Hawley," he said softly but firmly.

Cooper's eyes were filled with warning as he turned them on Brooks. "Let go of my arm, El, or you'll be next," he hissed.

"Ye ain't gonna come against me," Brooks said.

"That may be, but I aim to take this fucking scut's hair."

"You've put him under for certain, Hawley. There ain't no call for ye to raise his hair."

"I got to."

"No, ye don't."

"After what this bastard done, the son of a bitch..."

"He's a white man. He ain't no damned Blackfoot, and by God, ye ain't neither."

"You didn't stop me last time."

"Didn't have time to think on it then. I have now. And I figure ye ain't that kind of man."

Cooper hesitated. He had never taken a white man's scalp before, but he wanted to take this one badly. But in the next instant, the idea of taking the hair of a fellow mountain man suddenly bothered him. "Damn," he spit, letting Webster's face fall back on the frozen ground with a small thud. He looked at Brooks. "We should've left this son of a bitch in Slow Bull's village."

Brooks nodded. "Should have."

Cooper sighed. "I reckon you're right about not takin' his hair, El, but lettin' him off this way to roam with the Great Spirit instead of wanderin' aimlessly don't shine with this chil' the least bit."

"The Great Spirit ain't gonna have nothin' to do with this coon, Hawley. Nor God in heaven. Don't fret over that."

"What're we gonna do with him?"

Brooks shrugged, then kicked Webster in the side. Webster grunted softly. "Well, he don't deserve no decent burial, that's certain. No, sir, such doin's won't shine a'tall. But I don't know..."

"Let ze wolves 'ave 'im," Beaubien said. "I'll take 'im over zere"—he pointed to the woods where they had fought the Blackfeet earlier—"and leave 'im. Ze wolves and ze buzzards and coyotes can 'ave 'im. Zey pick 'is bones clean for sure, eh. Zhen shit out ze results."

"That suit you, Hawley?" Brooks asked.

Cooper wiped his knife on Webster's shirt, straightened, and slid the weapon away. He picked up his tomahawk and did the same. Suddenly he felt tired again and the pain of his wounds returned. He shuddered. The sun would be gone soon, and the temperature would plummet. "Reckon it does," he said wearily, stepping away from Webster.

Goes Far pushed forward, heedless of the men in her way. She carried Cooper's capote, and she helped him into it. He nodded thanks. With Goes Far at his side, he turned and started walking away.

"Hawley..."

He turned and faced Brooks again as the other men drifted off, Beaubien and MacTavish dragging Webster toward the fringe of the woods.

"I don't know how to say this exactly," Brooks started in a soft voice. "But..."

"Well, then just say it, dammit."

Brooks chewed on his mustache for a few moments,

then said hesitatingly, "I was thinkin'...through the past few days that...well, I ain't certain, mind you...but...well." He stopped, drew a deep breath, then said in a rush, "Well, dammit, I were thinkin' on it, and since I did, well, promise ol' Zeke I'd do it fer him should the need come, but, well, if she'll have me, I'll take up with Mornin' Song."

Cooper grinned and Goes Far smiled happily. She had worried about her friend. Sits Down would have watched over his sister but being too close to her would be unseemly in the tribe's eyes, so she had been prepared to suggest that Cooper take her in as a second wife, if that was the only way to keep her alive out here. Goes Far would not have liked it, even though she and Morning Song had become as close as sisters. But she would have done it. However, this would be much better. She liked Elson Brooks and knew he would take good care of Morning Song, almost as well as Zeke Potts had.

"What about Sits Down?" Brooks asked. "He's been around her much of the time."

"She's his sister, and he wants to protect her," Cooper said. He did not think it necessary to tell Brooks about the Nez Perce's words about a bad omen concerning Potts. "But tribal custom limits how much he can do, I reckon. Once he knows you aim to take her as your woman, you'll have no trouble with him."

Brooks nodded.

"It'll take a spell, though, El," Cooper said. "She's still got a heap of grievin' to do."

"I know. Well, maybe I didn't till you just said it." Embarrassment flushed his face.

"Goes Far'll let you know when it's time. Meanwhile, be around her, help her when she needs it."

"I will. 'Sides. it's just temporary. Ye know, just 'til we get to rendezvous or maybe back to her village. Then I can be shed of her."

Brooks looked fondly at Morning Song, who stood sadly in front of her lodge, her hair hacked short in mourning. Her face was pale with sorrow, but there was determination there in the set of her jaw, even though her eyes betrayed fear of what was to become of her.

Cooper saw the look, though Brooks did not know he did. He figured things would work out all right. "What made you decide, El? Other than ye'd made a promise."

Brooks smiled. "Man's got to do something to keep warm these nights," he said, though there was no seriousness in it. It was just an embarrassed way of saying he thought it right.

He looked over at Morning Song again, his face caring.

Cooper grinned. There would be the sounds of lovemaking coming from Potts's old tipi again before much longer.

ABOUT THE AUTHOR

Though it might sound strange for someone who has published more than sixty Westerns, John Legg was born and raised in New Jersey. An Air Force veteran, he has traveled much of the West, having been a newspaper copy editor for more then twenty-seven years in Phoenix.

He currently works for a major newspaper's editing center in Florida and has a BA from William Paterson College (now university) in Wayne, N.J. and an MSJ from the Medill School of Journalism at Northwestern University. He has two grown children and two young grandsons.

9 781639 774456